Tapping In
To
Murder

By

Bernie Ziegner

Rosstrum Publishing
Nashua, NH

Also by Bernie Ziegner

TIMBERLINE

PURSUIT

Death in Cedar Canyon

MISSING

Coming Soon

BUSHWHACKED

Tapping In
To
Murder

Rosstrum Publishing books are available at discount when purchased in bulk for premiums or promotions as well as for fundraising or educational use. Based on quantities, special editions can be created to specification. For details, contact the publisher.

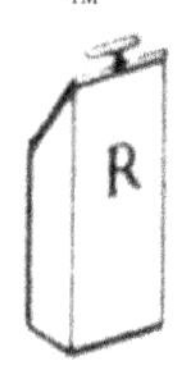

Rosstrum Publishing
A division of The Border Company, LLC
8 Strawberry Bank Road
Suite 20
Nashua, NH 03062-2763
RosstrumPublishing@gmail.com
www.rosstrumpublishing.com

ISBN number: 978-1-62570-045-2 Print
978-1-62570-046-9 Smashwords e-book
978-1-62570-047-6 Amazon e-book
978-1-62570-048-3 CD for PC print

Library of Congress Control Number: 2017933734

Manufactured in the United States of America
First Printing February 2017
1 3 5 7 9 10 8 6 4 2

Acknowledgements

I have tremendous gratitude and appreciation for the encouragement and help given by the Tyngsboro Writers Group in the writing and editing of this novel. Special recognition is given to Brian Hammer, Karen Johnson, Mike Johnson, and Joe Ross for their valuable assistance.

Thanks to Joe Ross of Rosstrum Publishing for editing and the many things publishers do. My apologies to anyone I may have left out.

All Errors are mine.

BZ

Chapter 1

IT WAS AN EARLY WINTER day in 2007, not at all unusual - a mix of rain and snow and cold. Jim Randolph drove south in a rented car from Poughkeepsie on US-9 into the Palisades region on the way to his hotel from a day at the company office. He wished he was still at his apartment in Philadelphia, but the company had sent him to the New York office to assist in a new project.

–

Maria DiCosta strained to see the icy patches on the dark road. She had left her parents' estate along the river in the Hyde Park area and sped along US-9 in her Jaguar, anxious to get to her business in Manhattan, Maria's Interiors, to prepare for a sales meeting the next morning.

Maria suddenly realized she was driving too fast for the black ice conditions and she let up slightly on the accelerator. While she normally drove this road well above the speed limit, she was suddenly frightened by the darkness, intermittent snow, and the slippery road surface.

–

"Crazy bastard," Jim muttered as a late model Mercury Marquis passed him and overtook the car in front, a Jaguar sports car. Jim watched in alarm as almost immediately, coming into a left-hand curve, the big car forcibly rammed the left rear quarter of the Jaguar.

"Oh God," cried Jim as he slammed on the brake.

The Jaguar spun onto the left side of the road, slid into a gravel area, and slammed headlong into a rock ledge, fifty feet from the road. The Marquis continued around the bend and disappeared.

Jim pushed hard on the brake. He saw the sudden burst of flames from under the left front fender of the Jaguar, and seconds later at the back wheel. Impulsively, he turned abruptly and shot into the gravel area where the burning car rested. He wondered if he could get the driver out before the whole thing went up in a ball of fire.

Jim's car skidded sideways into brush, saplings and rocks before stopping. Panic gripped him when he saw that flames enveloped most of the front of the Jaguar. He sprinted from his car hoping to reach the driver before they were both in a fireball. He saw flames at the rear wheel and thought he might only have seconds before the fuel tank exploded.

The driver's door didn't budge as Jim yanked on it. He kicked it in frustration and pulled upward while pressing a foot against the rear panel. The door came open suddenly, spilling him backward onto the ground. He scrambled to his feet, thanking God under his breath that the door opened. He saw a woman with her face buried in the collapsed airbag. He didn't get a response from her when he yelled, so he pushed the airbag out of the way and untangled her from the seatbelt and began to pull her from the vehicle. He strained to drag her limp weight away from the burning car. Grabbing her under her arms, he pulled and managed to move her about ten feet when he heard the alarming whoosh of a new burst of fire. He put all his energy into dragging her away, getting about thirty feet before the car exploded.

The shock wave made him stumble and lose his grip on the woman's arm. He recovered his grip and started to drag her farther from the burning car when there was another explosion. Jim staggered when a metal projectile ripped through his shirt and tore into his right arm. A section of flying window glass then felled him with a knock-out blow to the head. Jim collapsed unconscious on top of the woman.

—

A passing motorist, who saw the burning car, called 9-1-1, but did not stop. The first police officer arrived in twelve minutes and determined that both people were alive. He then called for backup. A fire-rescue truck arrived a few minutes later. Soon, patrol cars blocked the road and the scene became bathed in blue flashing lights. The fire department paramedics acknowledged that both victims were alive and went about preparing to transport the victims to a hospital. A second ambulance arrived and both victims were taken away. In the meantime, the fire crew worked to extinguish the flames.

The woman regained consciousness during her trip to Columbia University Hospital. She gave her name as Maria DiCosta. When the ambulance attendant asked for additional information about herself, Maria realized she was covered in blood. She cried out and began to sob and tremble. The attendant tried to calm her – telling her the blood was not hers, rather it belonged to the man that pulled her from the car. They would not give her his name.

Jim was stabilized at Columbia University Hospital. He was assessed with a concussion and loss of blood from the deep laceration on his arm. The next day, against medical advice, he was transported by private ambulance to Philadelphia at the request of his parents. During brief periods of consciousness, he was informed that the woman he helped had only minor injuries and would be released from the hospital the next day. He didn't know who she was.

Chapter 2

JIM'S PARENTS IMMEDIATELY arranged for their son's transfer from Columbia to Philadelphia Friends Hospital where they could look after him. Jim and his parents, desiring only privacy, asked both Columbia and Friends Hospital to maintain confidentiality on his identification and personal information. The staff at Friends readily agreed as Mr. and Mrs. Randolph were contributing members to the neurological research group. Jim realized with some angst the police report would have his identification. He deplored seeing his name in the newspaper.

—

Maria awoke the next morning to see her father sitting in a chair by her bed. His personal guard stood behind him and smiled as Maria opened her eyes. She looked at her father in alarm.

"Dad! You shouldn't have come down here. You're not well."

His lip quivered. "My little girl was in an accident. I had to see her." He turned to his companion. "Dom, help me up."

The guard helped Angelo DiCosta move his chair to be against the bed.

"They said you are being discharged this morning. How bad are you hurt?" Father and daughter held tight to each other's hands. Dom stood behind the frail man.

Maria smiled, looking at her father and Dom. “Thank you for coming down here, although you shouldn’t have.” She looked at Dom.

He shrugged. “Your dad insisted.”

“Tell me what happened,” said Angelo. “I want to know what happened.”

“Some big car slammed into my left quarter and sent me off the road. The car kept going, never stopped. The guy behind me stopped and pulled me out of the wreck before it blew up. That’s what the ambulance guy told me.”

No one knows who the big car belongs to?” He looked at Dom.

Dom nodded. “I’ll look into it.”

“My car is gone, Dad.”

“Forget the car. I never liked that car anyhow. Too dangerous.”

“Oh, Dad . . .”

“Who was the man that stopped and helped you?”

Maria shook her head. “I don’t know. I’d like to thank him.”

Angelo looked at Dom. Dom nodded again.

Maria was discharged from the hospital with bruises and numerous, but minor, cuts and scrapes to rest at her parents’ home at the Palisades. She hung up the phone as her father walked slowly into the sitting room of the large house. She worried about her father, 65, who was suffering with emphysema. He had deteriorated during a recent five year stint in prison.

“You have someone taking care of things in the city? Want Dom to go down there?”

Maria smiled and went to her father, hugged him and guided him to a chair. “Everything is fine, Dad. Really. I have all the help I need at the place. I’ll probably go back down there tomorrow. I’ll ask Dom for a ride.”

“Yes, I want him nearby wherever you are. The more I think about it, the more I don’t think this was an accident. Dom doesn’t think it was, either.”

Maria looked wide eyed at her father. “Why Daddy? Probably some drunk, driving too fast.”

He shook his head. “Maybe that’s what it’s supposed to look like. I have enemies.”

"Dad . . . this was on purpose?"

"I have a bad feeling. Dom is looking into it. Also, I want to talk to the young man that pulled you out of that car. I want to thank him. Also, I want to know what he saw."

"Who is he? Do you know? *I* want to thank him."

Angelo nodded, "Dom is getting the information. We should know later today."

—

Maria and her father received scant information from the police in their attempt to find Jim's identity and where Jim had been taken on leaving Columbia. Angelo DiCosta, not without resources, was eventually able to discover that Jim Randolph was transferred to Friends Hospital in Philadelphia. The hospital, however, refused to give out any information about Jim. From the New York City police records, they obtained Jim's address in Philadelphia.

The next day, Dom informed Angelo that Jim had left Friends Hospital, and was absent from his apartment, and not at his parent's home. Later, Dom found out that Jim was staying in a private-care center near his parents' home on the Main Line. Telephone calls to the Randolph residence were answered by a secretary who refused to release any information without her employer's approval.

—

Jim had asked his parents to help him remain anonymous; that he didn't want any publicity, just desired to get well and return to his job. After a month, all inquires stopped.

It was three months before Jim was released from the nursing facility. He was anxious to resume his position with his employer, SCCI (Secure Corporate Communications, Incorporated), and begin part time work in the Philadelphia office.

Chapter 3

SPRING HAD COME TO New York City when Jim moved from Philadelphia to the Clarion Arms Hotel in Manhattan. SCCI had a contract for the installation of a sophisticated communications facility in the Walker Building, being reconstructed in the Upper West-side by the DiCosta Construction Company. This building of twelve stories was being designed for business clients that desired the best electronic security possible to shield their business trans-actions from hackers, competitors, and spying agencies.

Jim spent the first morning at the job site getting acquainted with the building and overall plans for installation of the specialized equipment. The numerous DiCosta Construction signs around the base of the building had given him pause. His mind drifted back to the night of the crash at the Palisades. Although he had been told the name of the prime contractor at the orientation meeting in Poughkeepsie, it was now, with the construction signs every ten feet that he began to wonder. He tried to dismiss the thoughts, convinced there must be a hundred people in the city with the common name of DiCosta. But still, he wondered.

The building seemed like a formidable challenge as he walked through it, and he began to have reservations. Was he up to it? It wasn't so much the technical aspects of the job ahead, he thought, for he was confident of his capability. Instead, it was being in a blue collar construction environment that caused him to doubt himself. This was a totally foreign situation for him, different than the sedate life he enjoyed in Philadelphia. Jim stood at the edge of the third floor and looked out to the scene below, at the busy traffic and hoards of people, and then took a deep breath and turned back into the building. This would be a challenge.

After several hours surrounded with blue prints and technical manuals, he realized that the sophistication and complex nature of the facility would require much more study if he was to become an effective engineering manager of the project. At noon, he suggested to his colleague, Steve Arnold, that they break for lunch. Jim took an immediate liking to Steve, born and raised in Albany in a blue collar family, and an engineering graduate from RPI in Troy, NY. Jim appreciated Steve's straightforward response to questions, and honesty in admitting when he wasn't sure of something.

Jim turned to Steve. "So, where do you go for a bite to eat?"

Steve didn't hesitate. "Let's go to Henry's off Columbus Circle. It's got good food, and this time of day, abundant eye-candy."

Jim grinned. "Sounds like my kind of place. Do we walk there?"

"Yeah, it's only ten minutes away." Steve saw Jim reach for his jacket and frowned. "Leave your jacket here, it's warm out. Besides, you look pretty dapper in your polo shirt and khakis."

Jim hesitated. "I'm kind of self conscious about this ugly scar on my arm."

Steve shook his head. "Get over it. It's not ugly. It gives you character."

Jim chuckled. "Yeah, right."

-

Maria looked at Jennifer sitting across the booth. "I'm glad you could have lunch with me. Haven't seen you in weeks."

Jennifer smiled. "I'm glad you called. Happy to get out of the office for a while."

"You still with Randy?"

Jennifer scowled and slowly shook her head. "Dumped him a couple weeks ago. He was two-timing me with some bimbo from Brooklyn. Saw them going into the Carlton House one night."

"Sorry," said Maria. "He seemed like a nice guy."

"A real disappointment."

Maria lifted her Margarita to her lips and then hesitated.

"What's wrong?" Jennifer started to turn around.

"Don't turn around," Maria whispered. She put the glass down. Her heart thumped as she stared at the man coming toward her, approaching along the row of booths - a handsome young man in a wine colored polo shirt. She saw the unmistakable long scar on his right arm. "Could this be him?" she wondered aloud.

"Who?"

"Shh."

She turned her head and watched as he and his companion walked by with only a glance toward her. Her heart racing, she hesitantly called out his name.

"J . . . Jim?"

She saw him stop and turn to look back as he said something to his friend, who then continued to a vacant booth. Jim slowly walked back to stand by her booth.

A smile teased the corners of his mouth. "I'm sorry, I don't remember . . ."

"I . . . I'm Maria. Maria DiCosta." Her eyes welled. "You pulled me out of my burning car." She reached for his right arm and ran her fingers over the long white scar. "They told me you were hurt."

Jim smiled, his gaze darting back and forth between Maria and Jennifer. "I'm glad that you're okay."

"I tried to find you to thank you." She let go of his arm.

Jennifer cleared her throat.

"Oh, I'm sorry." Maria wiped at her eye with the back of her hand. "Jennifer, this is Jim Randolph. I told you about him."

Jennifer reached to shake his hand. "Really pleased to meet you. Maria has been looking all over for you."

Jim nodded, looked at Jennifer and then to Maria. "I was in Philly getting patched up. Then I worked at a job there for a while."

"What are you doing here, in the city?" asked Maria.

"I just started a new job with the same company." Jim turned to look back at his companion sitting alone several booths away. "I'm sorry; I better get back to my friend. I'm very happy to have met you. Please excuse me."

"Jim, uh, would you want to have dinner with me?" Maria looked boldly at Jim, her mouth open slightly.

Jim shuffled his feet and bit his lower lip.

"Please?"

He nodded. "I'd be happy to."

"Oh, that's great. Can you met me at Josef's, say at seven?"

"I don't know the city."

"Just tell the taxi driver, he'll know."

Jim smiled and started to walk away. "Okay. Seven it is."

When Jim was out of earshot, Jennifer looked at Maria with a broad smile. "Wow. That was amazing. But I think he's a little scared."

"Glad I finally found him. He saved my life."

"He's handsome, too."

"I did notice that." Maria grinned.

"Notice the tight buns?"

"Oh Jen, for crying out loud."

"Well, did you?"

Maria nodded and looked down at her Margarita. "Of course."

—

Jim and Steve ordered their lunch; Steve, a Reuben and a beer; Jim, a roast beef sandwich and a beer. Steve looked at Jim as the waiter walked away.

"I couldn't help noticing as I walked by – man, she is gorgeous."

Jim nodded. "Her name is Maria DiCosta."

Steve's eyes widened. "DiCosta?"

"Uh-huh. Why?"

"The prime contractor for the Walker Building is DiCosta Construction."

Jim shrugged. "I know but there gotta be lots of DiCostas in the city."

"Maybe, but DiCosta was a major mob figure some years back."

"The same DiCosta that's contractor on the building?"

"Yep. When the old man got outa prison, the bosses put him in charge of the construction company. He's an old guy now and probably just trying to stay clean."

"And what? You think this woman is related?"

"Might be," said Steve. "Read somewhere he has a wife and daughter."

They fell silent as the waiter brought their food and drink. Jim took a sip and looked at Steve. "Even if she is related, is that a problem?"

Steve shook his head. "Hell, no." Then he grinned. "Have dinner with her. Enjoy yourself."

Jim took another bite before looking at Steve. "What are you telling me?"

"Just wanted you to know, that's all."

Jim swallowed and reached for his drink. "What kind of place is Josef's?"

"It's an upscale place in the upper West-side. Reservation only."

"Hope they take a credit card," said Jim as he washed down the last of his hamburger.

"I'm sure. However, she invited you. It's her show."

"I shouldn't take the check and pay it?"

"If the waiter hands it to you, yes. But I'd be surprised if there was any check at all. I'm willing to bet she is a regular there."

Jim frowned. "Well, okay."

"You don't need to wear a tux." Steve grinned. "A long sleeve white shirt, nice tie, and a blue blazer would be perfect."

Jim suddenly looked up. "They're leaving."

"Let's wait a few minutes," said Steve.

"We need to get back. There's a lot of stuff I have to learn."

"Yep."

—

Jim stepped out of the cab in front of Josef's a few minutes before seven. He glanced around and then went toward the brass door that was opened for him by a uniformed doorman. He stepped into the foyer and was met by the maître d', an older man in a tuxedo.

"Good evening, sir. Have you a reservation?"

Jim couldn't see into the restaurant. "I think so."

The maître d' smiled. "Would you be Mr. Randolph?"

"Yes. I am."

"Please come with me." He led the way past his podium and they entered through heavy wood doors into the dining area.

"Wow," Jim whispered under his breath as he was surrounded by the opulent surroundings of mahogany, leather, and large green plants. The dining alcoves were all occupied with elegantly dressed couples and parties. The maître d' directed Jim to an alcove hidden by palms. Maria looked up and smiled. Jim felt his heart racing as the maître d' presented him to Maria.

"Sit down, Jim. Please."

"Thank you." He glanced at her half-empty margarita. "Have you been waiting long?"

Maria shook her head. "I had to escape from the office. Too many cranky customers." She smiled. "I'm sure glad you came. I so much wanted to see you."

"I'm very happy to see you and you're not suffering any aftereffects."

She looked at him wide-eyed. "I'm glad, because I didn't think you wanted to be found."

Jim grimaced and met her glance. "I'm sorry if I caused you or your family any discomfort. I was raised to keep a low profile. So, I avoided any publicity about the accident."

"But you stopped to help me . . .."

Jim nodded. "It was the right thing to do."

The waiter brought another margarita for Maria and bourbon on the rocks for Jim. Jim noticed there were no menus; instead, the waiter recited the supper dishes for the evening. Maria asked for the seafood medley and Jim chose a sirloin steak.

"They only have a few dishes for supper and it's different every day," said Maria. "But it is exquisitely prepared." She smiled. "You'll like it."

"I'm sure I will."

While they enjoyed their meal, Maria told Jim of her business venture, *Maria's Interiors*, on 5th Avenue near 61st.

"Sounds like a fancy location. Are you doing well?"

"Oh, yes. We're thriving. I have seven employees in the store and an installation crew of six guys."

"You do mostly commercial accounts?"

"Mostly offices of upper management people. I have a pretty good backlog."

"How did you get started in interior design?"

"I worked for an interior decorator for a year and then had the opportunity to go out on my own. There seemed to be more business, more customers, than the various decorator outfits could handle."

"Interesting."

Maria nodded. "First I put together a core team." She grinned. "Stole the best people I could find. Then, I asked my father for a start-up loan that I've since paid off."

"Wow. Congratulations. That's a real accomplishment."

"Thanks." She met his glance and smiled. "So tell me a little about yourself."

The waiter cleared the table and brought them fresh drinks. Neither Maria nor Jim cared for dessert.

"So tell me . . ."

Jim squirmed in his seat. "I'm 26 and an electronic engineer. Went to Drexel in Philly. I work for SCCI. I was transferred here to be the engineering manager at the Walker Building overseeing the installation of the communications equipment."

Maria looked at Jim. "The Walker Building, off of Columbus Circle?"

"You know it?"

Maria nodded. "Is SCCI a Philadelphia company?"

"Corporate offices are in Poughkeepsie. I was driving into the city the day of the accident."

Maria looked away. Jim noticed a slight trembling of her lip.

"I grew up on the Main Line in Philadelphia," he continued, My parents did especially well in real estate. They are conservative from way back."

"My dad and I tried for quite a while to find you." She held his glance. "I just wanted to thank you."

"Sorry about that."

Maria smiled. "I can't believe I actually found you and we're sitting here like this."

"I'm really happy just to see you're okay from the accident."

The waiter brought coffee.

Maria, quiet for almost a minute, looked at Jim. “The building you’re working in is being rebuilt by my father’s construction company. SCCI must be a subcontractor.”

“DiCosta Construction is your father’s company?”

She nodded. “You know about him . . . don’t you?”

“I’ve heard a few things since I got here.”

She toyed with her coffee cup before continuing. “He’s retired from his past life since leaving prison. He only has the construction company now and he runs it clean. He only bids on medium-sized projects like parking garages, strip malls, and office buildings.”

“Has to be a pretty good sized company.”

“Yes. His old boss has a financial interest in the company, in that he underwrites his loans. But, the lawyers manage to keep everything legal and the FBI hasn’t found anything to squawk about; . . . not yet anyway.”

Jim saw the frown come over her. “You don’t have to tell me anything. It’s okay.”

Maria smiled and looked at him for a few seconds before continuing. “I’d like you to feel comfortable with me. What I’m telling you is common knowledge. Ferrari owes him a lot for not talking at his trial and taking the prison time for him.”

“I don’t know much about those years,” said Jim. “I was in school and pretty busy.”

Maria nodded. “How was your steak? It smelled good.”

“Very tasty.” He didn’t want to tell her he barely tasted his food. He was struck by her beauty; her dark brown hair to her shoulders, her statuesque form and posture, and the warm sound of her voice.

“This is my favorite place for dinner. They prepare everything so perfectly.”

“It *is* a very nice place and this meal is awesome.”

After a short pause, she looked at him. “My dad’s getting up in years and in poor health. He took the rap for Ferrari. This allowed Tony to keep the organization together. My dad’s health deteriorated in prison. It’s about all he can do to run the construction company.”

Jim shook his head. “Has he thought about retiring?”

Maria shook her head. “No, he needs something to keep his spirit going. I imagine Ferrari will buy him out when the time comes.”

“Do you live with your parents?” asked Jim.

"No. I visit them often, though."

"Your mom? . . . She's well?"

Maria smiled. "She's fine. Acts half her age, what with parties and keeping dad from overdoing it."

"The construction company must keep your father pretty busy."

"It does, but he has people that keep things going. My dad and Tony get along well. Unfortunately, a guy named Mike McGregor is trying to force a wedge between Tony and my father. He doesn't hide his ambition, which is to take over the construction company."

Jim frowned and shook his head. "Can't Ferrari teach him some manners? He *is* the boss."

"Not so easy. Mike's the son of Tony's boss's sister. He has his hands full trying to control McGregor."

"The FBI . . . still giving your father trouble?"

Maria looked down at her coffee for a few seconds before replying. "The federal prosecutor was unhappy with my father going to prison for only a few years. Although they couldn't prove it, the prosecutor told the news people he was certain my father lied and took the rap for Ferrari. They're still trying to find a way to charge Ferrari and my dad with RICO violations."

"Maybe you shouldn't be telling me all this."

Maria put a hand on his. "I want you to know who I am."

"I like who you are."

She pulled her hand back to her coffee cup. "You're different – nice different."

Jim smiled. "Thanks."

The waiter returned and refilled their coffee. When he had moved away, Maria continued. "During my father's incarceration, McGregor began to take advantage of any weakness in the construction company, and make trouble where he could."

"What kind of trouble?"

"Suppliers that don't show up. Impromptu labor strikes for a phony issue. Always something. McGregor has some real cutthroat people on his payroll, people that I wouldn't want to meet in a dark alley. "

"Damn."

"I'm afraid something might happen to my father; just a bad feeling at this point. I've sensed being followed at times, and fear that McGregor's gang might try to get to me in order to destroy Dad. I sometimes have Dominic, one of my father's bodyguards, with me if I drive into the city late at night."

"And this Ferrari guy, he doesn't do anything about it?" asked Jim.

"His hands are tied. McGregor's mother is of the Salerno family, sister to Carmine Salerno and married to a McGregor out of Boston."

"Wow. I've heard of Salerno."

"He's not a nice guy." Maria hesitated then looked into Jim's eyes. "What actually happened at my wreck? What did you see?"

"I told the police what I saw."

Maria nodded. "Please."

"I was coming down from Poughkeepsie. The road had large patches of black ice and it was snowing intermittently. I saw you ahead in the Jaguar and slowed down."

"The ice had scared me," said Maria.

"At that time, a big Mercury Marquis came up behind me and passed me. He was just ahead of me for a few seconds, then he darted forward slamming into the back of your car. When you spun and ran off the road to the left, the Mercury took off and disappeared."

"I remember a big bump before I lost control."

Jim nodded. "That was the Mercury. I abruptly turned off the road and skidded, slamming into some trees and rocks about 100 feet to one side of you. I saw flames coming from under your front wheel well and hurried to your car. When I got there flames were coming out of the rear as well. Your door was stuck and I had to work at it to get it open. I got your seat belt off and started to pull you out of the car. I only got maybe thirty feet from the car when it exploded. I don't recall anything after that."

Maria had turned pale. "Someone was trying to kill me."

"I told all this to an officer at Columbia."

"Someone wanted to kill me." It was almost a whisper.

Chapter 4

JIM REALIZED HE HAD thoroughly enjoyed his dinner with Maria the previous night. He decided to wait a few days and then ask her out. As he walked back from a hamburger stand a few blocks from the Walker Building, his mind jumped back and forth from his job to Maria.

As he approached the Walker Building, his cell phone buzzed in his pocket.

"Hello."

"Jim. It's Maria. I'm glad I caught you."

"Yeah, the building is rather dead to cell phones."

"I wanted to ask you if you would like to visit *Maria's Interiors* after you finish work."

"You bet, but I won't be able to get out of here before five."

"That's okay," said Maria. "We're located on 5th Avenue just north of 61st. It's a short cab drive."

"Thanks for the invitation. I'm looking forward to it."

When he entered the lobby of *Maria's Interiors* he was favorably impressed with the brass and mahogany decor and tasteful furnishings. An elegantly dressed receptionist of middle aged greeted him. "I'm Elaine and you must be Mr. Randolph."

Jim smiled and nodded. "Yes."

Elaine brought him up a curving staircase to Maria's office. Maria turned from the large window and smiled.

"Welcome, Jim. Please, have a seat. Elaine, would you be kind enough to bring some coffee?"

Elaine smiled, nodded, and left the office.

Jim felt his heart quicken. She was beautiful with very little makeup, a light olive skin, and flowing brown hair. He openly admired her before realizing he was staring like a schoolboy. He sat at a small mahogany table as Maria closed her computer and joined him.

She looked at him and grinned. “Not what you were expecting?”

“I thought it would a classy place being on 5th Avenue. I wasn’t disappointed.”

“Thank you. Through there,” Maria pointed to a wall visible through the glass doors, “is where all the planning and business is conducted. I’ve a good team.”

“Where do you do the manufacturing?”

“Our crew of ten works out of a leased warehouse in mid-town. We rent trucks when we need them. It keeps our overhead down.”

“It looks like you’re doing well,” said Jim. He turned to look toward the office doors as a well dressed man entered with coffee service on a silver tray, placing it on the table.

Maria smiled. “Thank you, Walter.”

They sipped their coffee for a moment. Jim glanced often at Maria, enchanted by her presence, and the sound of her voice.

“I’m wondering. . . . How did you get started in this business?” Jim asked.

Maria leaned back and sighed. “I graduated from Columbia with a liberal arts degree. By then I had a real interest in interior design. I started working with my elderly aunt in her decorating business. My father had loaned her money to modernize and expand the business. When she passed away, a year later, I was very fortunate that she left the business to me.”

“Wow,” exclaimed Jim. “That’s quite a story and accomplishment, and a real cool address.”

“My clients are mostly condos and business offices. Of course,” Maria grinned, “my dad sent a few clients my way.”

“Lucky.”

Maria rolled her eyes and grinned. “Yep.”

A few minutes later Maria took Jim through the double doors outside her office. There were only a few people working in cubicles at that hour.

"Most people leave at five. We have eleven permanent staff in this section that do the design and manage the business. There are a couple of offices along this wall," Maria pointed to two enclosed offices, "where the accountants and sales people work."

Jim turned to her. "And you do all the marketing?"

"I used to, but I now have an experienced woman who helps me out."

They walked around the design area. Back at the main door, Maria put her hand on his arm.

"Join me for supper?" Before Jim could reply, she added, "Tony's is nearby and not too fancy."

Jim smiled. "Only if you let me treat."

Tony's was a small lounge that served a limited menu for lunch and dinner. They found an empty booth at the back.

Maria slid into the booth opposite Jim. "Kind of a cozy place, don't you think?"

Jim looked around at the small dining area with booths of dark wood and red leather. Several tables and chairs in the center of the room were elegantly set with linen and silverware. "There must be hundreds of these small places in the city."

"Oh, there are. But most are not this nice; just watering holes."

A young waitress with a neat and freshly pressed uniform came to their booth. "Welcome to Tony's."

"What's good?" asked Jim, looking at Maria.

"Tony always has roast beef, which is excellent. Of course, the hamburgers are really good, too."

"I haven't had a good hamburger in a long time."

"I'm going to have one," Maria grinned, "and chase it down with a Miller."

"Sounds good to me."

The waitress took their order and returned quickly with two draft Millers. Jim took a sip and set the mug on the table.

Maria looked at him. "So tell me, what was your childhood like in Philadelphia?"

Jim shrugged. "I got interested in electronics at an early age - always experimenting in the basement. I constructed radios and later played with computers."

"It kept you out of trouble?" Maria raised an eyebrow.

"As a kid, I enjoyed exploring the woods and nearby swamp. Spent a lot of time at the library, too. My parents kept me on a short leash, not much opportunity to get in trouble." Jim smiled. "How 'bout you?"

"I went to a private girl's school as a youngster. Not much chance for mischief there. My parents sent me to prep school for my high school years. I did well and had some fun, but nothing scandalous." She gave him a sly grin. "Had all the girls chasing you around the football field?"

Jim chuckled. "Hardly. I played baseball through high school, but never football. I wasn't attracted to it, and my parents really didn't want me to get injured."

"So, not too many girls?"

"I had several girlfriends in high school, but nothing I would consider serious."

"And in college?"

"I had two semi-serious relationships." Jim shrugged. "But when I didn't show more interest, they went their own way."

"Mom kept a sharp eye on me. If some dandy came to the door looking like a wannabe bad boy, she sent him packing."

"So, nothing serious?"

She shook her head. "Not in a long time. I've just kept busy."

"Dominic keeps an eye on you here in town?"

"He does. He'd give his life for my family. This thing with my crash has really upset him as well as my parents."

Jim turned grim. "Why would anyone want to run you off the road, maybe kill you? It's been bothering me."

Maria shook her head slowly. "Mike McGregor started to make moves against my father while dad was still in prison. McGregor is hell-bent on getting control of the construction company. Tony Ferrari has kept him under control, more or less, up 'till now."

"This McGregor guy sounds like a real piece-of-work."

"Ordinarily, Ferrari would have made him disappear long ago. But as I told you, McGregor is well insulated."

"So, Ferrari doesn't dare touch him?"

Maria scowled. "The family tolerates him, so far. But, he's been getting more aggressive lately, pulling his own jobs, not getting approval – just doing crazy things. His protection may come to an end one of these days."

Jim frowned. "So, it's this guy, McGregor, that tried to run you down?"

Maria shrugged. "I don't know. I'm sure Ferrari wouldn't want to hurt me; he and my father are good friends." She shook her head. "Could be McGregor is trying to force a wedge between my father and Ferrari."

"Your father has lots of security?"

She nodded. "His main security person, Dominic, is often in the city keeping an eye on my father's business and on my welfare. He stays in a nearby hotel, but never more than a couple days at the same one. I can always reach him on his cell phone, 24/7."

"I worry about you."

Maria reached across the table and put her hand on his. "Call me some time?"

Chapter 5

THE WEEKEND HAD NOT gone the way Jim had hoped. Art Wagner, supervisor from SCCI, had arrived on short notice from Poughkeepsie to spend the weekend going over the hundreds of design details of the communication system being installed in the Walker building. There had been only a short phone call to Maria on Saturday night as she had been entertaining a client. Art had driven back to Poughkeepsie Sunday evening, and Jim collapsed into his bed exhausted.

Jim stood at the edge of the fourth floor on Monday morning looking out into the empty space and the nearby buildings. He hoped his second week at the site would be more productive, and that he would get time to see more of Maria. Only a strip of yellow safety tape separated him from the emptiness beyond, as this spot was still being used to bring in supplies from the street below. Most of the twelve floors were still skeletal. The building had a temporary plastic tarpaulin wrap to protect the workers from the elements. This is the ideal time, Jim thought, for the contractor to install inter-floor wiring and communications apparatus; before electrical shielding and metal structures turned each floor into its own electrically sealed environment. It was this environment that he had to guarantee with exhaustive testing.

Jim knew the clientele signing a lease wanted a building with no exposure to sensors and electronic eavesdropping from within and from outside the building. Early interest in the building had been indicated by insurance and investment company inquiries.

Startled by a noise behind him, Jim turned to see two well dressed men walking toward him. *Who the hell are these guy*s, he wondered? When they were close to him, the older of the two men greeted Jim.

"Good morning. We are FBI and would appreciate a few minutes of your time." The two suits briefly showed IDs.

Jim looked at them suspiciously. "May I see that again?"

The older man scowled but they both showed their ID.

Jim nodded. "What can I do for you?"

"Jim Randolph?" asked the older agent. "May I call you Jim?" The younger man stared at Jim without expression.

"Whatever," replied Jim. "You are?"

"I'm Agent Jack Reed. My partner is Agent Wendell Somers."

"Jim, you are here working for SCCI, aren't you?" asked Reed.

"Yes, but you already know that," said Jim. "How did you get in here? The work site is a secured area."

"Agent Reed grinned. "We told your security folks we had to check on some reported irregularities."

"What irregularities?"

"What do you know about the DiCosta Construction Company?" asked Reed.

Jim shrugged. "Not much. Heard somewhere they were the contractor for this building."

Agent Somers looked at Reed and grinned. "Not much."

Reed looked at Jim. "Not much, huh? Well let me fill you in. Angelo DiCosta, of the old DiCosta crime family, has a daughter by the name of Maria."

Jim shrugged. "Oh?"

"Yeah. We saw you and her together the other evening, as well as in Henry's Pub, where she goes often."

"Wow. You guys are good."

"Uh-huh, we think so," replied Reed, not smiling. "What's your relationship to her?"

"Friends. We're friends."

Somers looked at Reed and grinned. "Friends."

"Well Jim, listen up. The DiCosta and Ferrari families are under investigation for racketeering, tax evasion, and other issues. These are your friends."

Jim shrugged. "Nothing to do with me."

"What do you know of the DiCosta and Ferrari family connection?" asked Reed.

"I'm a Philadelphia resident and not up on local issues."

"Okay, I understand." Reed smiled. "We'd appreciate your help by allowing us to monitor criminal activities in the building. We'd like to install monitoring devices. You'd be helping get criminals off the street."

Jim scowled. "It's not my prerogative, and any such order would have to come from management."

Reed shuffled his feet. "We were hoping to keep it low key. A few sensors to see if there was anything to pursue."

Jim shook his head. "If you want to pursue this bug thing, you need a court order before SCCI management would comply. And . . . this would likely be challenged in court in the privacy and contractual interests of clients in the building."

"Jim-bo is a regular lawyer," sneered Somers.

Reed stared hard at Jim. "I hear where you're coming from. I ask that you don't speak of this conversation with anyone."

"Only a court order can guarantee that."

"A regular fuckin' lawyer," mumbled Somers.

"I suggest you get on the right side of this investigation," said Reed, then added, "We'll be around."

Jim called Maria on his cell phone as he stepped out of the building during his lunch break.

"Jim? Nice to hear from you. How's your second week starting out?

"Better, I hope. My boss showing up for a weekend of work; wasn't something I planned on."

"So, you on your way to lunch?"

"I'm going down the street and grab a hot dog."

"Yuck. Can't you do better than that?"

"That's why I called – was wondering if you'd like to have dinner with me?"

"I'd like that a lot. Why don't I pick you up in front of your hotel at seven? Is that okay?"

"Seven is fine."

"You sound kind of tense," said Maria. "Anything wrong?"

"Not sure. I had some visitors this morning. Tell you about it tonight."

"Okay. See you at seven."

Jim sat down next to Maria and the cab started to move. “Can we go someplace we haven’t been?”

Maria looked puzzled, but then gave the driver directions. “Is there something wrong? You sounded odd before.”

He nodded toward the driver. “Wait ‘till we get there.”

A few minutes later the cab stopped in front of small pub. Maria passed the fare to the driver and opened the door. “It’s small but nice.”

They were seated right away. A waitress brought menus and took their drink order.

“Okay, so tell me,” said Maria. “What’s wrong?”

“The FBI was in the building and asked me questions about the DiCosta organization, and about Ferrari.”

Maria looked at Jim, her eyes wide. “What did they want from you?”

“They had seen us together. I think they hoped to scare me into telling them something.” Jim shook his head. “I didn’t tell them a damn thing. They weren’t happy when I refused to let them install bugs in the building, not that it’ll stop them.”

“I’m sorry they hassled you,” said Maria. “Those guys won’t give up trying to get my father and Ferrari in prison.”

Their drinks arrived and they gave the waitress their food order.

“Those two agents might be trying to entrap me . . . seeing as we’re friends,” said Jim.

Maria sat quietly for a few seconds. “Thanks for telling me. But, don’t worry about it. Just do what you have to. I think I know who those two agents are. They’ve been to my place, too.”

“They have?”

“Uh-huh. Not the brightest bulbs on the Christmas tree.”

“I got the feeling they’re serious about going after Ferrari through your father.”

“I often wonder if McGregor is a mole for the FBI. He’s totally without honor or scruples, and it wouldn’t surprise me if he’s giving them half-truths.”

Jim commented, “Maybe he’s trying to forestall criminal prosecution.”

Maria nodded. “He’s trying every which way to force a wedge between my father and Ferrari so he can maneuver for a piece of the construction company from Ferrari.”

“And the larger family puts up with this . . .?”

"So far." She scowled. "He seems to be counting on immunity because of who he is related to."

Maria lowered her coffee cup and looked at Jim. "I have to ask, okay?"

Jim nodded slowly. "Sure." He saw her lip quiver slightly.

"Are you worried about keeping company with me? I mean your job and parents, what they might think?"

"Absolutely not," he blurted and then added, "I like you – a lot."

Maria's eyes welled. She touched his hand. "You're rather special to me."

"The roast beef was great," said Jim as they walked out to the street. "Best I've had in a long time."

"They've been here a long time. It's a family operation."

"You could drive right by and not even notice it."

"I like the place," said Maria. "A friend took me here a while ago."

"Has roast beef always been their specialty?"

"There's one coming out of the oven every day. They don't serve much else except for a good salad bar."

A yellow cab pulled up to the curb and Jim opened the door for Maria. He told the next stop to the driver and the cab pulled away from the curb.

Jim glanced at the back window of the taxi several times.

"What's wrong?"

"There was a black car with dark windows parked across from the restaurant when we left. It pulled in behind us. Is it Dominic?"

Maria shook her head. "If *he* followed us, you wouldn't know it. Don't worry about it, I'm not." She took his hand in hers. "So, you're going to see your parents this weekend?"

"Uh-huh. Haven't seen them in a while. This is my second week at the building."

"I'll be at my parent's, also. I'll be helping her put on a small get together for some of their friends. It'll get me out of the city."

"I need to show up at my parent's once in a while, be a good son."

"Will you tell them about me?"

Jim squeezed her hand and smiled. "Of course."

The cab pulled to the curb at Maria's apartment.

"We're both going to have a busy week. I'll be going to my parent's place Thursday afternoon. Will you call me when you get back?

"I will."

She kissed him lightly on the lips and quickly left the cab. He waited until she disappeared into the building before giving the driver the name of his hotel. He looked again at the rear window but didn't see the car that had been behind them earlier.

The week went by quickly. Every day Jim scoured blueprints and equipment manuals learning as fast as he could the intricacies of the communications system. When Friday came, he was glad for a couple of days off.

Jim was met by his parents at the train station when he arrived in Philadelphia. His mother threw her arms around his neck and kissed him.

"So glad you're home."

"Happy to see you, Mom."

Jim's father, Edward Randolph, shook hands with his son. "I'm really happy to see you. You look good."

"Can we stop at my apartment? I need to pick up some clothes to take to New York."

They chatted about life in Philadelphia and the increased traffic and congestion that seems to be moving closer to the Main Line. They stopped at Jim's apartment for a few minutes and then drove to their elegant stone colonial house. He had grown up with his parents in the Main Line house and he had agreed to stay with them on this visit and keep them company. He would have rather stayed in his apartment, but he knew the selfish impulse would have hurt his mother.

"Same company, but a new job. So how is it in Manhattan? It's been two weeks, now?" asked Edward, glancing at Jim as he drove onto the Main Line property.

"It's a very big job, a twelve story building being built in town," replied Jim.

"Really? What is your responsibility?"

"I have to be keenly sensitive to the schedule. It's a very complicated communications system and I'm responsible for testing all of it."

Jim and his father continued talking about the job until they were seated in the living room and Jim's mother, Nancy, brought in a serving tray with coffee and cake.

"We let the maid have the weekend off, her daughter's birthday. Hope the coffee is okay."

Jim smiled. "I'm sure it is, Mom."

Nancy sat in a straight back chair and straightened her skirt. "Have you made friends in New York?"

"I haven't been there but a couple weeks, Mom."

"You haven't met anyone? You don't have any friends?"

"There are the guys I work with, sure."

"Any young ladies? Surely . . ."

"I uh . . . there's a woman I met that I like quite a bit."

Jim's mother looked at him wide-eyed. "Oh?"

His father turned to him and grinned. "That's moving pretty quick, I'd say." He glanced at his wife.

"Well, that's nice, son. Who is she?" Nancy twisted her fingers together and placed her hands in her lap.

Jim kept his gaze at the pictures on the mantle when he replied. "Her name's Maria."

"She . . . she's Catholic?" It was almost a whisper.

"I don't know, Mom. We never talked about it."

"Her parents . . . Italian?" asked Nancy.

Jim nodded. "Uh-huh."

"But, who *are* they?" asked his father, looking directly at Jim.

Jim squirmed in his chair. "Her father owns a construction company; actually, he's the contractor for the building I work at."

Edward frowned, seemingly in thought.

"Is Maria educated?" asked Nancy.

"Yes, mom," Jim sighed. "She graduated from Columbia, and owns her own interior decorating company."

Edward cleared his throat. "Are we talking about the DiCosta Construction Company?"

Jim glanced at his father. "Yes. You heard of them?"

Edward shook his head. "Heard of them? Yes. DiCosta and Ferrari. I remember hearing about them some years ago. They are mob affiliated."

Nancy stared at Jim. "Is that true? She . . . she's in a mob family?"

Jim shook his head. “Mom, she’s a great person. Sure, her father was imprisoned for a while, but he’s out now, and in poor health. The only thing he’s involved in is management of the construction company.”

Nancy shook her head. “She’s not the right girl for you.”

“You need to look at a good family,” declared Jim’s father. “There are families in the club . . .”

“Oh, for heaven’s sake. I just met her. We’re friends. Remember the accident at the Palisades?”

Jim’s parents looked at him silently.

“Well, she’s the woman who was in that wreck.”

Edward turned to look directly at Jim. “You can’t be involved in a mob family.”

“We won’t talk about it anymore. Okay?” said Jim.

His father shook his head, his lips tightly clamped.

Jim turned to his mother and smiled. “How are things with your garden club?”

Chapter 6

JIM HAD A BUSY SCHEDULE when he returned to Manhattan to start his third week. He spent as much time as he could with the books and drawings describing the engineering task of installing a state-of-the-art communications system. The more day-to-day issues often interrupted his concentration.

Monday morning, Jim sat at a computer on the 2nd floor studying manuals and checking computer programs.

“Hey, Jim.”

He turned to see Steve Arnold hurrying toward him across the empty concrete floor. Steve’s face was in a frown.

“Steve, what’s up?”

“Hate to lay this on you first thing when you’re back, but I don’t know what to do.”

Jim stared at Steve. “Uh-huh?”

“There’s two power transformers that have to come up onto this floor. The electricians need to wire ‘em up next couple days.”

Jim knew that the heavy transformers had to be hoisted by crane to the outside shelf on the 2nd floor. Each floor had an outside shelf for loading heavy components and equipment.

“So? What’s the problem?” asked Jim.

Steve shook his head. “It’s the same Local 321 riggers we always use, but now they’re telling me that McGregor’s people won’t let them hoist the transformers.”

Jim frowned. “What the hell’s his problem?” Jim had been informed the previous week that Local 321 was controlled by Mike McGregor.

Steve shrugged. "McGregor is down on the street. Says he wants his own boys to unload and raise the transformers to the 2nd floor shelf."

"Aren't they all from Local 321?"

"Yeah, they are. It's just that McGregor is trying to take over the local for his own purposes."

Jim stood up and blanked the computer screen. "Go down there and keep an eye on things. I have to make a few calls."

Steve started to walk away. "Okay, got it. Let me know what to do."

"Goddamn McGregor," Jim mumbled. He realized costs were being accrued as the drivers, riggers and electricians sat around in the dispute. The problem was between DiCosta Construction, and the McGregor dominated Local 321. Jim called his management at SCCI and informed them of the difficulties. He was told they would get back to him shortly.

"Yeah, sure," said Jim as he hung up. "How long's that going to take?"

He wondered if asking Maria for advice would be a good idea. After a few minutes he picked up the phone again and dialed her number.

"Good morning, Jim. How'd your trip go?"

"Oh, okay I guess. Parents are parents. They worry a lot."

"My name came up?"

"Lots of questions. You know parents . . ."

"It didn't go over too well, huh?"

"They know you are someone I care about."

Maria was quiet for a couple seconds. "Well, I'm glad you're back."

"I am, too. Missed you."

"I went up to my parents, also. It was nice."

Jim cleared his throat. "Maria, I have a problem here. I was wondering if you could advise me?"

"Why sure, what's wrong?"

Jim told her what was happening with McGregor's interference and asked her how she would suggest he handle the problem.

"Jim, don't worry. Just stall a little, while I make a of couple calls."

"I really appreciate it, any help at all."

"Take me to dinner?"

"Absolutely," said Jim.

Jim paced the empty floor, peering occasionally down to the street where the flatbed truck was parked and the driver and crane operator sat at the curb. Other men leaned on the truck and sat on the flatbed.

"Son of a bitch, McGregor," mumbled Jim. He looked at his watch. An hour had passed since he called Maria and SCCI. When he looked down at the street again, he saw a black limo pull up to the work site next to the flatbed truck. Jim watched as a sidewalk conference ensued. He thought he recognized Ed Marcello, the foreman of the DiCosta construction crew that he'd been introduced to the previous week. He was talking to who Jim thought was likely the delegates from Local 321. Jim didn't know which one was McGregor.

When the limo doors opened, a well dressed man got out and opened the rear door to let out an older man, also dressed in a suit. Jim could see the shine from their shoes. The driver stood behind the older man as he spoke to who Jim assumed were the union delegates or maybe even McGregor. After ten minutes of conversation, a sign was given to the DiCosta crane operator to begin the unloading and hoisting operation. A few minutes later, the well dressed men drove away.

Ten minutes later, Jim's cell phone buzzed in his pocket. He recognized Maria's number.

"Jim, I made a couple of calls. I think the problem will be solved soon."

"Thanks, I really do appreciate it. Actually, the problem got resolved just a few minutes ago. Some men drove up in a black limo and after a brief conversation, they drove away and the crane operators went to work."

"In the old days, this wouldn't have happened, and there was no real reason for it except McGregor wants to wrestle control of the 321 and get his personal goons involved in the construction of the building."

Jim hesitated. "I, uh, didn't know who to call. I called my boss at SCCI, but I haven't heard back from him."

"I called my dad, and he talked to Ferrari. Since McGregor is part of the Ferrari crew, Ferrari went down personally to the work site to straighten things out."

"He was the one with the bodyguard in the black limo?"

"Yes, that was him."

"Thanks again for your help," said Jim. "Saved me a lot of grief."

"Is it worth a dinner?"

"You bet. Pick you up at 7?"

"I'll be ready."

Jim asked the cab driver to wait while he went into the lobby and buzzed Maria's apartment.

"Be right down." The small speaker gave her voice a squeaky sound.

In a minute, she came to the lobby in black slacks and white blouse – a sight that stirred his blood. He gave her an approving glance.

"You look lovely."

She laughed. "You just missed me, that's all."

"I did miss you. Thought about you a lot."

She took his arm as they went out to the cab. The cab moved as soon as the door closed.

"Where we going?" asked Maria glancing at Jim.

"Someone swore that Norman's had a good supper menu."

"I heard of it. Never been there. Upper West Side?"

Jim nodded. "Yep."

"This place is kinda nice," said Maria as they were seated in a small booth. "You were well advised."

"This guy I work with, Steve, knows all the good places," said Jim.

"Small. Odd, there's no bar."

"They do serve alcohol, but it's always been known for the great food. They aren't open much past dinner time."

Maria smiled. "I like it."

"Here comes the waiter."

They placed their order and waited for their cocktails to arrive.

Maria cleared her throat. "You didn't say how it went with your parents."

Jim nodded slowly. "They're pretty stuck in their Main Line social structure, and not happy that I'm outside their sphere of influence."

Maria stared at Jim. "Is it that I'm a DiCosta?"

"I told them that I liked you and you were important to me."

Maria looked down. "But not blue blood enough."

"That was their point," said Jim. "But, they'll have to get over it." He reached across the table and placed his hand over hers. "You *are* important to me."

"Bet you say that to all the ladies."

Jim shook his head and grinned. "Not *all* of them."

She looked up, her eyes glistening. His hand was still on hers.

The waiter arrived with their drinks and a small plate of hors d'oeuvres.

The conversation went to the events of that day at the Walker Building. Jim told her of what he had seen and said again how much he appreciated her help.

"Did you hear from your boss at SCCI?" asked Maria.

"Yes. By that time, you had defused the situation for me."

"Ferrari will do as much as he can to help my father. They have been long time friends."

"Good friend to have," said Jim.

"Tony did caution my dad that McGregor had important friends and relatives, people that could give both my dad and Tony problems."

"I would think Ferrari would make him disappear."

"Not without the okay from the family," said Maria. "That isn't likely unless he really goes off the rails."

They paused in conversation while the waiter brought their food – prime rib.

"Boy, does this ever look good," said Maria. "And, I'm hungry, too."

Jim nodded. "I wanted to mention that my cell phone as well as the temporary hard line phones in the building are probably being tapped by the FBI."

Maria grinned. "Those two jerks?"

"It's the impression I get. They're trying to get something on Ferrari and your father. They said as much."

She nodded. "I know. It really upset them that my father took the rap for Ferrari."

"Best if we don't give them anything on the phone."

Maria smiled. "I won't."

"I was wondering. Why did your father take the rap for Ferrari? Was he forced to?"

Maria shook her head. "No. Tony had a lot to lose. His young children. His new organization. And his standing with the family. My dad was old and not well and thought that he'd save his friend."

"That's quite a thing to do," Jim acknowledged.

"There were other things, long ago," said Maria. "Tony warned my dad of trouble and probably saved his life." Then she added, "They go back a long way. Dad took the rap for a friend, a special friend."

"Ferrari looked after the construction company while your father went away?"

Maria nodded. "Uh-huh. Did a good job of it. My dad went into prison in bad health – heart trouble and diabetes. He deteriorated there. Lawyers managed to get his sentence reduced to three years out of the six due to his health." She smiled. "My dad is doing a lot better now with good medical care and being pretty much retired."

"I bet you and your mother are happy he's home," said Jim.

"We're elated. Mom and I visited him almost every week. We could see how he was deteriorating. It was very upsetting."

"But the feds – they don't want to give up?"

"No," said Maria. "They think they can drive a wedge between by father and Tony, and somehow get a hook into the family."

"I keep wondering if McGregor has been bought."

"If Tony thinks so, McGregor is finished."

Chapter 7

THE NEXT MORNING AS Jim watched the activities on the street from a work area on the second floor, he saw Tony Ferrari leaving the job site and get into a waiting limo. Immediately, two men left the building by a temporary hard-hat entrance and moved quickly to a car idling nearby. As the car with Ferrari left, the other car pulled in behind, about ten car lengths back. Both cars disappeared around the corner. Probably the FBI guys, Jim thought.

He walked back to the second floor communications room and the bay of equipment he was testing. When Jim unlocked the computer screen and keyboard, he saw a notice appear: *'Unregistered Equipment Detected. Reboot computer to allow scan of peripherals. Click OK to reboot.'*

"What the hell is this?" he mumbled. He had never seen the error message before on the system. The proprietary SCCI software had been developed to control the massive second floor communication hub, as well as satellite stations on each floor of the building. The specialized software had been designed to sense invasive malware, and unregistered hardware and to purge itself of viruses, and any non-native commands. It also searched frequently for any equipment nodes that were not there during boot-up of the control computer, as well as to search for unidentified equipment that wasn't registered in the secure registry log. Password protection of the control program existed at every level, not just at the entry point. At the moment, Jim had only his password in the system. It was locked out to all others including the SCCI office.

Jim decided to be on the safe side and check a few things before he rebooted the system. *Probably a glitch in the program,* he thought, *maybe from some electrical noise.* But he was cautious and did some checking. He had experienced a locked-up system before, but had attributed it to electrical noise from arc welding on the floor below. This time, however, the presence of the error message made him nervous.

Jim opened a new window on the computer screen. Here, he toggled through program indexes until he found the peripheral equipment listing that had been generated during the most recent scan, the scan that precipitated the error message. The listing went on for several pages. At the bottom of the last page he saw two entries that looked strange. They both had similar descriptors.

Unidentified Hardware P
Location: Level 2SE
Portal: unknown

Unidentified Hardware P
Location: Level 2W
Portal: unknown

"P? What the hell is P?" Jim mumbled as he pulled down a HELP menu and typed in the letter P. The response came back as: *A parasitic hardware entity - does not provide an identifying handshake when queried.* The computer had discovered two such items, one in the interface cable housing in the southeast sector of the second floor, the other in the west sector. He sat there staring at the screen.

"This is really odd. What the heck am I looking at?" he said aloud. Was it real, he wondered, or some sort of glitch in the software? He argued with himself about rebooting the computer; that if it was a glitch, it would likely go away. But then on the other hand, on reboot the scanning program might accept the two entities as "Unknown," and include it in the start-up registry. No, he had to find out what had caused this before he lost the opportunity on reboot.

Jim thought about the equipment layout. He had supervised the installation of the computers and modems and now wondered what had been tampered with. On the southeast corner of the second floor was a locked closet containing automated telephone equipment that interfaced from the internal building communications nodes to outside telephone and data lines and broadband connections. The small room made of concrete blocks had a combination lock on the heavy door. He had set the six-digit combination himself the previous week when he initialized the equipment. He tried the door, it was locked. When he punched in the code, he heard the lock open. Inside, he turned on the overhead light and began a systematic inspection of the equipment bay.

After twenty minutes he was satisfied that the equipment had not been disturbed. He ran the self-check routine on the local control computer without an error alarm. Puzzled, he closed the equipment cabinet and looked at the external fittings. A power line came to the equipment bay through a sealed aluminum pipe. It didn't look like it had been tampered with. Jim opened the wall-mounted box that was the interface from the communications equipment to the outside telephone, data and broadband lines. He stared at the myriad line terminals and coaxial cable connectors. He ran his fingers up and down the twisted-pair telephone connections as he inspected each terminal. Everything looked as it should. He saw that the connector panel was hinged and retained by two twist-lock fasteners. He loosened the fasteners and swung the panel on its hinge so he could look behind it.

"What the hell?" he said aloud. A small black plastic container was fastened to the back panel of the interface box with a glob of what looked like clear silicone adhesive. He counted six wires connected to the telephone interface panel.

"Holy crap, what is this?" He knew that it wasn't part of the standard equipment, for he had supervised the installation of the equipment on this floor.

He walked over to a wire basket on the opposite wall and pulled out the equipment manual. He opened the book at the computer table and flipped through the pages until he came to the I/O Interface section. He went to the terminal panel and saw where the strange box had been connected. Back at the table, he quickly determined that the black box was getting electrical power from the telephone system and that wires were connected to modem terminals within the equipment bay.

This has gotta be a modem of some sort, thought Jim. *It may be sampling information from several lines and routing it to someone.* He couldn't tell just then to whom in the building the lines were leased, but he would ask SCCI headquarters to look it up for him.

"Sons o' bitches!" he exclaimed as he recalled the two men getting into the car and leaving when Tony Ferrari left. Although he hadn't identified the two from his perch two stories above the street, he was now almost certain it was the same two FBI agents he had met earlier in the week. "Sneaky bastards," he mumbled. He doubted that they had a court order for this little operation.

Jim took a voltmeter from a drawer in the computer desk and tested each wire connection of the strange box until he found the connection of DC power. Jim felt no guilt when he pulled out a pair of long-nose pliers from a drawer and disconnected all but two pairs of wires from the black box at the telephone panel. He found several unused terminals on the panel and reconnected the wires to those. He didn't disturb the connections to the DC power and what looked like connections to the module from outside lines. This way, whoever was controlling the box could still send in commands. The black box would still operate, but would not send back any information.

Jim smiled and closed the equipment room. Before locking the door, he changed the combination on the lock. His work log would keep track of the codes.

He would request a door sensor be installed that would allow the date and time to be entered into the computer log for each entry and exit for each communications room and equipment module on every floor.

He walked across the second floor, empty of workers, to the equipment closet at the west side of the building. This equipment was part of the intra-office network that routed telephone and data signals between clients in the building. Other networked equipment was located on alternate floors. He entered the combination, heard the click, and opened the door to the small room. He went straight to the I/O Interface box on the wall and opened it. All seemed okay, until he pulled the interface panel back on its hinge. There was another black box glued to the back of the housing.

"Goddamn bastards," he mumbled.

This box was the same size and with the same outward appearance, and with wires connected to the interface panel.

He looked in the tool drawer of the computer desk and found a pair of long nose pliers and again rendered the monitoring setup useless by reconnecting the wires to terminals that never would be used. He wondered how the black box was keyed on and off, but then decided that it was probably 'on' all the time. He changed the combination on the door before closing it.

Back in the main second floor communications room, Jim rebooted the computer, and poured some coffee from his thermos while the screen showed the sequence going through a dozen pages of setup protocol. When the setup routine was completed, the expected menu page appeared. There were no error messages.

He stared at the screen, rubbing his face. He wondered; was it his civic duty to help the FBI catch their alleged criminal targets? “Sure hate being manipulated,” he said aloud. Was there a court order to install these sophisticated bugs? Who were they after? DiCosta? Ferrari? No, he wasn't going to get sucked into any clandestine activity. If they wanted to serve a court order, then he would have to obey it. In the meantime, he would see who the taps were intended for. He picked up the telephone and punched in the number for Steve Arnold at SCCI headquarters in Albany.

Chapter 8

JUST AFTER 2 P.M., JIM picked up the ringing phone.

"Jim, Steve here. I have the info you asked about."

"Great. What'd you find out?"

"The telephone lines on the terminals that you mentioned are assigned to the DiCosta Construction Company and Ferrari Enterprises," said Steve. "They have leased the entire 2nd floor."

"Really? . . . Who else is signed up in the building?" asked Jim.

"I don't know. However, we only have work orders to wire up sixteen office areas on different floors. I'll send you an e-mail tomorrow with all the info."

"How about I get a door sensor installed that would allow the date and time to be entered into the computer log for each entry and exit and for each equipment module on all floors."

"I'll have to get *that* approved. I'll do it tomorrow. Assume it's approved unless you hear otherwise. I'll get the changed work order down to the site right away."

"Thanks, Steve. That'll be a help."

"So what's going on?"

"Let me get back to you on that. I'm not sure if there is anything going on. Don't get anyone worried, yet."

"Okay. I'll send you that stuff tomorrow."

Jim hung up the telephone and sat at his desk for a few minutes in thought. He had called his parents earlier, letting them know that he was staying in the city over the weekend. He'd tour some of the museums instead of going back to

Philadelphia. There wasn't much there but a vacant apartment. The telephone rang again.

"Jim, its Maria. Haven't heard from you in a few days. I was wondering if you're staying in town over the weekend."

"Hi. I called my parents earlier, told them that I wouldn't be there this weekend. There isn't all that much for me in Philly these days."

"Well . . . could we do dinner together? Or do you have other plans?"

"No plans. Sure, I'd love to go to dinner with you. What time?"

"I'll pick you up at 7:30, okay? May I pick the place?"

He laughed. "Of course, but not too fancy."

"Know just the place. See you at 7:30."

Jim put the phone down, sighing. Was this why he had stayed in the city this weekend? He couldn't deny the excitement he felt knowing he would be with her again for a few hours. It seemed he was thinking of her more and more. She certainly was a desirable beauty, but there was something more. He shook his head and got up from the desk, making sure all the cabinets and the desk were locked before walking to the front elevator. Work had stopped; it was after 4:30. The guard let him pass through the door in the chain link construction fence, mumbling a 'good night' as the gate latched closed again. He found a cab idling nearby and headed to his hotel.

Alfred's was a small steak house near Columbus Circle. A tiny bar near the front entrance opened into the more secluded dining area. The charm of the wood paneled interior and red leather booths was accentuated by the small intimate lamps that cast a warm glow in each booth.

"This is nice," said Jim as they were led by an elderly waiter back to a booth.

"Alfred and his family run the place," said Maria. "They've been here for ten years."

The waiter took their drink order and promised to come right back.

"I'm really glad you called," said Jim. "It's nice to see you."

"Haven't heard from you in several days. Missed you."

"Sorry. I've been up to my ears in stuff."

"Here at work?"

Jim nodded and then smiled. “What’s new in the interior decorating business?”

“Well, we received three new contracts in the past couple of days. It’ll keep us busy for the rest of the year. How ‘bout you? Anything exciting?”

Jim frowned and shook his head. “Things aren’t right over there.”

Maria chewed her lip. “I expect some trouble with the unions. A power struggle has been going on for some time with McGregor. He’s been trying every way he can to gain control of the electricians and riggers. Don’t know how much longer Ferrari will put up with it.”

“Is McGregor on drugs or something?”

“I don’t know. One thing for sure, though,” Maria said, shaking her head, “If Ferrari or Salerno found out he was, his career would be over.”

“Who’s Salerno?”

“Carmine Salerno is Ferrari’s boss. He’s seventy years old and a tough guy from the old school. He won’t tolerate anyone using or selling drugs in his outfit.”

“Other outfits surely do . . . don’t they?”

Maria nodded. “They do. And make a lot of money doing it. But the old man won’t have it.”

Jim scowled and looked at Maria. “I’m thinking the Walker Building might be laced with electronic bugs.”

Maria’s eyes widened. “You found some?”

Jim scowled. “Found two. It might be FBI handiwork.”

The waiter brought their drinks. Jim ordered the roast pork and Maria, the Cobb salad.

Maria looked at Jim. “I wouldn’t be surprised if the FBI is sneaking around. They’ve never gotten over not putting Ferrari in prison.”

“You think that’s what it’s about?”

Maria nodded. “I know my father has done some unsavory things in the past, but now he’s just trying to run a profitable and legal business, and mind his health.”

“The FBI is probably looking to find a weak spot they can exploit,” suggested Jim.

Maria hesitated, but then quietly said, “I have to assume that my father sees that certain funds make their way through Ferrari to the family. It’s how it’s done.”

Jim nodded. “Bugs and wiretaps, FBI’s favorite tactic.”

"FBI and IRS have been harassing my father as long as I can remember. I have to keep good records, too. The IRS audited me last year."

"What bastards," mumbled Jim.

"I suppose they're hoping to trip up my father or Ferrari with tax evasion or RICO charges."

Jim looked up and frowned. "It's been done before."

"Of course. And Ferrari may yet fall into a trap. But my father is keeping straight books and has a good accountant and attorney." She bit her lip again. "I don't want him to get hurt, and he can't go to prison again – it would kill him."

Jim nodded, not sure what to say.

"Don't guess you had to worry about that out on the Main Line, huh?" A smile teased her face.

Jim shook his head. "Not really. My parents were strict and put me through private school. Summers, we all went to Maine for a month. Anyhow, I liked being by myself and reading or exploring the woods."

Maria grinned. "No girl friends?"

"There was one in high school and a couple flings in college, but nothing serious until I graduated."

"So what happened?"

"We were engaged, but I broke it off a year ago." Jim shrugged. "We just wanted to go in different directions. What about you?"

They both looked up as the waiter arrived with their meals. When he retreated, Maria looked at Jim.

"That looks pretty darn good. May I have a taste?"

"Sure" Jim cut off a piece of the pork roast.

She reached with her fork to stab the sample and tasted it. "Damn, that *is* good." She looked at her salad. "Well, maybe next time."

"What about you? Grew up at your parents' place?"

"Yep. Maybe not as conservative as your parents; but still, they kept me on a short leash."

"Public school?"

She nodded. "Through eighth grade. Then I went to a private school in Connecticut."

"From there to Columbia?"

"Yep. Business Admin. It made my parents happy that I stayed local."

Jim grinned. "You must have had guys lining up at your door."

Maria laughed. "Hardly. My mother wouldn't let me go out with most of the guys that came by. 'Morons' she called them. I didn't find the dating scene very satisfying."

They chatted about themselves through supper. They relaxed when the dishes were cleared and they had fresh drinks.

Maria smiled at Jim. "Question for you."

"Okay."

"Tomorrow afternoon my parents are having an informal lawn party. They'd like to meet you, and asked that I invite you. What do you think? Will you come?"

Jim's face broke into a large smile. "I'd love to. Thank you."

Maria took a small notebook from her purse and tore out a page. She drew a map. "It's really easy to find." She handed it to Jim.

Jim looked at it for a moment. "Up past the Palisades."

"It'd be nice if you could arrive between 3:30 and 4, as most of the guests will be there already and things will have quieted."

Jim nodded. "Sure. What would be proper attire?"

"It's informal. A sport coat and tie would be good."

"I appreciate the invitation. I hope I don't turn out to be one of those 'morons' your mother spoke about."

Maria laughed. "No chance."

Chapter 9

JIM ARRIVED IN FRONT of the DiCosta estate at 3:40 in the afternoon. All he saw was a long stone wall with a driveway entrance marked by stone towers and antique lamps. He noticed video cameras on nearby trees. On pulling into the driveway, he was stopped by a closed iron-bar gate at a stone guard hut. Jim rolled down the window as a man in a dark suit approached. He held what looked like a TV remote control in his left hand. On his lapel was a small microphone. A small ear piece was visible in his right ear.

"Yes, sir. May I help you?"

"I'm here at Maria's invitation," said Jim.

The guard looked at Jim for a moment, and then backed away out of ear shot. Jim saw that he was talking on his lapel radio. In a minute he returned to the car.

"May I see your driver's license, sir?"

Jim shrugged and reached in his jacket for his billfold. He saw the guard stiffen, but then relax as the billfold came in view. The guard cast a quick glance at the photo and then pressed a button on his remote unit. The gate rolled open.

"Thank you, sir. Please drive to the end of the driveway and park. The entrance to the lawn party is on that side of the house. You'll see it."

"Thanks." He gave the guard a quick smile.

As Jim drove slowly around the gate, he saw another video camera in a tree and another near the ground. "Spooky place," he thought.

The parking lot was full of SUVs and expensive sedans, a sharp contrast to his rented Ford Taurus. Jim noticed cameras overlooking the parking lot and the side of the large house, an old two-story stone structure dating to the late nineteenth century.

Jim walked along a flagstone path to a heavy wooden gate, leading to the rear of the estate. He heard the merriment before he passed through the gate. Then, he saw a swimming pool and cabana, and a row of decorated tables with food. There was a portable bar manned by a bartender in a tuxedo. A crowd almost obscured it from view. Small tables around the pool were occupied with some guests in swim suits and some well dressed. Jim was awed by the beautifully maintained estate that disappeared at the cliffs overlooking the Hudson River. He further noticed the estate was ringed with an iron-bar fence, and that video cameras scanned the entire grounds and the back of the house.

Jim saw Maria part from a crowd and come toward him smiling. She looked beautiful in a white blouse and patterned skirt. She came up to him, kissed him lightly and grabbed his arm.

"You look lovely."

"Come on you handsome man. My mom and dad would like to meet you."

Jim felt awkward meeting Maria's parents, as they smothered him in welcoming hugs and thanked him for helping their daughter. He was happy to meet them, yet felt embarrassed and uncomfortable.

Maria took his arm and graciously excused herself from her parents while she introduced him to several other guests.

"Your parents have some guards among the guests?" he asked.

Maria smiled, nodded, and then led him to one of the guards, closest to her parents.

"Jim, I'd like you to meet Dom, the friend I mentioned to you earlier. He's been my parent's personal guard for many years," and then smiling at Dom, "as well as keeping an eye on me."

Dom was an older man whose eyes scanned Jim quickly.

"Dom, this is my friend, Jim. I mentioned that he would be visiting this afternoon."

Dom nodded and extended a hand to Jim. "Pleased to meet you, sir."

"Dom, we'll be wandering around. I'll show him the river," said Maria.

Again, Dom nodded and smiled. He slowly wandered off, keeping to the interior of the crowd.

"I don't think he likes me much," said Jim.

"Oh, don't worry. He's just very protective. He's been our bodyguard ever since I was little."

"He's not the only one. I counted three others," said Jim.

"Dom is special, though. He makes the security decisions and the other guys work for him. A while back, my father saved his parents from losing their business. When they passed away, he joined my dad's crew. Sometimes he goes with me if I have to go into the city at night. I'm never afraid when he's with me."

"Your mother is a sweet lady. Your father is a bit intimidating, though."

"He's mellowed. His stint in prison and his illness . . . I guess it makes him look at things differently now. Don't be afraid of him. When it comes to me, he and Dom are very protective; . . . may seem to be a bit overbearing. You weren't too comfortable back there."

"I'm sorry. I didn't mean to offend anyone."

"No, you didn't. I saw that you were uncomfortable with my mom and dad smothering you. They mean well. It's the first chance they've had to thank you."

Jim shuffled his feet and gazed downward.

"There. I've made you uncomfortable again." She pulled him behind a large chestnut tree, wrapped her arm around his neck, and kissed him. They looked at each other, and then she kissed him again, a kiss he returned. "I'm getting to like you." She smiled, her eyes sparkling.

He held her close for a moment. "You're growing on me, too."

Her voice was husky. "I know. I can feel it."

"Uh-huh. We'd better keep walking."

At the far end of the grounds, Maria guided Jim to a granite bench that offered a panoramic view over the Hudson River to the hills beyond. She snuggled against him, his arm around her shoulder. Their conversation was lighthearted, but then Maria looked at Jim.

"What are thinking? You're worried?"

Jim nodded. "I wonder what's going to come of the FBI involvement at the Walker Building. Also, I have to wonder about the attempt to hurt or kill you in that car wreck. I have a bad feeling this is all related somehow."

"My father thinks the trouble is the loose cannons in the McGregor faction of the Ferrari crew. He says McGregor is an ambitious psychopath – someone who has been a continuing problem for Ferrari. However, McGregor has been protected by his connections further up the family tree."

Jim shook his head and sighed.

Maria continued. "McGregor looks at my father as an irrelevant impediment to his ambitions, and that the business crew my father employs and the projects he manages should be his. I'm afraid of him, more than ever."

"It's hard to predict what a psychopath will do. You really need to be careful."

"Dom says he'll be staying close to me."

They looked across the Hudson as she pointed out features on the New Jersey side. In a few minutes they walked back to the party where Maria introduced Jim to several guests as they made their way to the lavish spread of food. The centerpiece was a gurgling punch fountain, either side arrayed with dishes of shrimp and lobster and dishes of finger food. When they sat at a table with their dishes, they were joined by her parents, and Jim was kept busy answering a myriad of questions. Maria tried to interject some levity and change the subject.

As darkness fell, Jim announced that he would be leaving and graciously thanked Maria's parents for their hospitality.

Maria took Jim's hand and walked with him to his car.

"Think I passed the test?" asked Jim smiling.

"They definitely like you."

"Your father seemed okay with me," said Jim.

"I think they're both glad I didn't bring home some mob moron."

"I think the jury's still out with Dom though. Don't you?"

"Maybe. He'll be checking you out in the next few days. He'll tell me."

"He won't like the FBI following me around."

"I'll talk to him about that. He needs to know," said Maria.

At Jim's car, Maria turned to him, wrapped her arms around his neck and they kissed passionately. He held her close for a moment, before she gently pushed him away.

"I'm glad you came," said Maria. "It meant a lot to my parents . . . and to me."

Jim opened the car door and then turned to her. "I hope they like me."

"*I* like you."

He smiled and started the car engine. Maria was still waving as he turned down the driveway.

Jim felt good about having been there with Maria, and admitted that her parents seemed like nice people, if somewhat overbearing. Her father didn't seem the ogre that his reputation suggested; but then, much had happened to him.

A few minutes later, he noticed headlights behind him, keeping pace with his changes in speed. It seemed so bazaar that the FBI would go through this trouble to watch him. What did they expect to learn? He resented the intrusion into his life, and of being used.

It was forty minutes into town and the car stayed with him. When he turned into the side street to the garage, he no longer saw anyone following. He left the car in the parking garage and walked the short distance to the hotel. No one seemed to be watching him.

Chapter 10

IN THE MORNING, WHEN the cab stopped at the Walker Building work-site entrance, Jim was greeted by the two FBI agents he had encountered earlier. They asked him to accompany them to the FBI office for a meeting.

"I'm under arrest?" asked Jim.

"No, no. We just need your cooperation. Give us an hour and we'll have you back here right away," said the leaner, older man, Jim knew as Wendell Somers.

"What's it about? I need a lawyer?"

"You're not under arrest. We would just like to talk to you quietly, and hopefully you can clear some things up for us," said Wendell.

"I'm calling my employer first." Jim pulled his cell phone from his pocket and scrolled to the number for Art Wagner, his supervisor at SCCI. While he advised Wagner of what was happening, Wendell's partner, Jack Reed, waved, and a car pulled up to the curb.

"Jim, cooperate with them. See what they want. If it becomes troublesome, call back. Okay?"

"Okay. Thanks. I'll keep you posted." Jim closed his phone and got into the car.

"Hey, we got good coffee down at the office. Maybe we can even find you some stale donuts," said Jack grinning.

"What the hell is this about?" Jim groused his displeasure. "I've got *real* work to do."

"Just give us an hour," said Wendell. "We'll have a little chat at the office and you'll be back here in a jiffy."

They were soon southbound on the Westside Highway. After a feeble attempt at small talk, the agents gave up and stayed silent. They exited onto Chambers Street, and in a few minutes they entered the parking garage at 26 Federal Plaza, the FBI New York Field Office.

Jim was led into a small meeting room, joined by agents Somers and Reed and two other agents. Introductions were made. A middle aged man came in before the meeting started and introduced himself as Leon Freedman, supervisor in the RICO branch. He greeted Jim, asked if he wanted anything for refreshment, and then gave his speech asking for cooperation in bringing to justice members of organized crime. He said that Jim's civic duty was to help law enforcement wherever he could, for society needed the cooperation of its citizens to rein in the lawless element in the city.

After the introduction, Freedman left the room and the meeting was spearheaded by Somers. He mentioned that although this was not a formal deposition, it was essential Jim's answers be forthcoming. Wendell started the questioning.

"Where do you live, Jim, when you're not in the city?"

Jim gave his apartment address in Philadelphia.

"Do you travel frequently between your home and New York City?" asked Somers.

"I'll travel occasionally to Philly to see my parents."

"Will you always stay at the Clarion Arms Hotel here in Manhattan?"

"Probably," said Jim. "It's convenient, and has a special rate with SCCI."

At that point Jack Reed cleared his throat. "Can you tell us who owns the Walker Building?"

"I don't know. I have to believe that you do though."

Reed ignored the taunt. "Who is the prime contractor at the Walker Building?"

Jim shook his head and grimaced. "As you already know, it's DiCosta Construction."

"What do you do for SCCI at the Walker Building?" asked Reed.

"I supervise the installation and setup of the communication system."

"Who issued the contract to SCCI?"

"I don't know and don't care. You'll have to ask my supervisor, Art Wagner."

"How do you receive your work orders?"

"The Poughkeepsie SCCI office issues formal work orders on paper and e-mail."

"What is to be delivered or accomplished by SCCI under the contract?"

"Installation of a computer controlled secure system for in-building and out-of-building communication."

"When is the SCCI contract scheduled to be completed?"

"The initial work, setting up the communication nodes, should be done by Labor Day. The connection to each client will depend on occupancy."

Jack glanced at Wendell.

"Are we done here, or what?" asked Jack pushing his chair back.

"I have a few more questions," said Wendell.

"Marvelous," said Jack and pulled his chair back to the table.

"Who's signed up so far to lease space in the building?"

"I don't know, but I understand there are at least three."

"What's the relationship between DiCosta Construction and the Ferrari crime organization?"

"Why don't you tell me?"

"Is DiCosta Construction part of a crime organization?" asked Wendell.

"Not that I'm aware of."

"Is Angelo DiCosta involved in the day-to-day operation of the company? If not, who is?"

"DiCosta is not. The manager of the construction company is Edward Marcelo."

Reed and Somers exchanged glances.

"What's your relationship to Maria DiCosta?" asked Wendell Somers.

"What business is that of yours?" Jim resented the inquiry about Maria and resolved to tell them as little as possible.

"We'd appreciate an answer so we can keep our heads clear," said Wendell.

"We're friends."

"What occurred at the DiCosta estate when you visited there a couple days ago?"

"Christ, you guys are something."

"Well, we know you were there."

"It was a garden party. Best shrimp I ever tasted."

"Who'd you meet?"

"I didn't know anyone but Maria. I met her parents and a few other guests whose names I've already forgotten. It was casual."

"Who would have reason to follow you from time to time?"

"Other than you guys, I don't know."

Jack Reed spoke. "Would you be willing to help the FBI gather information at the Walker Building?"

"Only if issued a direct order from SCCI," said Jim, glaring at the two FBI agents.

"Would you facilitate certain technical tasks if SCCI was served with a warrant?"

"I would obey any court order."

"Will you agree to keep this conversation and all others with the FBI secret?"

"Again, only if court ordered."

Jack Reed looked at Jim. "The FBI has people working on examining everything DiCosta and Ferrari are involved in, and you can expect to have company at the site from time to time."

"See the foreman, Ed Marcelo. Otherwise, its all the same to me."

Wendell Somers looked at Jack. "We appreciate your frankness and thanks for coming down here. I'll take you downstairs to the garage. There is a car waiting to take you back to the Walker building."

—

Leon Freedman, supervisor in the RICO branch, sat at the conference table with Jack Reed and Wendell Somers.

"We've been screwing around here for years. What the hell have you two been doing? We spent thousands of hours in preparation and testimony in the trial of DiCosta and Ferrari, only to have the federal prosecutor accept a plea from DiCosta to a much lesser charge that also got Ferrari off the hook. You guys remember all that?" Freedman glared at Somers and Reed. "We have squat to show for it."

"We've been trying to drive a wedge between DiCosta and Ferrari. We're making some progress . . . with McGregor."

"Progress? I want evidence," said Freedman. "The stupid-ass prosecutor let DiCosta take the hit for Ferrari. I want to indict Ferrari if it's the last thing I do."

"Did this Jim Randolph guy give you any information? Is he gonna help us or what?"

"He'll take a bit more convincing, I'm afraid," said Wheeler.

Freedman glared at the two agents. "In the meantime, I have orders to wrap this thing up. There's not to be any additional funding after the current allocation ends in three months."

"Three months?" said Wheeler. "You shitting me?"

"Listen," said Freedman. "I've got orders from higher up. We have to wrap it up."

"Three months, Jesus," muttered Wheeler.

"Unless there is some illegal union activity or kickbacks at that construction site, there isn't much for us to do *but* wrap it up," said Freedman.

"What about that asshole McGregor? We keep him on the string?" asked Wheeler.

Freedman shook his head. "I can't get support any longer to keep him on. This project is due to end in three months."

Wendell looked at Jack and scowled. "Well, that sucks." Then he looked at Freedman. "We're heading back up town."

Freedman nodded.

—

Back in the Walker Building, Jim called Art Wagner at SCCI and told him about the interview at the FBI office. Wagner asked that he be kept informed of conversations with the FBI, but otherwise, Jim was not to worry.

Jim spent the rest of the day upgrading the software in the second floor communications room. When he ran the scanning program, he was pleased to not detect any unaccountable nodes. He checked the equipment bay to be sure it had not been compromised since he had changed the lock combination on the room.

Before leaving the building, he called Maria from a construction phone and told her he'd be going to Philadelphia for the weekend.

"Seeing your parents?" she asked.

"I'd like to soften them up a little about you and your family."

"That may be impossible."

"I'll work on it."

"I love you, Jim."

"I love you, too."

Jim walked across the lobby to the glass doors, glad the work week was at an end. Before pushing the door open, he was surprised to see a large black car pulled up to the curb. He stared at it for a second and realized it was a Mercury Marquis. There didn't appear to be any damage on the front passenger side. *Is this the same car? Could it be?*

As Jim stared at the car, a man walked up to the passenger door, opened it, and got in. *Ain't it that son of a bitch, McGregor? Never had a good look at him, but I bet it's him.* When the car started to edge out into traffic, Jim pushed open the glass door and focused his attention on the license plate. He pulled a ball pen from inside his jacket and wrote the license number on his palm. *Son of a bitch. That's got to be the car that hit Maria.*

The street was already quiet. Gone were the crowds that usually streamed by at the end of the work day. *Everyone gets out early on Friday*. He stepped out into the street and hailed a cab.

Chapter 11

JIM HURRIED INTO the hotel; he wanted to catch the 7 o'clock train. It took but a few minutes to pack, and then he stood at the curb and hailed another cab. In thirty-five minutes he was in front of Penn Station. He glanced at his watch. He had ten minutes. The ticket lines were short and in a few minutes he descended onto the main track level. He boarded the Philadelphia train, tossed his bag on the overhead, and took his seat. He absently gazed out the window as the train chugged ahead. Then he closed his eyes and felt the tension slowly leaving his body. The image of the damaged Marquis persisted. Was it the same car? He'd have to find out. But how? He thought of Maria. He adored her, and knew he didn't want to lose her. But her family; what of her family?

He had fallen asleep. He looked at his watch. The train would arrive at the 30th Street Station in a few minutes. He looked forward to a hot shower and a good night's sleep. He'd spend the night at his apartment, and then see his parents in the morning.

His parents picked him up at noon and they went home to lunch. His mother was very curious about Maria, not altogether approving. His father seemed more concerned with his safety at the work site; and, yes, not to get his name scandalized in the newspapers. What did Jim know about her family, he asked? Jim told them about the party at the DiCosta estate and his favorable impression of Maria's parents. After lunch Jim spent several hours alone, enjoying the peace and quiet in the garden of his parent's estate.

In the afternoon, Jim called a friend who worked at the DA's office in Philadelphia. Ben Lansky had graduated from Temple University, while Jim was finishing at Drexel. Their friendship continued well beyond their days of beer-drinking and carousing. Ben was now a respected attorney and lived with his wife in a townhouse east of Independence Hall. After some small talk and good-natured kidding, Jim brought up what was on his mind.

"Have you ever heard of DiCosta and the Ferrari's?" asked Jim.

"Heard of them? Sure. The Ferrari tentacles reach down here," said Ben.

"How so?"

"Well, he's got some cousins that run loan sharking here. He's got part ownership in a couple of spaghetti joints and a dry cleaner in the south side. They got them from guys that couldn't otherwise pay up."

"Pay up for what?"

"Whatever. What's with all the questions?"

"I'm working at a building site that is being put up by DiCosta Construction, but I think there may be some Ferrari involvement," said Jim.

"Hey, give me a few seconds, I'll see what I can find in our computer."

"Okay. Next subject. Do you think you could find the owner of a car with New York plates?"

"You don't want much," he replied, sarcastically.

Jim gave him the plate number and make of car.

"Come on, what's this all about? I'm sticking my neck out."

"Just some trouble at the work site. Guy named McGregor is a pain in the ass. I'd rather check my facts before I say much, okay?" asked Jim.

"I've got the DiCosta file in front of me. Gimme a second." There was a pause. "Let's see . . . A variety of federal charges were dropped in a plea bargain. He did a short stretch. There's a section here on his construction business, but nothing jumps out at me. Some pictures here of him, his family and his big house."

"That's it?" asked Jim.

"I don't see much. There aren't any outstanding lawsuits or complaints. Keep in mind, the FBI have *their own* files. It looks like he's been keeping his head down since he's been outa the joint. Let me pull up Ferrari, bound to be something there."

"I thought there'd be something," muttered Jim.

"Ferrari. Oh, yeah. Lots here. Let's see . . . It looks like there are on-going investigations by the FBI. There are some RICO task force codes here, but I don't know what they mean. Tony Ferrari has managed to avoid indictment, but it looks like the big guns are trained on him. The last task force code was inserted only two weeks ago."

"Does it mention anything about DiCosta in that file?" asked Jim.

"No, just the earlier thing when Angelo took the rap. Hang on, the license plate trace is coming up."

"How'd you get that from New York?" asked Jim.

"Ain't sayin', but I have it. You got a pencil?"

"Yep, I'm ready."

"Okay, it's registered to Michael Puzo at a place called the Shady Lady. There are six traffic tickets against this guy, all in Manhattan."

"Nothing else on him?"

"Hang on; I'm running him now," said Ben. "Come on, Jim. Tell me what is going on."

"I will, as soon as I've got my facts straight."

"Hey, here it is. Michael Puzo, a.k.a. Big Mack, age 33, 6'2", 250 pounds, hair black. I don't see any warrants, just the traffic tickets. Previous arrests are attempted murder, and assault and battery. Charges later dropped. Under known associates it mentions some Philly names I recognize, as well as Tony Ferrari and a Mike McGregor. That your guy?"

"Yeah, a real crazy," said Jim.

"Ferrari did three years out of six in Joliet when he was young for assault with deadly weapon. Don't have anything on McGregor."

"Ben, I really appreciate this info. I'll call you when I'm back in New York and have a chance to figure this out."

"It's good hearing from you. Stay out of trouble. . . . You hear?"

Sunday afternoon, Jim's mother put her coffee cup in the saucer and turned to look at him. "But she's not from around here – not one of us."

"That doesn't make her a bad person, mom," said Jim.

"How are you going to introduce her at the club?" asked his father. "Maria, daughter of a mobster? People are going to ask, you know."

"Jim," his mother spoke softly, "we just want what's best for you. For you to have a good life. Your father is right. People here will make an issue of it."

"Mom, if you met her, you'd like her."

His father shook his head. "I don't think that's the issue, son."

Jim pushed back his chair. "Thank you for dinner, Mom." He smiled. "It was as delicious as ever."

"Why are you running off?" she asked.

"I want to get an early train."

"Give me a few minutes and I'll drive you to the station." His father grimaced but didn't make any other comment.

Chapter 12

THE COMMUNICATIONS modules had arrived Monday morning in non-union trucks. Mike McGregor, still trying to wrest control of Teamsters Local 321, stood in the street in heated conversation with DiCosta Construction people.

Jim got out of the cab in front of the Walker Building and saw McGregor waving his arms and yelling. He heard a car stop behind him and turned to see who had arrived. He saw a large man with drooping jowls and an eagle-beak of a nose just before a fist slammed into the side of his face.

"Mind your own business, asshole, or you'll get worse."

Jim fought to stay conscious, but the second fist knocked him cold to the ground.

He woke up sitting on the sidewalk and against the building. Several workers from the building hovered around him.

Jim shook his head. "How long I been out?" He rubbed the side of his face.

"Hey, man. You okay?" said one man he didn't recognize. Another voice, "Want to call 9-1-1?"

He shook his head. "No. I'll be okay. Help me up."

Two men pulled Jim to his feet.

"Anyone know that guy?" asked Jim, not expecting anyone to volunteer a name.

The two men glanced at each other and shook their heads in unison. "Don't know him," said one.

Jim called the SCCI office in Poughkeepsie and reported the incident to Art Wagner.

"Did you go to the hospital? Get checked out?" asked Art.

"No. I'll be okay. My face is swollen, but there isn't anything broken."

"You oughta get checked out."

"I will if I start to feel worse," said Jim.

"I want you to file a complaint with the police."

"Oh, Okay."

A policeman had taken a report of the incident and departed.

"Waste of time," Jim muttered. Then pulled his phone from his jacket pocket and dialed Maria's number.

"Hi gorgeous."

"Hi yourself. You standing outside?

"Yep. Leaning against the building, getting some sun." He cleared his throat. "Ran into a fist this morning."

"What?"

Jim heard the alarm in her voice. "I'll be okay. Some guys musta been waiting for me to arrive. I heard a car pull up, but he decked me with two punches to my face before I knew what was happening."

"Oh my God! You're hurt, aren't you? Call the cops?"

"Face is swollen. It's pretty sore. Cop just left."

"Oh Jim, I'm so sorry."

"I'm gonna go to the hotel and get some sleep."

"I can reschedule. I can come over."

"Thanks. No, don't. I'm going to get some sleep. It's what I need."

"Wh . . . Why did he beat you? Who was it?"

"I don't know who it was. If anyone knows, they're not saying."

"Why did he do that?"

"I remember the jerk saying that I should mind my own business or I'd be getting worse."

"Jim, I'm calling Dom right now. I want him to know."

"I'll be okay. I need some sleep."

"I'm calling him. He has to know about it."

"Okay. I love you, gorgeous."

"Oh, Jim . . ."

Jim awoke early Tuesday morning and stood in the shower enjoying the warm flow of water over his face. The sight in the mirror was not encouraging; his was knotted with deep purple bruises.

He ate breakfast at the hotel. Each bite hurt his jaw, and he left half of the food untouched, but finished his coffee. Outside, he waited for a cab. He wondered; had McGregor seen him the other day writing the license number on his palm? A chill went up his back. Is this why he was attacked?

Before Jim's cab got to the Walker Building, he received a call on his cell phone. A police sergeant asked if Jim could come to the local precinct and look at a mug book, hopefully to identify the man that attacked him. Jim redirected the cab driver to the police station.

Jim sat at a table looking through books with hundreds of photos. He wasn't sure his brief glimpse of his attacker would be enough, but he kept turning the pages. The sergeant sat patiently as Jim flipped page after page. Ten minutes later, Jim stopped and pointed.

"That's him." He turned to the sergeant. "This is the guy."

The policeman looked where Jim had his finger. "You're sure about that?"

"Yes. This is the guy who hit me."

The sergeant pulled a notebook from his vest pocket and wrote down the particulars. "Michael Puzo, a.k.a. Big Mack."

"That's the guy," repeated Jim.

When Jim arrived at the Walker Building, he looked for the DiCosta Construction supervisor. He found Greg Matthews on the fourth floor watching the ground crew hoist a communications module up to the loading shelf. Jim held a short meeting with Greg to review the work schedule for the installation of the communications modules on the even numbered floors.

The afternoon was spent running acceptance tests on the second floor equipment installation. The tests went smoothly. No errors showed up on the control computer. He was glad that he had changed all the lock combinations on all the communication room doors.

Jim had called Maria and asked her to join him for supper at his hotel dining room. He still didn't feel normal and wanted to get an early sleep. When he returned to his hotel, he found the message light illuminated on the phone. The message was short. "Keep your fucking nose out of the labor."

At supper, Jim could see Maria was upset. She chewed on her lower lip as he related his earlier experience starting with seeing McGregor getting into the black Mercury Marquis.

"You didn't see the driver?"

Jim shook his head. "My friend in Philly said it belonged to this Puzo guy. You heard of him?"

"No. It's the guy that ran me off the road?"

"It was that car or one just like it. The damage had been fixed."

"And McGregor got in the car with him?"

"Yep. Those two know each other."

"I have to tell Dom," said Maria. "He'll know what to do."

—

Angelo DiCosta awoke on Wednesday, troubled by what Dominic had told him. His conversation with his daughter the previous evening had left him worried and anxious for Maria's well being. He knew if her friend, Jim, was being threatened, it was ultimately aimed at him. Angelo called Tony Ferrari after breakfast and asked for a lunch meeting at an old pizza haunt in Brooklyn that neither had been at in years. Tony agreed without inquiring further.

The two men greeted each other warmly and found a seat in a back booth out of earshot from other lunch patrons. They both declared they were hungry, so a large pizza was ordered with a pitcher of beer.

"Smells just like it did back in the day," Tony commented.

"Same old guy owns it; runs it with his son."

"You're looking good. I'm glad to see you doing well."

"Yeah, it's my daughter I worry about."

"Tell me about it."

Angelo related what Dominic had told him and emphasized that McGregor had been seen getting in a car that belonged to Puzo.

"Maria thinks it's the same car that ran her off the road, and that this guy Puzo was driving it."

Tony looked at Angelo and shook his head slowly.

"I'm afraid . . . afraid that Maria is going to be hurt or killed . . . to force a wedge between us."

Tony grimaced. "You and me . . . we're like brothers. . . . Remember that."

"Tony, if it was Puzo . . . ran my daughter off the road . . . almost killed her. If it was him . . "

Tony nodded. "If it *was* him, . . . he's done."

—

A hot shower and a nap was all he wished for Thursday afternoon as the cab stopped at his hotel. That was before he felt the phone buzzing in his pocket as he got out of the cab. He smiled when he saw Maria's number on the display. "Hi, was just thinking of you."

"Anything you can say out loud?"

"Probably best if I didn't."

"Why don't you come over for a drink? Maybe then you'll tell me what you were thinking."

"We could go out for a bite to eat afterward," suggested Jim.

Maria laughed softly. "We'll see."

Jim showered, shaved and changed his clothes. On the way to Maria's apartment, he asked the cab driver to stop at a liquor store where he picked up a bottle of Chardonnay. When the cab arrived at Maria's, he stepped out and looked around. Where was Dom, he wondered?

When Maria opened the door, Jim felt his heart skip a beat. She was dressed in a tight-fitting white blouse and Kelly green shorts. Her hair hung below her shoulders.

"You look dazzling," said Jim. He handed her the bottle of wine.

"Well, you can start by taking off that tie."

He started to undo the tie knot.

"And the jacket, too."

He handed Maria the tie and jacket, then stared at her as she left the living room. His heart beat rapidly. He hoped he wouldn't embarrass himself without the jacket to shield him. He couldn't dismiss the urgency he felt.

Maria reappeared from the hallway. "You haven't been here before. What do you think of my place?"

"It's really nice," said Jim. "But then you *are* a decorator."

"You *really* like it?"

Jim looked at the furniture and pictures and bookcase, and then gazed into the small dining room. "It works for me." Jim smiled. "I *do* like it."

"Have a seat while I pour some of this for us. What did you do today?"

"Trouble-shooting some computer errors. Boring stuff. Kept thinking about the guy punched me, and the big Mercury."

Maria scowled and shook her head. "I hope they put that car in a crusher . . . with him in it."

"Not my favorite guy, either." He rubbed his face. "I'm still a little sore."

"Dom told me dad was going to speak to Ferrari today. Find out what he could about this creep. See if McGregor was part of it."

"What happens then?" asked Jim.

Maria shrugged. "I keep thinking about a crusher."

"Someone else will replace him. . . ."

"Let's not think about that right now."

She carried two glasses of wine into the living room and placed them on the coffee table. As she sat down next to Jim, he put his arm around her shoulder. She turned toward him slightly, pressing her breast against him, her hand coming up to his face. Their lips met in a soft teasing kiss that quickly developed into a passionate embrace.

Maria pulled open Jim's shirt as his hands explored her body.

"Bedroom?" he moaned.

"No," she gasped as he pulled her blouse off her shoulder.

The wine glasses stood untouched.

The next morning as Jim got into a cab, he opened the Friday morning paper. When he turned his attention to page three, he saw the article, *Car and Body Pulled Out of East River.* He started to read and goosebumps ran down his arm. The short article mentioned that a vagrant had spotted the roof of a car just under the surface of the water and mentioned it to someone with a cell phone who called police. The article went on to identify the body in the car as Michael Puzo, a.k.a. Big Mack, a reputed mob figure known to the police.

Jim smiled and folded the paper as the cab approached the Walker Building. He was glad that Maria would not be threatened by him any longer. And, he felt a measure of satisfaction because of the beating Puzo had given him.

When Jim returned from a quick lunch, two suits approached him by the second floor communications room.

"Well, if it ain't the F.B. freakin' I. Why do I deserve such distinguished visitors?"

Agent Somers looked at Agent Reed. "Jerk-off making fun of us?"

Reed smiled as Jim approached. "Might be."

Jim stopped in front of the man and stood there unsmiling.

"We need to have a little chat. Won't take up too much of your time."

Jim stood there and didn't say anything.

Reed raised an eyebrow. "What was that little ruckus about the other evening out by the street? Your face still looks kinda purple."

"Not sure," said Jim. "I think he didn't like me."

"I can't understand that." Somers looked at Reed. "Can you?"

Reed grinned. "You gotta get a better class of friends, Jim."

Jim looked at Reed and then Somers. "That just occurred to me."

Reed shook his head. "All we're trying to do here is see if there is a connection between the trouble down on the street and this guy pulled out of the river last night."

"Who was that?"

"Of course you know. It was Puzo."

Jim shrugged. "No shit?"

"You were home all last night?" asked Reed.

"As you already know, I was indoors all night."

"Yeah, we know," said Somers, a crooked grin twisting his mouth.

"Did you have anything to do with the demise of Michael Puzo," asked Reed.

"I didn't kill him," replied Jim. "But I'm not sorry he's dead."

"We're not sure about you," said Somers. "Seems like you had a real motive."

"You *know* where I was yesterday and last night," said Jim.

Reed scowled. "Yeah, we know."

—

It was after five when McGregor entered the bar, nodded at the bartender, and knocked at the heavy back room door. Casey's was a workingman's bar wedged between a small parking garage and a rundown strip mall on the East Side. Its day had come and gone a decade ago, and now was a meeting place for McGregor's cohorts. Truck drivers and local laborers kept the place alive in the evenings. A few working-girls came and went on Friday and Saturday nights. But it was McGregor's generous contributions for the use of the back room that kept Casey's afloat. McGregor heard the heavy bolt slide and the door opened.

McGregor stormed into the room and went immediately to the large table near the back. Three men from Local 321 Teamsters, and two from the 4119 Electrical Workers were seated, with mugs of beer and a bowl of popcorn. McGregor pulled a folded newspaper from under his arm and tossed it at Marc Fontana.

"Page three. Read it," growled McGregor.

The table got quiet as Fontana opened the paper. McGregor glared at the men seated. He pulled out a chair as a kid came into the room from the kitchen with another pitcher. "Leave it," groused McGregor. The youngster did as he was told and beat a hasty retreat.

"All right," McGregor directed his question at Fontana. "What the hell happened?"

Fontana passed the paper to the guy next to him. "Shit. This is the first I heard of it," said Fontana. He shook his head. "Why did they do Big Mack?"

"That's what I want to know," yelled McGregor. "What the hell was he into? What the hell is goin' on that I don't know about?" McGregor's face turned a dark shade as he looked from one of the men at the table to the other. No one said anything. "Listen, goddamn it. You guys get your asses out on the street. Who the hell took him down? It weren't an amateur, that's for goddamn sure. Find out who. Find out what happened. Get back to me right away."

The men got up from the table and headed for the door.

"Fontana. Come back here," said McGregor.

He came up to McGregor. "I don't know anything, boss. I'll be asking around."

McGregor glared at him. "See that you do that. Someone takes out one of my best guys. What the hell?"

"I'll get back to you."

"Yeah. Don't make me have to come look for you."

The door closed with a thud as the men left. McGregor's fist came down hard on the table. "Goddamn it!"

He sat alone nibbling on a doughnut. It was unbelievable that someone had killed Big Mack. And then, to find him in that car. Why? Why go to all the trouble of putting Big Mack into that car? And then what? Drive it into the goddamn East River? Him and that car?

He recalled the mission he had sent Big Mack on. Hell, that had been months ago, he thought. It was to terrorize her, to send a message to her old man, to prompt the old bastard to give it up – sell out to *him*. No one had known about that; it had been their secret. Someone would pay, he promised himself.

—

"Walls are going up fast," Jim said to himself as he inspected the lower floors. A special construction technique was being used for the interior walls and ceilings in the designated secure area of each floor. Behind the drywall was a nickel alloy screen of $^1/_8$ inch mesh applied behind all wall and ceiling surfaces. This made the interior space a virtual sealed box to radio signals, except for the windows.

Jim was told the windows employed a soft polymer layer on the interior that would be translucent but absorb sound vibrations. Also, a screen mesh was embedded in the polymer. The only view through a clear window would be in the non-secure lobby areas of each floor.

Jim was pleased with the work progress. All communications modules were in place on each floor and were being wired by DiCosta electricians. Jim realized there would be a lot of pressure on him to complete the setup and testing, as the modules got connected to the system.

Chapter 13

THE NEXT FRIDAY MORNING, Jim was in the sixth floor communications room preparing to make the preliminary setup on the equipment. He spent an hour reviewing the manuals and the signed-off installation certificates. It was almost 11 o'clock when he began the test procedures.

Jim soon realized he had a major problem. Switching-sequence testing to acquire outside lines showed an unusually long delay in acquisition. Occasionally, an error message appeared on the computer screen:

Trunk connect not completed, timing sequence interrupt.

Repeating the test several times produced the same error message.

"Well, hell." Jim stood up and stretched. "Better check on 5 and 7." He closed the comm room door and locked it, then headed up the stairs to the seventh floor.

The equipment in the seventh floor comm room had not yet been initiated or tested, so Jim spent a half hour testing for a proper installation before running tests. The first test sequence completed without an error message. Jim stopped the test and went to the fifth floor.

The equipment in the comm room of the fifth floor went through the initiation procedure without any difficulty. Jim sat back in front of the control computer and pondered the problem. He knew, the problem was isolated to the sixth floor comm room – or was it?

Jim realized the communication nodes on each floor connected directly to the automated routing and control equipment on the second floor, which then connected to outside lines and broadband connections using computer controlled priority codes. He abandoned further testing of the fifth floor equipment and instead went downstairs to the second floor trunk line module in the locked concrete comm room. He saw no evidence of unauthorized entry into the locked room. He turned on the display for the control computer and checked the access log. No computer entries had been made since the door switches had been installed the previous weekend.

When he pulled up the test page for the sixth floor circuits, the same error message appeared: *Trunk connect not completed, timing sequence interrupt.* When he did a manual disconnect of the sixth floor circuits at the computer and repeated the test, the error message disappeared.

"Damn," he mumbled. "The trouble has to be between the sixth floor and the input to the trunk module here in this room." He shook his head. "It's going to be a long day."

Jim went back to the sixth floor. There he found a footstool allowing him to reach inside the space behind the ceiling tiles. He followed the cable from the comm room, across the ceiling space, to the junction box mounted on the outside of the elevator shaft, just inside the secure area. He stared at the box, its cover secured with a number of screws. It didn't look as if anyone had disturbed it; but then, who knows, he wondered.

He sprinted back to the comm room, grabbed the tool box and ran back to the elevator. In the tool box was a socket set and he reached for the $^{3}/_{8}$ inch driver. In a minute he had the panel removed. He knew immediately there was an unusual item in the junction box. A black molded plastic module was adhered to the housing wall. On closer inspection, Jim discovered every outgoing line from the sixth floor was tapped into the foreign module. Initially unseen, Jim discovered another module attached to the side of a large conduit, a thin pair of wires running behind the pipe and into the junction box terminating in the strange black module.

"What the hell is this?" exclaimed Jim.

He studied the configuration of wires carefully. He saw that one thin wire was glued to the concrete wall surface with a glob of silicone.

"Damn. That's got to be an antenna." Jim stared at the junction box. "How do they get power to this thing? Not batteries . . ." That's when he recognized it. A clamp-on magnetic coupler had been placed around power lines running through the junction box. "Well, kiss my ass. This is really slick. It's self powered from the power line. No dummy, this guy . . . whoever he is." He realized the well-hidden installation would not be easily detected except for the degraded performance noted on the computer.

"These two modules transmit all the information present on all the outgoing lines using a small radio transmitter," he muttered. "This has to be FBI. Who else?"

Then Jim laughed out loud at the futility of the installation. He knew, when these floors were completed, there wouldn't be any radio signals leaving the well-shielded areas. All outgoing calls, fax transmissions and internet traffic would be encrypted communications over optical cables.

He reconnected all the module wires he had disturbed to a single unused terminal. It would take some time, he knew, for anyone to get to the box to correct it. In the meantime, he would ask that the junction box housing be modified to allow a padlock; maybe not foolproof, but a deterrent at least.

He didn't feel as if he was working against justice, if indeed the FBI had installed the sophisticated taps. Instead, he thought all the surreptitious activity was focused on retribution against the DiCosta elder, not against the main troublemakers of the day.

Jim walked down to the second floor communications room and started the test routine again on the computer. He smiled when the computer went by the previous spot where the error message had appeared and continued with the test sequence.

Has to be the FBI responsible for this, he thought. *But, I'm sure those two jerks didn't install this stuff. They had help.*

Jim stared at the screen as the test sequence proceeded. "Damn it," he exclaimed. "It's got to be someone in the construction crew – some electrician. I have to find out who is helping the FBI."

He wondered whether he should ask Greg Mathews, the foreman of the DiCosta crew at the building, about identifying an electrician. By the time the test sequence had completed, he had made up his mind to not trust anyone with what he was thinking. Instead, he called SCCI and asked for them to e-mail a list of the DiCosta employees at the site, since all of them had been registered at the beginning of the contract with SCCI.

When he later perused the list of employees, there was one name that stood out, Marc Fontana, a supervisory electrician. He had met the man while supervising the installation of a power transformer on the second floor ledge. Jim had seen him recently working inside the elevator shaft. The other electricians named on the listing were not likely experienced enough to manage an installation of the complexity he had found.

Jim closed the communications room and left the building. Outside the main door, he pulled his cell phone from his jacket pocket and called his friend, Ben Lansky, in the Philadelphia DA's office.

"Ben. It's Jim Randolph."

"Yeah, how you doin'?"

"I have a quick question. You up for it?" asked Jim.

"Oh, what the heck. Give it to me."

"Would you look up a Marc Fontana on your bad-boy lists and see if he pops up?"

"Hang on . . . What's he done?"

"I'm not sure yet."

"He doesn't show up locally. Let me try NCIC."

"Appreciate it, Ben."

"Yeah, well, what kind of trouble you getting yourself into?"

"Working with a rough crowd at this building site."

"Whoa! Here we go. Your boy served 12 years in Leavenworth for robbery and assault on a FBI agent in Chicago."

"Really? He's working as the lead electrician at this work site – a union member."

"Musta turned over a new leaf. Says here he's a master electrician by trade. He doesn't have any other arrests."

"Thanks. This is helpful," said Jim.

"So what's he done?"

"Don't know yet. I have more checking to do."

"You be careful with this guy."

"Thanks. I'll be in touch." Jim closed his phone. Had the FBI recruited Fontana, put muscle on him because of his record? Could he have it all wrong, he wondered? Maybe it wasn't Fontana. He'd better be careful in investigating this, he mused.

If it was Fontana, Jim pondered, he didn't want him to end up like Puzo. It could happen if the wrong party found out Fontana had been exposed. He'd be a liability to the FBI, maybe to McGregor as well, since he affectively controlled the Electrical Workers Local 4119.

Jim went with Maria that evening to her favorite pizza place, a small storefront near the East River. Their small talk kept coming back to the troubles at the Walker building. Jim didn't mention his suspicion of Marc Fontana, he wanted to be sure. They agreed to spend Saturday together and just hang out.

It was after nine when the taxi pulled up in front of her apartment building. She kissed him and opened the door. Jim put a hand on her arm.

"I'll walk you up."

She smiled. "That'll be nice."

When they entered the lobby she greeted the guard. "Good evening, Fred."

"Ms DiCosta . . . there were two phone calls that came into the lobby earlier; he asked for you."

Maria and Jim looked at each other. "Did he give a name . . . or a phone number?" she asked.

"No. I asked, but he hung up both times."

"Thank you Fred."

"Think it was Dom?"

Maria shook her head. "He'd call my cell phone. No. Something odd about this."

At the fourth floor, they turned down the hall toward Suite 404.

"Do you want to call Dom?" asked Jim. "Have him look around?"

"I'll give him a call in a few minutes."

Maria put her key into the door lock, turned the brass handle, and pushed the door open. Facing them just inside the doorway was a well dressed man with a gun and wearing a ski mask.

"Get in here. Both of ya."

Maria gasped. "Who . . . who are you?"

"What the hell you doing here?" challenged Jim. "Get the hell out."

As the door closed with a clang of the lock, the gun man grabbed Maria and tossed her like a rag doll against a lamp table. She cried out as the table toppled and the lamp crashed to the floor.

When Jim lunged toward the gunman, the man swung viciously and slammed the gun into the side of Jim's head. He fell to the floor, blood running down his face and crawled to Maria. "Are you hurt?"

"I'm okay," she mumbled. She grasped his arm, never taking her eyes from the masked intruder.

The intruder waved the gun at Jim and ordered him to stand. As soon as he stood up, the intruder punched him in the face, followed by a blow to the stomach. Jim staggered but stayed on his feet. The intruder glanced at Maria and then pushed Jim to the wall, ordering him to face it. He pulled flex cuffs from his pocket and began to fasten them on Jim's wrists. That's when Maria leaped. A golden letter opener glistened in her hand. The intruder started to turn, his pistol coming around, but it was too late. With a banshee-like yell, Maria drove the saber-shaped tool into his neck.

Jim turned and grabbed the man's gun arm. The shot went wild; the small caliber bullet went into the drywall. The man dropped the pistol and clasped a hand on the letter opener. The blade came free and blood spurted against the wall and across the beige rug. In slow motion, he fell to his knees, then forward onto his face. Blood spurted and pooled on the rug.

Maria and Jim held each other and stared. The blood stopped spurting.

"Call 9-1-1," he gasped as he bent to check on the man.

But Maria stood there, mouth agape, wide eyed, staring at the intruder. Jim fumbled for his cell phone and dialed 9-1-1. He gave the operator the address and then went to Maria, gently pulling her against him. She was shaking.

"Oh, God. Is he dead?" Her voice shook. "Did I kill him?"

He held her for several minutes, calmly talking to her, reassuring her that she had saved them both.

When there was loud banging on the door, Jim opened it. Two policemen rushed in, two others stood outside the door. All had their weapons drawn. Jim and Maria were told to sit on the sofa. One officer called someone on his radio while another officer told a third that the man on the floor was dead. The same officer made a call on his cell phone.

Jim held Maria against him.

Tears ran down her face. “I killed him,” she whispered.

In minutes two detectives, a man and a woman, arrived with two paramedics. Twenty minutes later, the medical examiner came into the room. Jim watched as countless photos were taken, a chalk outline was made, and many tape measurements made. The paramedics removed the body when the medical examiner left.

The two detectives informed Maria and Jim that hey would have to stay somewhere else for a day or two as the suite was now a crime scene. But first, they would have to come to the police station for an interview.

“Are we under arrest?” gasped Maria.

“The ADA will determine that,” said the male detective. “But for now, you both need to come with us to the station for an interview.”

“Can I bring some clothes?”

The female detective replied. “I’ll go with you and you can get some clothes, but we’ll go to Police Plaza as you are.”

Maria looked at Jim. “I need to call my lawyer and Dom.”

Jim nodded. “Yes.”

Chapter 14

WHILE THEY SAT IN a police car and the officers conferred by the building, Jim called his office and left a message to inform his boss of the situation. Maria left a message for Dom.

They tried to understand what had happened and why. Maria looked at Jim. “Are we going to be arrested?”

“I hope not. It was self defense.”

“I killed someone.” Maria stared at Jim.

Jim reached for her hand. “You saved my life.”

“I don’t understand why all this happened.” Her lip trembled.

“The guy never said what he wanted.”

Maria shook her head. “He didn’t search for anything. Nothing looked disturbed.”

Jim gasped. “Was he there to kidnap you?”

She shook her head again. Her eyes filled and she wiped at them with the back of her hands.

“It had to be that bastard McGregor. It had to be,” said Jim. “The son-of-a-bitch is moving against you, your dad and Ferrari. It’s *got* to be him.”

Maria wiped her eyes again. “I don’t know, but I’m scared of how my father will react when he hears about this. I’m afraid he’ll overreact, and play right into the hands of the FBI.”

Maybe that’s it, thought Jim. *That’s their plan.*

Maria and Jim were informed that they were not under arrest, but as a man had been killed, certain formalities had to be observed. The Miranda rights were read to Jim and Maria and they were led into separate interview rooms. Both were fingerprinted and photographed. Each was tested for gunshot residue (GSR). No blood was found on either Maria's or Jim's clothing. The detectives acknowledged that blood spatter from the victim of the stabbing had been away from the pair, splattering on the wall and rug.

The interview was held at midnight when an ADA arrived. Dom and Maria's lawyer had arrived a few minutes earlier. Jim waved his rights to representation, but Maria insisted that her lawyer be present in the room during questioning. Maria and Jim told identical versions of events which corresponded well with the police reports and that of the coroner. When Maria asked for the identification of the intruder, the ADA hesitated and then looked at her notes.

"We have him as Gerry Scalia."

"A local thug," mumbled the lawyer.

Maria shook her head. "Never heard of him."

"You sure you don't know him?" asked a detective.

"She said she didn't know him," replied the lawyer.

The detective scowled, but didn't pursue it. The interviews continued with numerous questions and challenges by the ADA. The lawyer for Maria interceded to blunt intimidation. The ADA inquired repeatedly as to why the attack had taken place. Maria stated she didn't know and didn't voice any suspicions. An hour later, the interviews ended. Jim and Maria were cautioned to keep themselves available as further inquiry could be expected.

It was almost 1:30 in the morning when Jim and Maria were allowed to leave the police station. The lawyer lagged behind to finish details, while Maria and Jim walked into the lobby.

"What the hell?" uttered Jim.

Standing in conversation with Dom was FBI Agent Jack Reed.

"What're you doing here?" demanded Jim.

"I got ears – hear things."

Maria went to Dom who put an arm around her and led her to a couch.

"So, what the hell you doing here?" asked Jim.

"You can't stay outa trouble, huh?"

Jim scowled. "I don't need this right now. What do you want?"

“Just a couple things. I was outside the room. I heard what you said, but really, why was the guy in her room?”

Jim shook his head. “Don’t know. We just don’t know.”

“Could it have something to do with Ferrari?”

Jim shrugged. “Don’t know. Why?”

Reed got close to Jim and in a low voice said, “Because we made this guy, Gerry Scalia, to be a real bad-ass that hangs with McGregor’s guys.”

Jim looked at Reed with surprise. “Never heard of him.”

“This guy has a mile-long rap sheet, but rape and assault on women isn’t on it. He steals cars, raids warehouses, transports stolen goods . . . stuff like that,” said Reed.

Jim shook his head again.

“I gotta believe this thing with Maria was a means to an end,” said Reed. “Maybe to make trouble for her old man?”

Jim was getting impatient. “When you figure it out, let me know.” He walked away to join Maria and Dom.

Dom shook hands with Jim. Maria asked, “What’d he want? Interview?”

“No.” Jim scowled, “FBI. He was trying to tie the assault to your father, Ferrari, or McGregor. I didn’t tell him anything.”

Dom nodded. “They’re always looking for a crack in the armor.”

Maria took Jim’s arm. “Dom said dad is going nuts. I gotta call him.”

Jim nodded. “Okay.”

“He’ll be glad to hear that you weren’t hurt,” said Dom. “But he ain’t gonna sit still for this.”

“I’ll call him soon as we get back to the hotel.” She looked at Dom. “I’m staying with Jim while my place gets renovated. They’ll start tomorrow. Take a few days.”

Dom looked at Jim and nodded slowly. Then he looked at Maria. “I’ll be close by.”

Maria smiled. “Thank you.”

Later in Jim’s hotel room, Maria had a long conversation with her father. Jim stepped out into the hallway to give her privacy. He looked down the long hallway and spotted a man near the far end. He leaned against the wall and looked in Jim’s direction frequently. Was he waiting for an elevator, Jim wondered? But after several minutes he knew that the man was not interested in the elevator. Jim started walking toward him. Well before Jim came to him, the man disappeared around the nearby corner. Jim hurried to the corner and looked down the other hallway, but there was no one in sight. Had that been a cop, he wondered? Or was it some goon? FBI? Jim turned and went back toward his room. He turned and looked back, but there was no one. *Something doesn't feel right.*

Inside the room, Maria was still talking on the phone. Jim turned the deadbolt and then set the safety latch. He saw Maria frown. When she put down her cell phone, she turned to him. "Why are you doing that?" She pointed to the door.

He told her about the man in the hallway. She wrapped her arms around him, her face against his chest. "What is happening?"

"Did you calm your father?" he asked.

"I convinced him not to overreact. That it's probably what his enemies want him to do."

"Did he know the bad guy?"

"No. He points the finger at McGregor. Says the guy's been trying to make trouble for quite some time. Ferrari knows he's got to watch his back."

"He's sure about Ferrari?" Jim asked.

She didn't hesitate in replying. "Ferrari owes him. My father isn't a threat to him."

"And McGregor, he's got big friends?"

"Uh-huh. Family connections."

"That's probably what keeps him alive," said Jim.

Maria gave him a small grin. "I'm sure." She picked up her cell phone again, opened it, and punched a speed-dial button.

"Dom? Are you nearby?"

She nodded. "Uh-huh. Would you mind checking out the hotel? Jim spotted someone loitering in our hallway. He disappeared when Jim approached him."

She turned to Jim. "What did he look like?"

"White guy. Medium height. Gray hair. Ill fitting suit." Jim shrugged.

Maria repeated the description, and then listened. "Okay. We really appreciate it."

Maria closed the phone. "He'll check the place out. Said to stay put until he called back."

Jim nodded. "Sounds like a good idea."

It was an hour later when Maria's phone rang.

Jim watched her expression as she talked, presumably with Dom.

"Uh-huh." She nodded several times. "Appreciate it. Thanks."

She disconnected and looked at Jim. "Dom said that he saw no one in the hotel that aroused his suspicion. He was on all floors, as well as the restaurant and lounge downstairs." She raised her hand when Jim started to speak. "He did see two guys he figured as FBI sitting in a car by the side street entrance to the lounge."

"FBI?"

She nodded. "He was real sure."

Jim looked puzzled. "What the heck is going on?" He shook his head and sat down on the sofa. Maria sat next to him. He brought her close, nestling her against his chest.

"There's a couple of things going on, I think," she said. "First there's the FBI trying to get something on my father, and they're trying to get you to help them."

"Fat chance."

She smiled. "Then there's McGregor. Dad said he's a dangerous psycho and that Ferrari would have gotten rid of him long ago, except for the family. Ferrari is sure McGregor is trying to cause a rift between him and my dad by what he's doing at the construction site, and also by having something bad happen to me. He's pulling together a bunch of guys loyal to him. They pay scant attention to Ferrari."

"Something bad ought to happen to him," said Jim.

"Ferrari told my father he'd take care of McGregor when the time came. Said to stay away from him."

"He's responsible for your crash, I'm sure of it."

"Yeah," she nodded, "I believe it."

—

Casey handed McGregor a newspaper when he came in.

"Casey, how ya doin'?"

"Okay." Casey continued wiping the bar. "Say, you might want to look on page two."

"Okay. Thanks." McGregor went into the back room. The young waiter brought in a pitcher of beer and quickly retreated. McGregor scanned the first page and then flipped to page two. When he saw the headline near the bottom of the page, he rose out of his seat and slammed both hands down on the table.

"What the hell?" he bellowed. "Gerry Scalia dead?"

He could hardly believe it. He knew Scalia as a street savvy and productive guy, one of the best break-in talents he had. He pounded on the table.

"Goddamn it all to hell!" he roared. He reached for his cell phone.

McGregor recalled that Fontana had reported there had been nothing on the street about Big Mack. His police friends had told him they were as puzzled as anyone. There was only one way Big Mack could have been hit, he thought, and that was with the complicity of Ferrari and maybe even with some of DiCosta's people. A single person didn't do this, he felt sure. But why? Had DiCosta figured out what had happened at the daughter's crash? Had there been a witness?

"Goddamn!" A chill went up his back. He had nearly forgotten. There *had* been a witness - that asshole giving his union guys trouble at the work site. Yeah, now he remembered. What the hell was his name? He re-read the article. Yes, there it is; Jim Randolph.

"Son of a bitch," he mumbled. "DiCosta's daughter and him. Son of a bitch!"

He punched in Fontana's number.

"Hey Marc, call me back on the house phone. You know where I am. Use the scrambler." He closed his phone and went to a house phone on a shelf next to a CD player. He made sure the scrambler unit was turned on. When it rang he picked it up.

"Marc, did you read this about Gerry Scalia? It's in this morning's paper."

"Haven't seen the paper, yet," said Marc. "What happened?"

"That goddamn DiCosta bitch killed him. She killed him!"

"You shittin' me?" exclaimed Marc. "*She* did it?"

"Yeah, s*he* killed him. Paper says she and her stud-muffin came home and found him in her place. We had planned to scare the shit outa her. But then that asshole, Randolph, showed up and it went bad. I still can't believe it."

"Who the hell you talkin' about?" said Marc.

"That SCCI guy out at the Walker Building. Christ, you musta seen him there."

"Yeah. Yeah. I know who you mean. He's been a pain in the ass around there. He won't go with the flow. Cocky bastard."

"Damn it, Marc. I've lost two good guys the last couple weeks. What the hell?" said McGregor.

"You figured out anything on Big Mack?" asked Marc.

"I've just been thinking about that," said McGregor. "Just dawned on me the asshole Randolph was the guy that witnessed the accident on the Palisades. He's the guy stopped to help her. Now, that's too much of a coincidence for me. Can you believe that son-of-a-bitch cost me two guys? Can you believe that shit?"

"This guy's been big trouble."

"I can't believe this is happening," said McGregor. "We must have a leak somewhere."

"I was wondering about our two jerk-off FBI friends," said Marc. "I know you and them got some deal going; but I gotta tell ya, I don't trust them."

"We're moving the stuff into the building later tonight," said Marc. "Is there anyway that those two dick-wads could know this?"

"Don't see how," said Marc. "But we'll be extra careful."

"Goddamn it, we screw this up and it'll go bad for us."

"I'm on it."

McGregor hung up.

Chapter 15

JIM REVIEWED THE installation of radio frequency shielding, electrical wiring, lighting, communications cables, and drywall panels. He made sure each floor was essentially a shielded box to prevent unwanted electronic signals from either leaving or entering. Inspection of the seams between shielding panels and at electrical junction boxes concerned him and he paid particular attention to these features. Once the drywall panels were installed, he knew it would be nearly impossible to find any electrical leaks without ripping the walls apart. When each floor was completed, Jim expected SCCI to send a contractor into the building to make radiometric measurements of signal leakage.

The time to plant bugs for FBI surveillance, Jim realized, is before the drywall panels are installed. The workmen cast a wary eye at Jim's presence with flashlight and notebook. Jim knew there was at least one worker among them doing the FBI's bidding.

The next morning, riggers brought a flatbed truck with a large air conditioning unit to be installed on the second floor ledge. Since the second floor contained more communications equipment than any other, additional cooling capacity was needed. The auxiliary air conditioner was not part of the original work order. The need for it had been determined recently by the engineers at SCCI.

Jim had to go outside to sign for the equipment before the crane operator would unload the truck. As on previous occasions, the air-condition equipment was brought to the work site by a non-union rigger associated with the equipment manufacturer. Jim expected some objection by the union workers at the building. After he signed the papers and turned back to the building, he saw several men walking up to him.

"Still using non-union truckers, asshole?" called out the man in the lead.

Jim gasped from a hard fist to his back and staggered forward into the speaker.

The lead man drove his fist into Jim's stomach. "You're a slow learner, man."

Another blow, to his kidney, and he doubled in pain, falling to his knees. Through tear-filled eyes, he looked for help. But, no one came forward. He saw the three men that had accosted him walk away toward the main street.

After a minute, Jim managed to stand. He saw that the crane operator and truck driver were readying the air conditioner for its lift to the second floor. The workmen didn't seem to see him, or were afraid to help him.

-

"You got hurt again? Jim, what are you going to do?" Maria was upset on hearing of the altercation.

"I'll ask my boss if he'll hire some cops. I doubt he will."

"Why not? You can't keep on like this."

"Are you in your car?" asked Jim.

"Uh-huh. Half way to my parent's place."

"Please say hi for me."

"I will." She hesitated. "I'm going to ask my dad and Dom about what's happening to you. There's got to be something they can do. I love you, Jim."

"I love you, too."

-

The following morning when Jim got out of the cab there were some men in a huddle at the corner of the building. McGregor separated from the group and walked quickly toward Jim. His men followed but stayed back a few yards.

"You're the scab asshole giving my guys trouble." McGregor was within a foot of Jim's face. He lowered his voice. "You got your nose in other people's business."

"Back off," said Jim.

McGregor pushed Jim hard with both hands on Jim's shoulder. "How'd you get Big Mack killed?" He pushed Jim again.

Jim heard cat calls from the men behind McGregor.

"Back off. I don't have time for this," said Jim.

"Who'd you have working for ya? You and old man DiCosta, is that it?"

McGregor hit Jim hard with a fist to his shoulder. Jim stumbled but stayed on his feet.

"I'll be comin' after you." This time his fist landed into Jim's stomach, doubling him over.

Two construction site guards came out of the building and stepped between McGregor and Jim. They got Jim inside the building safely.

"Thanks, guys," panted Jim. "Dom send you over?"

"Yeah. Just started this morning. We'll call him . . . let him know. See what he wants to do."

"Okay and thanks again," said Jim as he started toward the elevator.

Jim rested in the second floor communications room for a few minutes and then called his supervisor and reported the incident. Afterward, he worked with Marc Fontana and the other DiCosta Construction electricians to install the auxiliary cooling unit. None of the men talked about the earlier incident. Later, he went back to the communications room to reboot the computer and run tests. He checked the door to make sure it was locked. The looks he got from Fontana had made him nervous.

Jim worked late into the evening preparing a technical report to SCCI. In was almost 8 o'clock when a power outage occurred in the building. Twin gas-driven generators installed at the rear of the building had not yet been integrated into the building's electrical system. Although a pallet of UPS power backup components had been delivered, the items had yet to be installed; thus, the computers went dead. There was no one on the second floor except Jim. He found the flashlight in the desk drawer and made his way to the opening at the ledge. There he could see the windows of buildings around him were illuminated. He placed a call with his cell phone to the power company and was told that there was no service interruption in that area, that it had to be a problem in the building. His next call was to Dom advising him of the strange power failure.

Dom advised him, "Stay put. I'll check it out."

Fearing something was wrong; Jim went inside the second floor communications room and locked the door. He was in total darkness except for his flashlight. He made himself comfortable on the floor using seat cushions and several collapsed cardboard boxes and formed a place to lie down. He stayed quiet, and turned his cell phone to *vibrate* only.

Jim heard nothing for thirty minutes. His heart skipped a beat when someone tried the door, but couldn't defeat the security lock. He heard a male voice, "Let's go before someone gets the lights back on."

There was a pounding on the door, like a big fist, before a different voice yelled, "Hey! Anyone in there? Power failure, better come out."

The first voice said, "There's no one here. He must be downstairs by now."

The second voice said, "Yeah. Lets just take a quick look on the other floors. Be a shame to miss the guy."

The first voice laughed, "Yeah, a real shame."

Jim wasn't sure, but the first one sounded like Fontana.

Jim checked his watch when the electronic equipment next to him came to life. It was 8:45. He hadn't heard anyone since someone had tried the door. He wondered if they had really intended to find him and beat him up . . . or worse. What the hell for? What was going on? He was uneasy. Had it been the issue with the truck driver, he wondered? McGregor had said he'd be coming after him. Was he now a target?

Jim stepped out of the second floor comm room and locked the door. The equipment would be going through a lengthy boot-up procedure following the power failure. He would have to see about getting the UPS power components installed immediately. In a few more weeks, the gas-powered auxiliary generators would automatically take over in a power failure. The empty floor was dimly lit by a scattering of temporary hanging lights. Jim walked to the front stairs and listened and, hearing nothing, walked down to the lobby level. There was no one around except for the night guard.

"Dom called. Said you were in the building."

"Yeah, stayed upstairs until the power came back on," replied Jim.

"I walked around this level with my flashlight, locking the doors out back."

"Seen anyone?"

"There were two guys working out back. Don't know who they were."

"You didn't see them leave?"

"No. They coulda left out back. The doors are only locked for entry, not exit."

Jim nodded. He waved and went to the front door. He'd catch a cab at the curb.

The next morning the SCCI boss asked Jim to help the crew doing the radio frequency leakage tests because the overall schedule was starting to slip. There were three tenants ready to move in, including the new headquarters for Ferrari Investments and the DiCosta Construction Company.

Jim found Greg Mathews, the DiCosta foreman on the 4th floor. He reviewed the schedule and discussed the morning's problems of the street below.

"Jim, I gotta tell you, my men are being intimidated by McGregor's people."

Jim nodded. "I know."

"I'm pretty certain they plan to cause work stoppages or worse – cause DiCosta to default on the contract, and hopefully soon be out of business."

"I've come to the same conclusion."

"McGregor will probably do whatever it takes to accomplish this. Your name has been mentioned. You better watch your back."

"Yeah, I'm aware of that. By the way, Greg, have you been approached by the FBI here in the building?"

"No, but I've seen a couple men in suits I assumed were feds."

"They haven't talked to you?" asked Jim.

Greg shook his head. "Not yet. What're they up to?"

"They have a vendetta against DiCosta and are trying to get him on whatever they can."

Greg shook his head. "I've never seen the old man."

"I wouldn't be surprised if the FBI and McGregor are working to the same end, but for their own reasons. I'd appreciate a heads up about any trouble if you see it coming."

Greg nodded. "Okay." He walked away shaking his head.

A secure area verification procedure was to be implemented as each floor of the building was completed with the EMI shielded walls, floors and special windows. Part of the test required Jim to test each area using his cell phone. In all cases he found cell phone communication was not possible; no signal bars registered on the phone display.

The businesses moving into the building required the best in electronic communication security. SCCI was contracted to facilitate this with secure land-line, cable and satellite communication. Ordinary as well as encoded transmission methods would be employed in communicating with outside facilities. The comm center on each floor would act as a local router, enhancing the confidentiality of business transactions. The tenants on each floor subscribed to a safe business environment, free of espionage from internal or external threats.

Jim saw three policemen with Greg Mathews in the lobby of the building as he was about to leave. Greg introduced them as off-duty police hired by DiCosta Construction to provide additional security. Greg assured Jim that, together with the day shift guards, round-the-clock patrols would now be implemented.

Jim called Maria and was surprised she was still with her parents. "Is something wrong?"

"Dad got sick last night. I wanted to make sure he'd be all right."

"I'm sorry to hear that. Will he be okay?"

"The doctor adjusted his heart medication and he should be improving."

"I hope so. Please give him my best."

"Thanks. I will. Oh, by the way, there should be additional guards at the building."

"I saw three new faces. Tell your father, I really appreciate it."

"Sure. What's new with McGregor?"

"More trouble, but that's not exactly new. When will you come back to the city?"

"Tomorrow afternoon. The contractor finished work in my apartment. I'll call you when I get in. I really miss you."

Jim smiled to himself. "I miss you too," and he meant it.

When Jim arrived at the building entrance the next morning, the guard informed him that the same two FBI agents were in the building somewhere. They had a warrant to search for illegal aliens.

"What bullshit," said Jim.

The guard nodded and shrugged. "I have a new guy tagging along with them."

"What are they really after?" Jim asked himself aloud.

He stopped at the second level comm room. Since the communication infrastructure was now completed on levels 1, 2, 3 and 4, he had to set up an automated scan and calibration sequence that would verify network performance and integrity at eight hour intervals, and after any power interruption. He knew he had a busy day ahead and hoped that the FBI agents wouldn't waste a lot of his time.

It was less than an hour later when Jack Reed and Wendell Somers, the two FBI agents, came to the second floor comm room. Jim looked up as they stood in the doorway. He shook his head. "What now?"

"How ya doin'?" grinned Somers.

"Busy as hell."

"Well, we're trying to keep up with all the goings-on around here. Your name keeps popping up," said Reed.

"I'm popular."

"Yeah, that must be it. Why do you suppose McGregor is making so much trouble? Ain't you all working for the same mob?" asked Somers.

Jim looked up and scowled. "As you already know, I work for SCCI."

Somers waved his hand. "Yeah. Yeah. You're contracting to DiCosta. Isn't McGregor part of the Ferrari mob – same as DiCosta?"

Jim shook his head. "Mob? That's *your* terminology."

"Yeah, whatever," said Somers. "What's McGregor trying to do?"

"You guys always ask questions that you know the answer to?"

Somers smiled. "Just tryin' to understand."

"When you figure it out, let me in on it."

Reed spoke up then. "A word of caution, smart-ass. You get mixed up in these little feuds; you could end up hurt when the bullets fly."

Somers followed up. "DiCosta can't last much longer. It's a question of whether he gets it from the likes of McGregor, or we get him up on charges."

Jim looked at Somers. "What charges? Christ, he's an old sick man. What the hell do you guys want?"

Somers shook his head. "Like I said, it'll be us or someone like McGregor."

"In the meantime piss-off and let me do my work."

"We'll be around," said Somers.

Reed pulled his cell phone from his pocket. "What?"

The two agents walked away.

Twenty minutes later the two agents returned.

"Hey hotshot. Got a question for you."

Jim recognized Somers' voice and turned in his chair. "What?"

"How's this building designed? I mean, we've been on all levels and I can't work my cell phone inside the main areas. It works fine in the lobby area of each floor. What gives?"

Jim scowled. "Like I said before, you guys don't ask questions you don't know the answers to. What are you doing in this building anyway? There isn't any illegal labor or what ever bullshit you put on the warrant. So what are you after?"

Reed nodded several times, looked at Somers. "How about you tell us what this building is designed for? It ain't a regular building."

"You'll have to ask the owners. I just put in the electronic systems that SCCI is under contract for."

Undaunted, Somers plowed ahead. "So this building is going to provide electronically secure space? Nothing gets out? Nothing gets in? Every communication comes through your equipment here?"

Jim looked up at Somers. "Like I said, you guys got all the answers." Jim shook his head. "You already looked at the building permits and plans, so who are you kidding?"

Somers kept going. "So who needs this kind of building? NSA renting space here?"

"You've already seen the applications for occupancy. What's the big deal?"

Somers face turned grim. "Why do these companies have to conduct business in such a secure environment? What are they afraid of?"

"Beats me. How 'bout I finish my work?"

Reed smirked. "There isn't anything *totally* secure."

Jim turned to him and grinned. "That's what keeps SCCI in business."

The two agents walked away without comment.

Jim was sure the FBI believed only a direct bug on the internal data and voice lines would yield them any information. And, if this was the case, they would have to send their monitoring signal out of the building over the same lines as was used by the customers in the building, or feed it to a radio link outside of the secure areas. Jim knew it would be possible as he saw and defeated their earlier attempts. He would have to be vigilant, less SCCI lose customer confidence and accounts.

Chapter 16

JIM AND DICOSTA FOREMAN, Greg Matthews, ran into each other in the lobby at noon. They started in friendly banter, but then turned to their angst with McGregor.

"I'm surprised he's lasted this long," said Greg, "but his mother is of the Salerno family and married to a McGregor out of Boston."

"I can't stand the bastard."

"He's a hothead and a druggy, and thinks he's owed the world. He's got no respect for the organization."

"And they put up with that?"

"Ferrari doesn't want him around, although organizationally, McGregor reports to him."

"And Ferrari's hands are tied?"

Greg nodded. "For now. He'd have to have the okay from the old man, and that won't happen until Salerno has had enough."

"McGregor is making all kinds of trouble here."

"Yeah. Ferrari is aware that McGregor traffics in drugs, and he's afraid that will bring the feds down on them at some point."

Jim shook his head.

"Ferrari doesn't allow drug trafficking, but can't control McGregor."

"There's a lot of money in drugs."

"Neither DiCosta nor Ferrari deal in drugs as a sanctioned activity. Ferrari claims to make a lot of money on the traditional rackets."

"I better get back to the damn computer. Lots to do today."

Greg nodded. "Yeah, me too. I'll be up on the fifth floor for a while."

Jim worked late after the SCCI crew completed installation of comm ports throughout the second floor secure area. After a while, he thought he heard voices coming from the back of the second floor. Jim waited until he heard no one and then went out onto the second floor service ledge located adjacent to the elevator shaft housing to look around for what might have been going on earlier.

Jim saw the door to an electrical distribution cabinet slightly ajar. Looking inside, he found a stash of two-dozen plastic baggies in a cardboard box. *Cocaine, no doubt.*

He was puzzled. Why hide the stash there? Not much of a hiding place. Could this be a setup? It's obviously there for someone to find, but for whom? The idea of a setup troubled him.

He pondered what to do. Should he tell the off-duty police security guards? Call his boss? Call the DiCosta foreman? Was this a drop for someone to pick up? Was it a setup for the cops to find to create a problem for DiCosta? What was going on? The whole setup seemed bizarre to Jim.

He couldn't call anyone from his own phone; the FBI was probably listening to it. He'd have to find a public phone.

Jim locked up the second floor comm room and left the building by the front door. He told the guard at the desk he wanted to get something to eat. The guard nodded, grunted, and kept reading the newspaper.

Jim walked up the block about a dozen doors to a small hamburger place. There he used a now rare pay phone on the inside wall.

"How is your dad? He's going to be okay?"

"He's resting well. The doctor changed his heart medicine. You working late?"

"Uh-huh. I need to talk to you. Can you meet me in front of your building?"

"Sounds mysterious. Give me ten minutes."

"Okay. Thanks." He hung up the phone and went outside to hail a cab.

At Maria's building, he asked the cabby to wait. When Maria came outside, he told her what he had found, and of the concerns he had about the strange situation. Her face grew stern, her lips squeezed tightly. She told Jim to dismiss the cab and that she would call Dom. He was staying at a hotel nearby.

Jim paid off the cab and they stood against the building and waited for Dom to arrive. She slipped her hand into his. "Jim, I'm afraid for your safety. This trouble is against my dad and the company, but you're right in the middle of it."

"I'm more angry than afraid. There's been a lot of trouble from the McGregor goons and those FBI guys. It seems sometimes like they're all working together."

She squeezed his hand and leaned closer to him. "I'm afraid for you. You're in a dangerous position."

A black sedan stopped at the curb. Dom got out and went to talk with Maria and Jim while the car and driver waited. Dom listened to Jim tell his story and asked a few questions. He was in quiet thought for a minute, and then he asked Maria to go to her apartment and stay there. He told Jim to get in the car and the two of them would go back to the Walker building. Maria hugged and kissed Jim, begging him to be careful.

When Jim and Dom arrived at the building, they got out of the car. The driver was told to keep the car moving, but not to go far, and to listen for his cell phone. The desk guard stood up.

"I'll have to ask your friend to sign in here. We're tightening up the visitor procedures."

"Sure," said Jim. "I'm glad to see we're doing that. "Mr. Caruso works for the contractor."

As Dom signed the sheet, the guard gave him a hard look. Dom was dressed in a dark tie, white shirt, dark trousers, and a burgundy windbreaker. He presented a no-nonsense business attitude.

"You guys gonna be awhile?"

"We'll be checking some electrical work," said Jim. "Shouldn't take too long."

The guard nodded and they passed through to the front stairs, and then up to the second floor.

Jim walked Dom around the secure area and showed him the comm room and explained briefly the concept of secure communications for the would-be occupants. Then they walked to the rear of the building where the doorway to the stairs and the service ledge were, as well as the freight elevator doors. Jim listened for a moment but heard no one on the other side of the doorway at the stairwell. Dom pulled a gun from under his jacket and as Jim turned the door handle to unlatch the lock, Dom pushed it open. The stairwell at the second floor level was empty.

Jim pointed to the power connection and large breaker closet. Dom opened the steel door. Sitting on a shelf was the shoe-box sized container with the baggies of white powder. Dom put his gun back under his jacket and took out his handkerchief to pick up a baggie. He pushed the plastic bag against the sharp edge of the steel door, poking a hole. Careful not to leave any prints, he let some of the powder fall onto his finger. He tasted it, and then turned to Jim.

"It's cocaine. Not prime stuff though." Dom dropped the baggie back in with the others.

"What should we do? Why would someone put it here?" asked Jim.

Dom didn't answer right away. Then he looked at Jim. "I think come tomorrow morning, when the crew gets to work here, FBI will raid the place. Whoever put this stuff here will call the FBI in the morning. They'll find this stuff and close the place down for who knows how long while they search every nook and cranny. I think this may be a ruse to get the FBI into the DiCosta business, maybe hassle the old man, and maybe even arrest him."

"Shit! What're we gonna do?" asked Jim.

Dom shook his head. "This isn't your fight. But if this is McGregor's doing, and we get rid of this stuff, those guys will be looking at *you*. You understand?"

Jim nodded slowly. "They'll think I stole it?"

"Sure." He paused. "Unless . . ."

"What?"

"Is the ground floor door on this stairwell visible from the alley behind here?"

Jim shook his head. "No. There's a cement-block wall around the back to keep people away from the emergency generators. There's a big double gate for access to the freight elevator, the dumpsters, and to this stairwell."

A thin smile appeared on Dom's face. "Okay. I'll take this box of stuff down the stairs. I'll check if anyone is in the area. If it's clear, I'll toss the whole thing in the dumpster."

Jim looked puzzled. "Is that gonna work?"

"If it's like I think, and the FBI and cops comes here in the morning, they at least won't find anything incriminating *inside* the building," said Dom.

Dom turned to Jim. "Stay here. I'm going down to the first level and toss this box in the dumpster. I'll be right back."

"Okay."

A few minutes later they said 'goodnight' to the guard at the front desk and left the building. Dom called his driver on the cell phone. The car appeared in four minutes and a few minutes later, Jim was at his hotel. His room looked undisturbed, but he still felt the nervousness of the past hour. When Maria called, he cautioned against talking about what had happened on the telephone. They made small talk instead, saying that she would be seeing Dom the next morning. She promised to take Jim to dinner the next evening.

When Jim's taxi approached the building the next morning they were stopped a half block from their destination by police cars, fire trucks and a bomb disposal van blocking the street. Jim saw several FBI jackets among those at the building. Jim left the cab and rushed to the building, but was prevented from entering by a police officer putting up yellow tape.

"You can't go in there. Stand back behind the tape until we clear the scene."

"What the hell is going on?" said Jim. "I work here."

"I told you to get back. Now do it."

Jim took a few steps toward the yellow tape. "What's going on in there?"

The officer scowled. "Bomb threat. Now move it."

Jim ducked under the yellow tape and watched the confusion at the front of the building. *Dom had been right*, he thought, *shit hit the fan this morning.*

Impatient to wait for the building to be searched, Jim pulled his phone from his pocket and called Dom. When he connected Jim heard, "Are you okay?"

"Yes. Cops and FBI all over the front of the place. They won't let me in."

"Yeah. Relax. Watch the show. It'll be a while." Then Dom hung up.

Jim stuffed the phone back in his pocket, turned and walked up the street to a bodega for coffee and something to eat. How long would it take to search a near empty building, he mused. He had noticed a K-9 van at the scene and wondered how long it would be before the cocaine was discovered in the dumpster. He was on his second coffee when his cell phone buzzed.

"Hi Maria."

"Are you okay?"

"Just having some coffee here while I wait for the cops to clear the place and let me in. They say it was a bomb threat."

"No kidding, a bomb threat?"

"That's what the cop told me."

"I guess they'll do a thorough search of the place, huh?"

"I expect they will," said Jim. "Are you at work?"

"Uh-huh. I have a client coming in a few minutes. Just wanted to hear your voice, wanted to know you were okay."

"Thanks. Love you."

"Love you too. Be careful."

It was a little after ten when the building was deemed safe and the yellow tape was removed. When Jim entered the building, the lobby was empty except for the guard at the desk.

"A lot of excitement here this morning," said Jim.

"Christ, it was like an invasion. Cops and dogs and FBI all over the place."

"Yeah, I couldn't get in. They find anything?"

The guard shook his head. "Not inside. One guy said there were some drugs outside in the back. Who knows? I'm just glad they're all outa here."

"So everyone is out of the building?" asked Jim.

"I've sent Hank upstairs to clear all the floors. He'll call me if he sees anything odd."

"Okay. I'll be on the second floor."

The guard waved and Jim went to the stairs to start his day in the comm room. The contractors would be sending the work crews back in the building as soon as the guard finished his inspection. In the meantime he'd have a few minutes of peace.

He was twenty minutes into data-error tests when Jack Reed and Wendell Somers cast a shadow in the doorway to the comm room.

Jim looked up. “Heard you guys were here. Did you have an exciting morning?”

Jack Reed replied. “Some guy phoned in a bomb threat to the locals. They alerted us and we joined the party.”

“And a good time was had by all?”

Reed scowled. “Don’t be an asshole.”

“So what did the cops or you guys find? Anything?”

“The *building* was cleared,” said Reed.

“Yeah, what’s that mean?”

“It means, smart guy, that we found some drugs out back in the dumpster,” said Somers.

Jim shook his head. “I can’t quite picture you two guys dumpster diving.”

“Wasn’t us. Cops sent their dog in there and came up with some stuff.”

“And what, you guys here to mop up after the heavy work is done?”

“You got a mouth on you,” said Somers with some venom.

“Anything you want to tell us?” asked Reed.

“I don’t know anything about drugs. I don’t know why anyone would put that stuff in the dumpster. What the hell for?”

Somers was nodding his head. “Yeah, we wondered that ourselves.”

Reed spoke up. “You better watch your back if you’re messing with these guys.”

“Which guys are those?” asked Jim.

The two agents turned to leave. “Don’t get in the middle of this thing,” cautioned Reed.

It was after 6 p.m. when Jim finished the scheduled tests, locked the second floor comm room, and went down to the guard desk. He waved and started toward the building entrance. The guard called out to him.

“Hey, Jim. There were a group of union guys milling around a few minutes ago at the corner of the building.”

Jim raised an eyebrow. “Seen them before?”

The guard shook his head. “Didn’t recognize them. Don’t think they work here. I already called Dom.”

"Thanks."

Just then, Jim's phone buzzed.

"Jim, Dom just called and said he'd be driving us," said Maria. "We'll be there in a few minutes."

"Okay. See you in a few."

When Dom arrived in a black sedan, Jim pushed open the glass doors and stepped out of the building. He saw three rough looking men at the corner of the building. They didn't make any threatening moves as Dom opened the car door and stepped onto the sidewalk. Jim joined Maria in the back of the car.

Dom dropped Jim and Maria at an out-of-the-way restaurant run by a friend of his. He promised to be nearby.

"What's wrong?" said Maria. "You okay?"

Jim shook his head.

"More trouble at work?"

"Almost every day, there's something."

"McGregor is trying to get my father and his company implicated in illegal activity."

"I think the bastard might be working with the FBI," said Jim.

"That is very likely. The FBI probably has a few things to use as leverage with him."

Maria nodded. "Dom has his network of spies and tells my father what's happening." She looked at Jim. "I'm worried about *you. You're* in a dangerous position if McGregor sees you as being involved more than as a worker for SCCI."

"I don't know what he's thinking," said Jim. "He's a nasty guy."

"I love you and I wouldn't want you to get hurt in this stupid union squabble."

"I love you, too" said Jim. "I can't bear to think of anything happening to you or your family."

They talked for another hour; slowly enjoying their meal, before Maria called Dom. Maria said she had to be up early in the morning to meet with a potential client who had an early flight to London.

She kissed Jim, "I'll make it up to you," and she left the car at her apartment. Jim smiled thinking of all she could do to make it up to him as he continued to his hotel. The car with Dom sitting in front continued to Jim's hotel.

Dom turned to Jim. "You going to be okay? I can wait."

"No, I'll be fine here. Thanks for picking me up."

"Not a problem. I'll be headed up to the Palisades."

Jim got out of the car and watched it pull away and into traffic.

As he entered the foyer, two men grabbed him and pulled him outside. The larger man grabbed Jim and pinned his arms behind him. "You're makin' it real hard for yourself, asshole."

The other man slammed his fist into Jim's face and then a blow to his abdomen. "Stop meddling in union business, or we'll be back." Another blow caught Jim on the side of his face. "You got that?"

Then the men were gone. Jim staggered to the building wall, gasping for breath. His breath came in painful gasps. Jim stumbled into the hotel, dismissed attention from the maitre d', and went to bed.

Chapter 17

GREG MATTHEWS, THE DiCosta foreman, approached Jim as he arrived at work. “What the heck happened to you?” He stared at the bruises on Jim’s face.

Jim scowled. “I was mugged at my hotel.”

“Damn,” exclaimed Greg. “Have anything to do with the FBI swarming us the day before?”

Jim shrugged, “Don’t know.”

Greg volunteered that Marc Fontana, his lead electrician, had mentioned overhearing part of an FBI conversation about finding packets of cocaine in one of the dumpsters.

“Strange place for drugs,” said Jim.

Greg nodded. “I wonder if Marc’s involved . . . somehow.”

“It crossed my mind.”

“Hey, if you need any muscle, let me know. One or two of us are usually around.”

“Thanks. Appreciate that. Guess I better get upstairs.”

The second floor comm room was larger than the comm rooms on other floors, because the data and voice signals from the comm centers on the other floors were routed through this facility, where connections were made to outside cables.

Jim was automating the tests through each cable to the comm room computers on each floor. An efficient and accurate test routine was essential to avoid any system down-time for the building clients and for SCCI.”

Tests to identify equipment malfunction, interference, and clandestine signal-monitoring were being designed for periodic scanning of the system. Clients in the building would be expecting electronic security that would protect their businesses.

Jim had found no recent incidents of covert tapping of phone or data lines. In checking the clandestine components he had deactivated earlier, he'd found them as he had left them; no doubt abandoned, he thought. He removed two of the modules and put them in his desk drawer. Then he began looking for new intrusions.

He doubted the FBI agents were doing the actual secret installations, and wondered if McGregor's surrogates were being used instead. It was just a suspicion, just a feeling, but he had the sense that the FBI and McGregor were working together.

Jim wondered if the FBI was using what they had on McGregor to get his cooperation in installing bugs in the building and making other trouble. He knew enough about McGregor to not put anything past him in his quest to control the DiCosta construction business. His protected status in the organization gave him cover for unsanctioned trouble making.

Just after lunch, Greg Mathews appeared at the second floor comm room door.

"How's it going?" asked Greg.

Jim glanced at him and shook his head. "Strange goings-on at some outgoing lines."

Greg came closer to peer at the computer screen. "Like what?"

"Signal loss," said Jim. "I'm getting an inordinate amount of signal loss in some of the lines going outside the building."

"You can tell from that gibberish on the screen?"

Jim chuckled. "Yep. It's not gibberish if you know what to look for." He pointed to data on the screen.

"Hey, reason I came by is there are other men with those two FBI guys that spend time here. They wave warrants around and say they're looking for contraband and illegal immigrant workers."

Jim looked up at Greg. "These other men, they don't have FBI jackets or badges?"

Greg shook his head. "Casual dress and briefcases."

"Where did you see them?" asked Jim.

"Here, on the second floor."

"Doing what?"

Greg shrugged. “Didn’t follow them around. I only saw them on this floor, none of the others.”

Jim frowned. “I haven’t seen these guys.”

“No. They arrive just about the time I’m leaving for the day. You’re usually gone by then.”

“You see the warrants?”

“They showed them to me; but hey, they looked okay to me. But I’m no expert.”

“You need to make sure you or someone you trust goes with them or follows them around.”

“Okay.”

Jim stared at the screen and shook his head. “Damn, I’m sure of it now. I just reran the test. I’m getting some signal loss on the outgoing lines.”

Greg looked perplexed. “What does it mean?”

“Well,” he looked up at Greg, “Line connections could be bad.” He hesitated. “Or, there is some sort of tap on them.”

“You mean like to listen to conversations?”

“That, yes, and to pick up data signals.”

“But how? Place is shielded,” said Greg.

Jim shook his head. “I don’t know. Not yet.”

Greg stared at Jim.

“What?”

“Maybe I watch too much TV,” said Greg. “But, I’ve seen these FBI turkeys going in and out of the building next door, the Empire Investment Trust. When I do my walk around before going home, checking the gates and all, I see these guys going in and out of that place.”

“No shit?”

Greg’s face tightened. “Yeah, the thing is, some of McGregor’s guys also go in and outa there about the same time.”

“Did you tell Ed Marcelo? He *is* the manager of DiCosta Construction, after all.”

“I mentioned it.”

“What’d he say?”

“Nothing really. He seemed distracted. I’ll tell him again.”

Jim leaned back in his chair. “What the hell is going on?”

Greg shrugged. “Are they in cahoots? The FBI always had it in for the old man and this company.”

Jim shook his head and scowled. “McGregor working with the FBI to bring down DiCosta? Could be.”

“McGregor is one mean son-of-a-bitch,” said Greg. “I wouldn’t put anything past him. The FBI might be trading some underhand work for dropping charges they have against him.”

Jim said, “McGregor’s guys get in here and put in eavesdropping hardware for those FBI pricks?”

“How would they do it?” said Greg. “This place is supposed to be shielded tight.”

“Nothing is ever 100 percent,” said Jim. “Have you seen any odd boxes or gadgets recently installed anywhere on this floor?”

Greg shook his head. “My electricians have been up on the fourth floor all week. This floor has been pretty empty.”

Jim scratched his chin. “Suppose they installed an infrared transmitter somewhere on this floor and it gets received over in the Empire Investments building.”

Greg’s eyes opened wide. “Really? They could do that? What? Like a TV remote?”

“It’d be a lot more powerful. It could be hidden somewhere and an optical fiber with a tiny lens poked out of a hole somewhere would do it.”

Greg shook his head. “There aren’t any holes in these walls. No way.”

Jim looked at Greg. “It wouldn’t take much. But, where is the infrared transmitter? That has to be probably as big as a couple packs of cigarettes. And the sensors, where the hell are those? Gotta be between this computer and the big-ass cable pipe leaving the building.”

“Well, before I go home, I’ll have a look around, now that I know what to look for,” said Greg as he walked away.

Jim brought a cable tester up from the locked storage area on the first floor. His normal tests didn’t indicate the type of flaw evident in the slow performance of the system. It took too long for the computer to acquire the test-data stream on some of the lines, barely within specification. Somewhere the signal was being attenuated. The additional equipment should provide enough detail to estimate the distance to the cable flaw.

It was slow going. He could only test one outgoing line at a time. When Greg appeared at the door to the comm room, Jim had only tested three lines.

"Whatcha doin'?"

"Testing each outgoing line that shows any suspicious behavior," said Jim. "Did you see anything interesting?"

Greg shrugged. "Down by the freight elevator. Not the stairwell, the other side." Jim looked up at him. Greg handed him a small object. "What do you make of that?" asked Greg. "There are several lying on the floor next to the air conditioning unit, like maybe somebody dropped them."

Jim looked up from the object in his palm. "It's an optical fiber lens ferrule. It goes on the end of an optical cable."

"No shit?" asked Greg. "Looks like someone dropped some of them out back."

Jim grimaced. "I can tell you one thing; we do not use these anywhere in this building."

Greg raised an eyebrow. "Somebody does."

"The lines that leave each floor are encoded coming into this comm room. They go through this central router here in *this* comm room and leave the building encoded," said Jim. "There are lots of lines, but only some of them show this anomaly of acquisition time. I've tested three of them so far. What it shows is that about 150 feet along these cables, there is an impedance perturbation and signal loss."

Greg grimaced and rolled his eyes. "If you say so."

Jim nodded several times. "Yeah, it shows me that about 150 feet away from this very spot someone has probably tapped these lines in some way."

Greg replied. "These lines all go over the false ceiling along with the power lines. At the outside wall is a big sealed terminal box where the service company lines come in."

"Well, it doesn't take a lot of work for someone to lift the ceiling panels. Question is; where's the optical fiber leaving the building? It's got to be aligned to some receiving spot on the Empire Investments building."

What do you want to do?" asked Greg.

"Don't you want to go home? Your day's been over for some time," said Jim.

Greg shrugged. "Ain't living at home right now. Staying with a friend."

Jim nodded. "Sorry."

Greg shrugged. "I can stick around – off the clock." After a moment, Greg said, "Tell you what. I'll go downstairs and get the plans for the wiring in this ceiling. I'll be right back."

Jim went back to testing.

Jim had been thinking about the electrician he had seen working by the elevator some time ago. He recalled that he had viewed Marc Fontana with some suspicion, but had not pursued it. Jim was still thinking about it when Greg reappeared with the plans.

"I'll go lift some ceiling tiles and see what's up there," said Greg.

Jim nodded. "Greg, a while back I saw Marc working by the elevator. At the time, I wondered if he could have planted any of those bugs I found."

Greg frowned. "Why do you suspect him?"

"Maybe I'm way off, but I *was* suspicious at that time. You tell me he's okay; then I'll drop it."

"Shit." Greg gave Jim an angry stare. "He's a good electrician, works hard."

"I'm probably way off," said Jim.

"Damn it, I'll check him out, just to be sure." Greg took the plans and left the comm room mumbling.

Jim wondered if he should have kept silent.

Greg found a stepladder and set it up where he thought 150 feet of cable from the comm room would be. He pushed the ceiling tiles away to expose the cable runs. The cables lay in ladder-type trays where the cables were readily observable between the supporting rungs. However, the top layer of cables was close to the ceiling and would require an inspection mirror to be seen. At first glance, nothing seemed amiss. He exposed more of the cable run in both directions and examined the cables with his flashlight. *What the hell am I looking for?*

He had chafed at the accusatory tone of Jim's suggestion. But now, he played with the thought as he looked at the cables. Marc was a good worker, but what did he really know about him? It wouldn't hurt to check.

The cables exiting the second floor comm room and going to the outside of the building, all lay in a tray running across the ceiling to the outside wall. With so many cables, Greg despaired at finding anything. There was insufficient clearance for him to put his head up high enough to see the top of the cable tray, so he ran his fingers back and forth along the smooth cables, feeling for anything unusual.

He recalled that Marc had often asked for overtime work. He assumed that he needed the extra money and usually complied with his request. Maybe I'd better look into this further, he thought. Then his fingers touched an unexpected item.

He felt the shape of it, and smiled. "Son-of-a-bitch," he muttered.

He explored the item with his fingers; plastic, he thought. He felt a thin cable attached to it, and it lay on the cable tray in the direction of the exterior wall. Soon his probing fingers found two more. He cursed the fact that he couldn't see them from his position below the cable tray. Each item was about an inch in diameter and it encircled one cable. He reached a few feet farther along the cable tray but didn't find any other odd devices. Greg put the ceiling tiles back in place and returned the ladder to where he had found it. Gathering up the blue prints, he started back to the comm room.

So far, Jim had noted eight cables that exhibited odd test results. He stared at the information on the computer screen.

"Hey, you still awake?" Greg had returned with a grin. "Got some news for you," he added.

"Got eight suspicious cables, so far," said Jim.

Greg unfolded a plan on Greg's keyboard. "See where I've got it marked?"

Jim looked up. "What did you find?"

"I looked around like you said, at the 150 foot spot. I couldn't see the top of the cable tray, but I found three odd items using my fingers."

"How odd?"

"Well, they're small plastic rings that encircle just one of the small cables – three of them."

Jim looked at Greg wide eyed. "Really?"

Greg nodded several times. "There may be more. I felt the little wires coming off these things; they were running with the cables toward the building wall."

"Wow. I think you hit the nail right on the head," exclaimed Jim. "Magnetic couplers."

"What do they do?"

"They can be used to sample magnetic fields in the cable."

"If you say so," said Greg. "You got something to think about anyway. Do you want me to stick around?"

"Go on, get the hell out."

"You sure?"

"Thanks for your help. I really appreciate this."

"What are you gonna do?"

Jim rubbed his chin. "You know, there's got to be at least one, maybe several laser transmitter modules up there somewhere or maybe behind a drywall panel."

Greg looked at Jim without speaking.

"What?" said Jim.

"Would they give off some heat, you think?" asked Greg.

"If it's what I think it is, a laser transmitter, it would give off lots of heat, at least body temperature," replied Jim.

Greg smiled. "I got a friend in the fire department. I'll see if I can borrow their thermal imaging camera."

"Really?" said Jim.

"I think so. However, my friend may want to come here with it, not let it out of his sight. It's way expensive."

"Well, that'd be okay. It probably wouldn't take long to find those things, assuming they are being powered up."

"See you tomorrow," said Greg. He turned and left.

It was almost noon the following day when Greg and his friend showed up at the second floor comm room where Jim was working. "Jim, like you to meet Fred. He's the firefighter I mentioned yesterday."

Jim stood and they shook hands.

Fred held up the camera unit for Jim to inspect. "This is an infrared camera that takes stills or video. I think it'll do what you want."

"Wow. This is slick. I appreciate you taking the time to come over here," said Jim.

"Hey, not a problem. Just show me where to look."

The three men walked into the empty second floor area and Greg pointed to where the cables ran. Fred adjusted the camera to compensate for background interference.

"Okay. I'll walk down the cable run to the outside wall, see if I spot anything," said Fred.

There was nothing indicating a heat source until Greg got to the outside wall. There, two bright spots appeared in the image, one larger than the other, just slightly right of where the cable run ended, within a few feet of a window casing.

Greg pointed to the wall panel where the bright spots appeared. “Hey, this panel isn’t a drywall. It’s a removable plastic and fiber panel that gives access to a bunch of cable terminations.”

“Yeah, it looks different.” Jim ran his fingers over the panel surface. “Feels different, too.”

The three men took turns looking at the image on the infrared camera display. “Not much detail,” mumbled Jim.

“No. About all we can tell is that there are two warm objects behind this panel. We’d have to remove it to see what it is.”

Greg looked at Jim. “I can pull that panel off in a couple minutes. What do you want to do?”

Jim looked at the two men. “I have enough for now. I need to find where the optical fiber leaves the building. Fred, thanks for coming over. This is great.”

He smiled. “Glad I could be of help. I’ll be going before someone misses me.”

Jim shook hands with Fred. While Greg walked Fred down to the building entrance, Jim studied the installation of the window carefully trying to ascertain how an optical fiber ferrule could be installed to transmit to the nearby Empire Investments building. He was almost certain what was behind the panel, but he’d have to remove the panel to satisfy his curiosity.

Greg appeared as Jim went back to the comm room. “What do you make of it?” Greg asked.

“Even without taking off the panel, I’m sure there’s a laser transmitter there, and maybe the other hot spot is some sort of switching unit.”

Greg wrinkled his brow.

Jim continued. “Yeah, I count eight perturbations on the computer. You found three. If there are indeed eight, then a switching unit could be used to sample each line on some programmed basis. When you get a chance, can you look for the other five magnetic couplers they have up there?”

“Yeah, sure. Maybe tomorrow morning early. Should I be disconnecting them?”

Jim nodded. “Yes, please. Just unhook them from the cable they’re on,” said Jim.

“Yeah, but won’t they know that they’ve been discovered?”

Jim nodded. “They’ll definitely know.”

Chapter 18

BEFORE CLOSING THE comm room that evening, Jim wrote a report detailing his findings and his suspicions about the taps on the eight lines and e-mailed it to his supervisor. He didn't mention anyone's name. Outside the building, he called Maria at her business and asked her about having dinner.

"Sure. I know a quiet, come-as-you-are place that has excellent food and comfortable booths."

"Sounds like my kind of place."

"Great. I'll call Dom and let him know where we'll be."

"Can I pick you up in thirty minutes?"

"I'll be ready."

—

"How'd you find this place?" asked Jim when they were seated at Eddy's.

"A client took me here for lunch some months ago. Never been for dinner though."

The lounge was half full with a few sitting at the bar. Jim appreciated the dark wood and leather seating. The high seat-backs offered privacy. An older man in a pressed uniform approached with menus. They placed their order and were soon discussing the intrigue at the building work site.

Jim explained that someone tapped the comm lines. "What I found required a level of sophistication that the average electrician wouldn't have."

"You think the FBI is doing this?" asked Maria.

"It's possible that they are responsible for it, but some other people are doing the actual work."

"McGregor's people?" she asked.

"Very likely."

Maria scowled. "He certainly would do it if he could get something in return, like the feds dropping any charges they have against him."

"He's gotta have some tech savvy people from what I saw."

"I'm sure he can find them. Maybe a telephone company technician?"

Jim nodded. "That's also possible."

Maria looked at Jim, reached across the table and put her hand on his. "I'm sorry you got beat up the other night. You're getting too close to this and you're in real danger. McGregor won't hesitate to eliminate any interference."

Jim nodded.

"My dad told me to ask you to back away and let Dom take care of things."

"I appreciate his concern, but I have a responsibility to make sure my company performs on the contract. I will try to avoid McGregor, but it's getting more difficult."

Maria sighed. "If the FBI and McGregor are working together, it's to destroy Ferrari and my father. Dad makes sure his business is run legally, and Ferrari doesn't interfere with him. Ferrari does get a piece of the action, though; that's how it works. The people that work for my dad are good men, as far as we know. Of course, that might be wishful thinking."

The waiter brought their drinks and the steak dinners arrived ten minutes later.

"Do you know Greg Mathews, the foreman?"

"Heard his name, but never met him," said Maria.

"He and I suspect that Marc Fontana is a McGregor operative. He's a good electrician, that's not in dispute. It's the circumstantial evidence. Greg is checking into him."

"I can ask Dom if he knows anything about him. The only guy from the construction company that I met is Ed Marcello, the business manager. He's been at the house several times."

Jim nodded.

"I only want my dad to live his remaining years in peace. I realize he caused his share of troubles in the past before he went to prison. Now, he's not a well man, battling diabetes and heart disease along with emphysema. He only wants to be with his family and be left in peace."

"I understand," said Jim. "I guess Dom keeps things going well for him."

"He does. I'm very grateful." She gazed into Jim's eyes. "I was wondering if you've said much to your parents about me and my family."

Jim smiled. "I have, but they have some rigid conservative ideas."

"Uh-oh. They don't like you seeing an old mobster's daughter?"

"I told them you were more than an acquaintance."

Maria gulped. "You did?"

"I said you were a very special person to me and that I love you."

"Really? What did they say?"

"They're stuck in the old society and worry about my future," said Jim. "They wish for me to stay within their circle."

Jim saw her lip quiver slightly. He held tightly to her hand.

"I love you so much," she said, just above a whisper, a catch in her throat.

—

Jim held the door open for Maria as they left the restaurant. He saw the black Town Car parked at the curb. Just then, the passenger window opened and Dom beckoned them to get in.

Jim opened the back door and he and Maria seated themselves in the spaciousness of the limousine. The glass window behind the driver went down with a hum, and Dom's face turned toward them.

"What's wrong?" asked Maria.

Dom looked at Jim. "You know a fireman named Fred something?"

Jim felt a knot in his chest. "Yes."

"He was beaten pretty badly earlier. Cops found him alongside his car behind the fire station."

Jim stared at Dom. "Why? Who would do that?"

Dom shook his head. "Greg called me, said he was helping you with something?"

Maria stared at Dom. “Is he . . .?”

“He’s alive, but he’ll be in the hospital for a week or more.”

Jim nodded, turned to Dom. “Fred helped Greg and I look for hidden heat sources with equipment from the fire station, looking for eavesdropping components.”

“Someone figured it out,” said Dom. “Someone didn’t like him helping you discover their undercover work. This is a definite message to anyone else even thinking of going against McGregor.”

“You’d think the bastard would just kill me, get me out of the way,” said Jim.

Dom shook his head. “He won’t push it that far. He remembers what happened to Big Mack.”

Jim replied, “Greg and I suspect the electrician, Marc Fontana, of being a McGregor operative.”

“What have you got?” asked Dom.

“It’s all circumstantial right now, nothing concrete, so far We’ve seen him leave work and cross the street to Empire Investment Trust on several occasions. Also, the two FBI guys that come around; I saw them come and go from that building.”

“What do you think is going on?” asked Dom.

“I suspect the FBI has a listening post in one of the rooms. It’s a bit of a stretch, but we think McGregor is doing the dirty work for the FBI in exchange for consideration on charges against him.”

The car started and blended into the flow of traffic. Maria held Jim’s arm as they made their way to Maria’s apartment. The car stopped just past the entrance.

Dom turned to face them, looking at Jim. “For now, leave whatever spy stuff you come across as you find it. I want to hear from Greg on this. Also, I’m going to scout the building across the street, see who’s coming and going and I’ll get some pictures. You just keep doing your job and ignore things for now. I’ll get back to you. Might be a week, maybe sooner.” He looked at Maria. “Both of you, be careful. Call me when you get into your apartment. I’ll wait here.”

Jim and Maria got out of the car and went into the building.

—

They sat together on the sofa watching the nightly news on the TV. Jim couldn't stop thinking about the firefighter in the hospital. "I feel responsible for Fred . . . the fireman. He only wanted to help."

"It's terrible, especially for his family," she said. "Dom will make sure they're okay while he's in the hospital."

"I hope he'll be okay."

"You have to be careful," said Maria. "The same could happen to you."

Jim hugged her. "I've been careful. But someone knew Fred was helping Greg and me."

"But why hurt him?" asked Maria.

"Like Dom said, as a warning to others."

"Life is pretty cheap with those guys," said Maria. "I always hated that about them."

"I keep wondering if all of this is because of FBI vindictiveness, their making a contract with the devil," Jim mused.

"After Ferrari's and my father's trial, there were a lot of angry FBI people."

"Some still want to get your father behind bars and they might sanction underhanded activity by outside contractors."

Maria nodded slowly.

Jim stayed with Maria that night. They lay together on the sofa, watching the TV until passion suggested the bedroom. He awoke early to find Maria already had the coffee made. Her scent and warmness were a tempting distraction, but she said that a customer would be at her office early. He left for his hotel room to shower and change.

Jim recalled that Dom had cautioned him; but yielding to his stubborn streak, he decided that he would disengage all of the eavesdropping sensors from the lines, and not compromise Greg any further. He saw no one on the second floor and moved rapidly to drag the stepladder under the panels he had marked earlier. He pushed aside the ceiling tiles and felt along the cables until he located and disconnected the eight sensors he had detected. He reinstalled the tiles, put the ladder back against the wall, and went to the nearby second floor comm room. There, he rebooted the computer to let it look for indications of spy equipment. The boot-up procedure was flawless. "Wonder how long before they do something else?" he thought.

Later that morning Jim received a call from his supervisor, Art Wagner, at SCCI, giving him the news that Ferrari Enterprises and DiCosta Construction would start moving into the secure area on the second floor, possibly as early as next week. They would be the first tenants in the building. In the meantime, building management would move into the first floor.

Jim was asked to qualify the communications facilities on the other floors as quickly as possible. Jim brought Art up to date on the spy hardware situation, and was told in no uncertain terms that the first and second floors had to be secure at all times.

"How ya doin'?"

Jim, startled, turned to see Agents Somers and Reed standing outside the door of the comm room. Reed grinned.

"What is it now? Got a warrant or something?"

Reed turned to Somers and sneered. "He's not very friendly today."

Somers stepped closer. "Thought we'd come by and see how you're doin'."

"What? You just waltz into the building anytime you please?"

"Sure," said Reed, "We got all kinds of paperwork. Want to see some of it?" He started to reach into his jacket vest pocket.

Jim scowled. "Spare me. What *do* you want?"

"We were in the neighborhood," said Somers "Just wanted to see how things were progressing. Anybody move in yet?"

Jim looked up at Somers. "No, but then you already know that. Don't you keep an eye on things from across the street?"

Reed looked at Somers.

"He's smarter than he looks," said Somers.

"Yeah, I hear he's an electronic wizard," said Reed.

"No kiddin?" responded Somers.

"Uh-huh," said Reed. "I heard he's making a really secure place here. Makes you wonder why, huh?"

"Yeah," said Somers, "I heard that he actually found some bugs." He looked at Reed, "Believe that?"

"Bugs, huh?" said Reed. "Maybe somebody's after DiCosta."

Somers grinned. "Our pal here is making a nice safe place for DiCosta and Ferrari to do their business." He glanced at Jim. "You really think any place is secure?"

Jim looked up at their sneering faces. "You really got a hard-on for those guys, don't you?"

"Hey, they aren't nice people," said Somers.

"DiCosta paid his dues," said Jim.

"Did he?" said Somers. "We don't think so. He skated by taking some minor rap for Ferrari. No, we're not done yet."

Jim shrugged.

Somers' face darkened. "You're in this up to your ass, aren't you? If you're not careful, there'll be a lot of grief in it for *you.*"

Jim waved his hand in dismissal. "Get the hell outa here. I've got work to do."

Somers nodded, and he and Reed walked away.

Jim, troubled by the injuries to the fireman and the threat from the FBI agents, went looking for Greg. He found him taking inventory of electrical supplies near the elevator on the sixth floor. Greg smiled and looked around quickly as Jim approached across the empty cavernous floor. Jim noticed the nervousness and wondered what was spooking him.

"Hey, what's up?" greeted Greg.

"Just want to let you know, I'm going to activate the combo locks on the doors to the secure area on level-1 and 2. Until the clients get moved in, I'll be the only one with the combination."

Greg nodded. "Well, we're done there. My guys are up on 7 now and should be up on 12 in a couple weeks." He raised an eyebrow. "What'd you decide about the ceiling bugs down on 2?"

Jim grimaced. "I disconnected them all, eight altogether. I don't think it went over well. The two dickheads paid me a visit this morning."

"FBI?" asked Greg.

"Yeah," said Jim. "Obnoxious pricks."

Greg stared at Jim. "What'd they want?"

"They got under my skin. I let them know I knew they were using the building across the street as a lookout."

"That probably wasn't too smart," said Greg.

Jim shrugged. "It probably wasn't. I got the feeling they knew we found all the bugs, and they didn't sound happy about it. What could they say though?"

Greg stared.

"Oh, they said I could get hurt if I stuck my nose where it didn't belong."

"I think you should believe them. I didn't like having to face Fred's family." Greg hesitated. "Also, last night I got a call. Wasn't too friendly. Guy said he knew I had been helping you find bugs, and suggested that I should mind my own business."

"Who was he?"

Greg shrugged. "Probably one of McGregor's guys."

"I'm sorry. Shouldn't have got you involved," said Jim.

Greg shuffled his feet, looked at the floor. "If they wanted, they could get me kicked out of the union. Make it so I couldn't find work in the city. Bastards."

"Greg, just back off. Let them think you're a good boy. I'd appreciate it though, if you didn't let them in on what I'm doing."

"No problem. I won't give them anything."

Jim turned to leave. "Take care."

"Yeah, you too," replied Greg.

Jim pondered his workload as he went back to his computer at the second floor comm room. He knew there couldn't be any flaws in the communications performance when the tenants, Ferrari and DiCosta, moved into their offices. Also, he thought, there was the pressure of getting all the comm nodes working up to the 12th floor. Should he request some help? No, his boss would send some green kid, and he'd spend all his time training him. Jim sat down at the computer and reviewed the schedule. The trouble was the bugs had slowed him down.

Jim and Maria met at a nearby pizza restaurant for a quick supper.

"I have to go back this evening," said Jim. "Gotta run tests of the first floor comm nodes, and make sure the few phone and data lines in the basement are functioning."

Maria nodded. “I understand. I should go back to the office, too.”

“How come?”

“Happily, business has grown quite a bit in the past year. Even with the sales person I hired, I still need to schedule suppliers and work in the shop.”

Maria saw the worried frown on Jim’s face.

“How are things at the building?” she asked.

“Right now it is schedule pressure to make sure I have the two floors ready for occupancy. Also, those two FBI jerks hassled me this morning.”

“What’d they want?”

Jim shrugged. “Just rattling my cage. I’m sure they know I found some of their bugs.”

Her face darkened. “They never give up.”

Jim grimaced. “Is there anything at all they could be looking at regarding your father that could land him in trouble?”

She looked at him for a moment, and then shook her head. “No. When he got out, he made an agreement with Ferrari that he would run the construction business clean. Ferrari was okay with that since he owed my father big-time.”

“So Ferrari keeps his activities away from DiCosta Construction?”

She nodded. “Yep, there’s no tie-in. I’m certain of that.”

“Where would your father be vulnerable? I mean, the FBI must think there’s something.”

Maria frowned. “You said the other day, that maybe the FBI was having McGregor doing their dirty work. I got talking about that with Dom, and he agrees that it is highly likely. He said he’d snoop around to see if he could get a lead on it.”

“Does he think the only way your father could get in trouble would be if McGregor and the FBI set him up - framed him?”

She nodded. “Yes.”

“I wonder how that would happen?” said Jim. “There are so many ways . . .”

Maria shrugged. “I’m afraid of what another round of indictments would do to him. He’s my father. I don’t want to lose him.”

“Then, we can’t let that happen. I’ll get together with Dom during the week and see what he thinks,” said Jim.

Maria smiled and reached for his hand and held it for a moment. "You're a good man."

That evening, back at the computer in the second floor comm room, Jim set up an automatic test routine to verify the performance of the comm nodes on the first floor and basement. In the meantime, he dwelt on what Maria had said at dinner.

What could the FBI do to have DiCosta indicted? The litany of old charges against DiCosta had been dropped after the old man's confession. New charges would have to be developed and put before a grand jury; maybe some sort of frame-up involving drugs, or fraudulent business practices, or even larceny. But how? He thought about the earlier roust with the planted cocaine at the rear elevator. They'd been thwarted then, but would they try again with a similar ruse?

Dom called Jim from the lobby late in the evening. Jim went downstairs to meet him and sign him in as his coworker. In the second floor comm room, he offered Dom a folding chair. Jim sat in front of the computer keeping an eye on the testing routines as they spoke.

"I've got pictures of the guys going back and forth between here and the building across the way," Dom said as he pulled out his digital camera, turned it on, and handed it to Jim. "Recognize anyone?" he asked.

Jim nodded. "This guy is an electrician, works for Greg. This other guy, I've seen around. He must work for Greg, too." Jim shook his head and scowled and changed the image. "These are the two FBI jerks."

Dom nodded. "They're easy to spot. Anybody else?"

Jim shook his head. "No. I don't recognize these other two. Don't think I've ever seen them."

"Tell you what. Can you load these images into the computer here?"

Jim nodded. "I got one of those universal card readers."

"Great," said Dom. "Take this card out and download the images. When you get a chance, ask Greg who these guys are, and why they're going back and forth across the street. This usually goes on after work hours. Okay?"

"Sure," said Jim. "Say, I wanted to ask you. . . . Remember the coke we found before? Out by the back elevator?"

Dom nodded.

"What's to stop them from trying something like that again?"

Dom looked at Jim and slowly nodded. "How is this place secured right now?"

"The secure area on each floor has combo door locks," said Jim. "Currently, only the first and second floors are secured with my own combination. The other floors have a combination set by Greg for his guys; that includes the basement."

"So nobody gets into the first and second floor unless you let them in?" asked Dom.

"Not in the secure areas. The front stairs and the back stairs connect each floor, but the secure areas require access codes, as do the elevators. As the other floors get finished, I'll secure them as well. When a tenant moves in, they set their own combination."

At the end of the following workday, Jim went looking for Greg. As the first and second floor secure areas were now barred to anyone without the security combination, he started with the ground floor, hoping Greg hadn't left yet.

Jim saw him chatting with the guard. "Greg, got a few minutes before you leave?"

Greg sighed. "Didn't you get me in enough trouble? I'd like to get out of here on time for once."

"I want to show you something. It'll only take a couple minutes," said Jim.

"Fine. Let's go."

They went up the lobby staircase, and Jim unlocked the second floor secure area.

"So, what is it?" asked Greg.

Jim unlocked the second floor comm room and woke up the idling computer.

"So what's the big urgency?" Greg said.

Just then the first image came on the screen. "Know this guy?" asked Jim.

A frown formed on Greg's forehead. "Yeah. Sal Costello." He looked at Jim. "Why's his picture on your computer?"

Jim raised a hand. "Hang on. How about this guy?"

"What the hell? That's Joe Faust. What's goin' on?"

"These guys work for you?"

"Yeah. Been on my team over a year. Why?" Greg's voice had turned hard. "I want to know what's goin' on."

Jim looked at Greg. "These pictures were taken as the two guys went into the building next door. They were seen going in there after hours several times - the same building the FBI and McGregor have been seen entering."

Greg frowned. "What the hell are you sayin'?"

"What do you know about these two? Why would they be going over there? Come on, Greg. You know the trouble McGregor and the fed pricks are giving us here. I can't just ignore this."

Greg shook his head. He pulled a chair up to the computer and sat. "Look. I had to take these guys on. I mean, they're good workers and all. It's that I was *told* to take these guys into my crew."

"The union?" said Jim. "But McGregor doesn't control *your* Local, or does he?"

"Who knows?" said Greg. "I figured they were plants for some reason. I wasn't sure why, but I thought maybe they were here to rip off supplies."

"Did they?" asked Jim.

Greg shook his head. "Not that I'm aware of."

"Then what? They're McGregor's guys, right?"

Greg sighed. "Probably. Like I said, they do their work well." Greg paused, scratched his chin. "Twice now, I ran into these guys accidentally. Just the other day I overheard one of them mention having to do something out of town that night. They clammed up when I joined them."

"Marc Fontana is part of this group, right?" asked Jim.

Greg nodded. "He was the one talking."

"Damn," said Jim.

"I don't know what to think," said Greg.

"You must've suspected something."

Greg shrugged. "I've seen them together down at Murray's a few times, tossing back a few. Never gave it much thought until the other day."

Jim looked at Greg; saw the deep frown. "What does your gut tell you? They're up to *something*."

Greg slowly blew out his breath. "You said that McGregor was probably doing the dirty work for the FBI, trying to undermine DiCosta. I gotta believe that asshole also has his own program as well to get rid of DiCosta."

"So we really don't know what they're up to," said Jim. Greg nodded.

Chapter 19

JIM CALLED MARIA before leaving the building, but she told him she had to wine and dine a client. That evening he found himself sitting in Angel's diner - a hole-in-the-wall place a block north of the Walker Building. Greg had mentioned it as a quiet place with decent food. Jim had bought the late edition of the *Daily News* and opened it as the waitress walked away with his order. *A real scandal sheet*, he thought, as he looked briefly at each header.

On the front page, above the fold, an article caught his attention. *Two Murdered in Scarsdale Mansion Robbery, $4.4M in jewels, bonds and currency missing.* The article told of an elderly couple coming home in the early morning hours. They had apparently surprised some burglars, according to the police. The bodies were discovered by the maid when she arrived at 9 o'clock that morning. Friends contacted by the police, along with information from the maid, placed the value of the heist at over $4.4 million. No one had reported anything suspicious in the neighborhood, nor had anyone heard any shots. The police were not releasing any more details.

The waitress brought his supper and Jim put the newspaper on his seat. When he finished and the waitress refilled his coffee cup and cleared the table, he continued looking through the paper. He glanced up when the door opened. It was the two men whose photo he had shown to Greg on the computer. He dropped his glance back to the newspaper. They took seats at the counter, joking with the waitress and placing their order. Jim wondered if they knew him, if he had been pointed out by someone. He decided to wait and see their reaction when they got up to leave. He leafed through the paper another time, and finally the two men got up to leave.

Jim kept his gaze cast downward, but saw that one of the men had seen him. He poked the other on the arm and said something Jim couldn't hear. The second man edged toward the door, the first nodded toward Jim. A chill went up Jim's back as both started back toward him.

Jim looked up as both men slid into the booth across the table from him. The dark haired man smiled. "How ya doin'?"

Jim shrugged. "Okay. What's up?"

"Randolph. You're Jim Randolph, right?"

"Yeah. Who're you?"

"I'm Sal Costello," he said smiling. Nodding to the man beside him, he said, "This is Joe Faust." Faust wasn't smiling.

"I'm supposed to know you guys?" said Jim.

"We seen ya in the building. You're that security guy, right?"

"I work for the communications company, SCCI." Jim didn't like where the conversation seemed to be heading.

Sal glanced at Joe. Joe didn't respond; his eyes followed the waitress. Sal looked back at Jim. This time the smile was gone. "Guys tell me you're checking their work. These guys know what their doin'. They're union electricians."

"I don't have a problem with their work. My job is to make sure the communications are working right."

"We don't like it when you piss all over our work."

"Just doing my job," said Jim.

Sal looked down at the newspaper, and noticed the Scarsdale article. He glanced at Jim, and then pulled the paper toward himself. He looked briefly at the open article and then slid the paper to his pal. Joe casually looked at it, but in a few seconds he went back to staring at the waitress. Sal glanced at Jim. "Bad things happen, huh?"

Joe nudged Sal with his elbow. "I gotta get goin'."

"Yeah, me too," Sal echoed. They slid out of the booth. Sal turned to look at Jim, pushed the newspaper toward him.

"You take care now, ya hear?" Then they were gone.

The following morning, the two FBI agents were waiting for Jim in the lobby of the Walker building. Jim shook his head as they approached. "What now?"

"Wanted to give you another chance to consider which side you're on," replied Reed.

"I don't take sides," said Jim.

"We think you do," said Somers.

"I don't care much what you think."

Reed nodded. "We heard about some of the company you keep."

"What company is that?"

Somers grinned. "You might get yourself incriminated in something."

"Gosh, I guess I better be careful, huh?" said Jim, scowling.

The two agents looked at each other, shook their heads, and walked off.

Jim found Greg getting off the elevator near the lobby.

"Going up?" asked Greg.

"Yeah, lots to do today."

"Did you run into the two FBI guys?" said Greg.

Jim nodded. "Yeah. They threatened me with some bullshit."

"They didn't say anything to me."

"It might be wise if you kept some distance between yourself and the bad guys. If something goes down, the feds could sweep you up in their net."

Greg scowled. "Assholes."

"Have you been threatened by any of McGregor's guys?"

Greg shook his head. "No." He started to walk away. "Gonna go out for some coffee."

Dom joined Jim and Maria for a pizza that evening. The conversation went to Maria's father. She looked at Jim, "My dad has been talking to Ferrari about selling him the construction business."

"Really?"

Dom nodded. "It would allow him to truly retire without obligations to the organization. Keep this strictly to yourself. Any hint of this to McGregor could motivate him to a hostile takeover of the business. He has enough men at his beck and call to cause some real trouble. He wouldn't want Ferrari to get the business – he wants it."

Jim nodded. "Of course. I understand."

Dom continued. "The bottom line here is for DiCosta Construction to complete the contract for the Walker building, at which point Ferrari would likely buy the business outright."

Jim looked at Maria and then to Dom. "I don't know what McGregor and the FBI guys are planning."

"Just need you to keep your eyes open," said Dom.

Chapter 20

A SMALL BLUE CAR PULLED up and stopped in front of the gate to the DiCosta estate. A man in a suit stepped out of the stone guard shack and looked toward the car. Several seconds later a uniformed man got out of the car and came up to the gate. The guard approached slowly, one hand in his jacket pocket.

"What can I do for you?"

The uniformed man held his identification up for the guard to inspect. "I'm with Johnson Certified Messenger Service and have a message to deliver to Mr. DiCosta."

The guard stared at the man. "You have what?"

The man sighed. He held up a pale yellow envelope. "A message. I have to deliver it in person to Mr. DiCosta."

"Leave it with me. I'll get it to him."

"No sir. I have to deliver it in person and wait for a reply."

The guard stared at the messenger, and then pulled his cell phone from his pocket. "Yeah, it's Bruce at the gate. Tell the boss there is a messenger out here who wants to personally deliver an envelope." The guard listened for a few seconds. "No, it's Johnson Certified Messenger Service." A few more seconds went by. "Okay." Bruce put his phone back in his pocket. He looked at the messenger. "An escort will take you to the house."

A golf cart came from the house and stopped at the guard shack. Dom got out of the cart and talked with the gate guard for a few seconds. Then the gatekeeper opened the gate. The guard frisked the messenger and nodded to Dom. Dom looked at the messenger. "Get in the cart. I'll drive you to the house."

Dom stopped in front of the house, got out, and asked the messenger to wait. Dom went into the house and spoke with DiCosta.

"This guy is a certified messenger. He has an envelope that he is supposed to hand you and you sign for it. Should I send him away?"

"Some sort of summons?"

"Don't think so. It is a plain envelope with the courier's logo on it."

"Well, hell, see what's in it."

"The guy said he want you to read and reply to the contents. Those were his instructions."

"Open the damn door. Let's see what the hell it is."

Dom pulled the door open and gestured for the courier to come in.

"I'm required to hand this to Mr. DiCosta and wait for a reply."

DiCosta came from behind the door and stared at the young man. "Who the hell are you?"

"Sir, I'm a courier from Johnson Certified Messenger Service." He held out the envelope. "Are you Mr. DiCosta?"

"Yeah." He took the envelope and handed it to Dom.

Dom tore off the seal and removed a sheet of paper and handed it to DiCosta.

He read the message, and without expression handed it to Dom. The message read:

> *Mr. DiCosta: I am offering to buy DiCosta Construction for three million dollars. The money can be deposited wherever you desire. The transaction can be consummated in the public area of The Oaks Country Club. I urge serious consideration of this offer and I await your positive response by return messenger. To me, the value of the enterprise will decrease as time goes on, and be worthless by year's end. M. McGregor.*

DiCosta showed no emotion. He looked at Dom, tilted his head toward the courier, and then turned on his heel and walked away.

The courier stuttered, "Sir, I . . . I was told to wait for a reply."

Dom shook his head. "There is no reply," and gestured for the courier to get in the golf cart. They drove to the gate in silence.

As the courier was set to leave through the gate, Dom handed the man a twenty dollar bill. "Mr. DiCosta does not have a reply."

Dom and DiCosta sat in the garden, each with a cold beer. DiCosta stared into the distance. "What the hell is happening? I can't believe the stones on that piss-ant. Where's he get that kinda money?"

"We shoulda been done with him some time ago," muttered Dom.

"Why now? Why in such a hurry? And, three mil? Where the hell he getting three mil?"

"Sounds like somebody is backing him, but the business is worth two-three times that."

DiCosta looked at Dom. "I need to know what's going on."

Dom nodded. "Okay to do what I gotta do?"

"Yeah. Don't get me any legal trouble, though."

Later, they discussed DiCosta's plan to sell the company to Ferrari when the building contract was completed. DiCosta admitted he didn't have the energy and good health to be an aggressive businessman, and Ferrari could compensate him adequately, giving DiCosta an additional financial cushion for his remaining years and to take care of his family when he's gone.

"I like the idea of selling to Ferrari," said Dom.

"Should put an end to McGregor's aspirations."

Dom shook his head. "I don't know. It will at least make him show his cards in any move against you."

DiCosta looked at Dom. "He wouldn't have any reason to move against me if the company is sold. I'd be totally out of it."

"I don't know. I'd feel better if I knew who was backing this buyout ploy."

"I'm going to meet with Ferrari, talk this over."

Dom grimaced. "McGregor's fixation on your company hasn't been a secret. He's been bragging that he's going to take it over some day. However, this is kinda sudden."

“This is bizarre. Who does business like this?” said DiCosta.

“I really wonder who’s backing him, and why.”

“Find out.”

Chapter 21

DICOSTA MET FERRARI at Mike's Diner in the Bronx to go over the McGregor situation, as well as the future of the construction company. Mike's was chosen, since both knew the place. And since they had not been there in many years, it was unlikely to be bugged.

The frumpy waitress brought menus, water and cutlery. They both ordered the blue plate special of chicken fried steak and coffee. The meal arrived quickly. When the waitress came by a second time to ask if all was okay, Ferrari handed her a five dollar bill and said he'd summon her if they needed anything. She stuffed the money in her apron pocket and walked away without comment.

Ferrari put down his coffee. "I'm the first to admit the bastard is a loose canon. The real problem, however, has been the attention he draws to the organization, attention from the FBI and local cops."

"How about what happened up at Scarsdale?" asked DiCosta. "He have the stones for something like that?"

Ferrari nodded. "Sure. He's a psychopath. He just does whatever pops in his head. Trouble is he doesn't do it for the family. I never see a nickel. And yet, anything goes wrong, it's the family the FBI comes looking at."

"You think McGregor is the ring leader? Hard for me to believe."

"I'm told he is."

"What're we gonna do with him? He's overdue."

Ferrari nodded. "I'm afraid the family is gonna have to get hurt bad before they do anything about him."

"So *if* he has some of his guys pulling robberies, where's all the stuff? Who's fencing it for him?" asked DiCosta. "You can't hide high-end goods for long."

"I got people looking into it. My best guess is he's dumping it out of town, probably in Jersey."

DiCosta shook his head.

"McGregor is acting like a separate organization and the boss still won't do anything about it. What I'm afraid of is the police arresting one of that gang, and they all point the finger at me."

"At some point, we gotta cut him loose," said DiCosta. "You *gotta* know that."

"Yeah." Ferrari nodded. "I have to wait until I have real proof. McGregor is the cousin of Capella's wife."

"McGregor probably has a following that's only after the fast buck."

"I know, there's some guys unhappy with Salerno's edict. But, he's from the old school and won't tolerate headline grabbing activity – murder, robbery, pimps and drugs. He always tells us, there's big money in protection, political graft, leveraged real estate trades, gambling, and bookmaking. It's traditional, and as long as he's alive, that'll be the way it is."

DiCosta nodded. "I've always been okay with that."

"Yeah, I know. Just saying . . ."

"So we wait a while?"

"Yeah. We wait."

Ferrari shook his head. "If it wasn't for the gravy, this'd be a sorry excuse for a steak."

"Yeah. The gravy makes this road kill passable."

"Things haven't changed much. I wonder how they're still here."

"Probably won't be for long."

The two men sat through dessert and more coffee, and the conversation turned to the sale of DiCosta Construction to Ferrari. The subject had come up before, but now both men seemed ready to make arrangements.

Ferrari took a sip from his coffee. "I'm thinking $15 million in cash and securities, and two pieces of undeveloped commercial real estate in the Upper East Side could be managed without any legal hassles."

DiCosta nodded. "Sounds generous."

"You earned it. But, I'll need you to complete the contract on the Walker Building as part of the deal."

"Not a problem," said DiCosta. "It'll get done."

Ferrari reached across the table and the men shook hands.

"I'll send my accountant to your place when you're ready. You and he can prepare a complete proposal. I'll need that."

DiCosta nodded. "What about staff?"

"I'd be inclined to keep Ed Marcello, your business manager, and make him general manager. Some purging of the construction work force will be needed to get rid of McGregor operatives."

"Marc Fontana, a good worker, I'm told, is really suspect in McGregor's subterfuge."

"Yeah, we'll need to talk about him."

"So what's the status of the SCCI contract?" Ferrari asked. "McGregor has been screwing things up?"

"He's been a problem. Mostly annoyances, except for him stirring up the unions when a non-union delivery driver shows up," said DiCosta.

"Maybe best if you insisted these out of state riggers use union drivers. It could save us a lot of hassle and unneeded attention."

"Yeah, I think you're right. Save money in the end."

"How's the contract going?" asked Ferrari.

"Pretty much on schedule. This guy, Jim Randolph, is doing a good job."

"Good . . . good."

"In addition, building management arranged for a maintenance contract, also with SCCI. That'll be part of any tenant lease agreement."

Ferrari nodded. "I understand four floors are currently under agreements."

"Yes. The other floors are in negotiation and should be finalized in a couple months."

"You'll give me a list of the probable tenants and contact people?" asked Ferrari.

"Sure. Send it to you tomorrow," replied DiCosta.

"What do you know about these tenants?" asked Ferrari, raising an eyebrow.

"The management company sets up the leases. They do all the investigative work, but it's mostly to be sure they're financially sound. I looked at the pending list the other day. Seems like they are investment firms, bank holding companies, and insurance companies. Actually, I never heard of any of them. Also, there are two accounting firms."

"Then there's you and I."

"Yeah. Two floors are ready for occupation at this time."

"No government connections?" asked Ferrari.

DiCosta shook his head. "Not that I'm aware of. The owners of the building are several Wall Street types. Their offices are in lower Manhattan."

"I'm glad you told me how special this building is," said Ferrari. "Putting my organization in there would make us all quite a bit safer. Seems like every other week the goddamn FBI comes around my office with some kind of warrant. They've got to be getting some leads from wiretaps or illegal eavesdropping. Moving into this building ought to slow that way down."

"I still worry," said DiCosta. "Those bastards haven't stopped trying. That Randolph guy has found all kinds of snooping devices hidden away. We'll have to have experts come in later and sweep the place."

Ferrari nodded. "Say, what about the security of information leaving the building? I never really understood how that all works. Do you?"

DiCosta shrugged. "The SCCI people gave me a presentation last year, but who remembers?"

Ferrari grimaced. "I want to know how the info is kept secure that we send out of the building to customers, or whoever."

"What I recall is that voice and data communication is encoded, but requires the customer to have the proper decoding or unscrambling equipment and code."

Ferrari shook his head. "Is this practical?"

"Sure. I saw a demo. Once it's installed and your people understand it, it's pretty simple. I wish I had it, back in the day."

Ferrari smiled. "Reminds me. What about that Randolph guy? Is he a troublemaker?"

DiCosta shook his head vigorously. "No. Ain't true," he said. "He's found the bugs in the building and has been working well with my crew chief. And, my daughter worships him."

Ferrari smiled. "Well, that's worth something."

"He's a straight arrow."

Ferrari sat back from the table and placed money on top of the check. "I got it."

DiCosta slid out of the booth. "Thanks."

Ferrari looked at him. "Get this all ironed out, and we'll get together at Portebello's. Have us a celebration with the wives. We haven't done that in a while."

DiCosta smiled and nodded. "That'd be swell. Maybe bring Maria and her friend?"

"Yeah, sure," said Ferrari.

Chapter 22

JIM WALKED TO THE ELEVATOR while reading an article in the morning paper. Another jewelry robbery had been reported, this time in New Rochelle.

"What's up?" Greg Mathews was trying to exit the elevator.

"Oops, sorry." Jim stepped aside. "Says here, another jewel heist last night."

The elevator door closed as the two men stayed in conversation.

"I ran into Ed Marcello last evening on the way out. He said he thought two members of the construction crew have been recruited by McGregor."

"Really? Makes you wonder what McGregor's been up to," said Jim.

"He's been making trouble around here for quite a while. His gang probably doing bad shit elsewhere as well."

"Makes me wonder about these recent high-end robberies, like last night," Jim commented.

Greg shrugged. "Pretty sophisticated for these guys. Don't you think?"

"I don't know. Maybe. It looks like the kind of shit these guys might do."

Marcello told me that he's long suspected Marc Fontana of being complicit with McGregor's hoodlums, and now he includes Peter Rankin."

"I don't know him," said Jim.

"Peter Rankin, apprentice electrician. Works for Fontana."

Jim shook his head. "I hear you, but I don't know about all that. What's the proof?"

"Ed said he recently saw a black SUV stop behind the building and Fontana get into it. He stayed for a minute or less, and then he returned to the building with a metal box. As the SUV drove away, he handed the box to Rankin. They then disappeared into the building."

"It wasn't locked?" asked Jim.

"Apparently not or Fontana had a key."

"What was Marcello doing out there?" asked Jim.

"He was inspecting the installation of the generators. Those guys didn't see him."

Jim shook his head. "Greg, if these guys think you're privy to what they're doing, they'll likely come after you and maybe kill you."

"I know," said Greg. "I think about that. It's scary."

"Murder is serious shit."

Greg nodded. "I know."

Jim was completing the certification tests in preparation for tenant occupation of the first and second floors, as well as the basement. Sitting at the computer in the second floor comm room, his thinking drifted onto what could happen if McGregor decided he was a threat. Also, what would McGregor do when he found out that DiCosta was selling the business to Ferrari? Would there be violence? These issues troubled him, left him unsettled as he gazed at the data streaming across the computer screen.

SCCI headquarters in Poughkeepsie had advised him there would be a technician assigned to permanent duty at the Walker Building when the construction contract with DiCosta was completed. The secure communications rooms on each floor would only be accessible by SCCI personnel. At that time, Jim would have a choice of several assignments within the city of New York. Also, he was eligible for assignment to other cities if he chose. Jim's parents had encouraged him to work in the Philadelphia area if possible, and he had given that some consideration. He did miss their company and the company of a few of his friends. Working for a while in other cities had seemed attractive, but that was before he had met Maria.

He had to stay in the city until all the tenants moved into in the Walker Building and secure communications were established for each of them. That meant likely another two months, maybe longer, he thought.

Jim called Maria as he was leaving the building. "Hi. Are you in your office?"

"It's been a hectic day. I'm still at a customer's office. I can't get back for a couple hours. What are you doing?"

"I called because I kinda miss you."

"I miss you, too."

"That's what I was hoping."

"I interviewed a potential salesperson this morning. I'm thinking of hiring her."

"You sure could use someone to take some of the work load."

"Business is growing faster than I had anticipated. I do need some help."

"I'll let you get back to it."

"How are things for you?"

"Just the usual. Trying to get everything running right for the tenants to move in."

"By the way, Jim, Dom has a partner now. You probably won't see him much, but he'll be around. His name is Albert Malloy. My dad beefed up the security crew."

"That is a good move. I worry about you running around all the time."

"Dad is worried, too. But we're both concerned about your safety as well."

"Thanks. It does get a little hairy at times."

"I'll try to catch up with you tomorrow. I have to run."

"Love you. Take care."

"Love you, too."

Well, he thought, he'd walk over to Norton's diner, a greasy spoon a few blocks west.

He spotted Greg as he approached the guard station. "Greg, want to join me for supper?"

"What? You buying?" He smiled broadly.

"Hadn't planned on it," replied Jim, shaking his head.

"Where you going, up to Angelo's place?"

"No," said Jim. "Over to Norton's."

"Okay. What the hell. Gotta eat somewhere."

Greg and Jim sat in a booth away from the doorway. They made their supper selection and the waitress brought coffee for Jim and a Coke for Greg.

"I was over to the union hall yesterday," started Greg.

"Where's that?"

"In Brooklyn," replied Greg. "The headquarters of Electrical Local 4119 and Riggers Local 321 share a two-story row house in Brooklyn."

"Was there some kind of union meeting?"

"No. I went there to change my deduction for the pension."

Jim looked at Greg. "Was there a problem?"

"There were quite a few strange faces milling around outside McGregor's office."

Jim looked at Greg, waiting for him to continue. When Greg hesitated, Jim prompted him. "What about those guys? What were they doing?"

"Looked like they were hanging at McGregor's office, waiting for him to open his door, or to come talk to them or something."

"Is that unusual?" asked Jim.

Greg dropped his voice to a near whisper. "Something's up. I could feel it. When I went near them, they all got quiet."

Jim shrugged. "What do you make of it?"

Just then the waitress brought their supper, refilled Jim's coffee, and walked away.

Greg continued. "I was sitting just inside the insurance office doing the paperwork and I picked up little bits of the conversation in the hallway. At first, I didn't pay a lot of attention, but then it started to get interesting." Greg took a bite of his supper and chewed.

"You gonna keep me in suspense all night?" asked Jim, grinning.

"Shit, I don't remember all I heard, but I got the impression they were getting ready to hit several places. The guys out in the hallway seemed to be the leaders, and each had a crew working for them."

"They didn't say where they were going?" asked Jim.

Greg shook his head. "I didn't pick that up. But, I heard talk about big equipment, trucks, cranes, bulldozers; stuff like that."

Jim stared at Greg for several seconds. "Oh shit."

"Yeah. That's what I heard. Mean something?"

Jim nodded several times. "DiCosta has warehouses with big equipment, stuff he uses on his jobs."

Greg's eyes opened wide. "Shit. You think . . .?"

Jim shrugged. "Maria told me her father rejected an offer McGregor made for his business."

"Yeah? McGregor offered to buy it?" asked Greg.

"Yep. It was a pissy offer, and besides, DiCosta wouldn't have sold it to him for any amount of money."

"And what? You think that McGregor might try to just take it?" asked Greg.

Jim nodded. "I'll get a hold of Maria tomorrow."

The next morning Greg arrived at the building entrance as Jim got out of the cab. "Hey, did you get a hold of Maria, like you said?"

"Not yet. I should though." He pulled his cell phone from his pocket and pushed Maria's speed-dial button.

It rang three times and then he heard Maria's voice. "Jim, what a nice surprise."

"Hi. Where are you? Did you get back to the office?"

"I got a call last night and had to dash down to Newark."

"You okay?"

"Uh-huh. It's going to be another long day. I just made a presentation to a large travel agency that moved here from New York. It'll be a big account if we win it."

"Oh, you will. You're the best."

"Thank you, appreciate the confidence. What have you been up to?"

"I'm here with Greg. I mentioned him to you."

"Yes, I remember."

"Don't want to go into the whole story on the phone, but we think your father could be in for some real trouble."

There was a moment of silence before Maria replied. "He . . . he's in danger?"

"Maybe. At least his machinery and equipment is from what I gather."

"Can I have Dom call you? Would that be all right?"

"Sure. I'll keep my phone turned on."

"Oh, Jim, what's happening?"

"Let's talk when you get home. Love you."

"Love you, too. I'll call when I get back. Bye."

Jim heard the click and he closed the phone.

Greg raised an eyebrow.

"She says that Dom is going to call me. He's their security guy."

Greg nodded. "Yeah, I met him. He was walking around the building one day." Greg grinned. "I challenged him. He introduced himself."

Jim nodded. "Nothing much gets past him." Jim felt his phone buzz.

"This is Dom. I'm on my way there. Where are you?"

"I'm at work. I'll be on the second floor," said Jim.

"Forty minutes."

Jim looked at his phone. Dom had clicked off. He looked at Greg. "Forty minutes."

Jim saw Dom as he approached the second floor comm. room. Dom glanced at Greg and Jim, and then asked them to start at the beginning with what they knew.

A few minutes later, Dom thanked Jim and Greg, and pulled his cell phone from his pocket. Jim watched as Dom made several calls just out of his hearing. Then he abruptly said goodbye and left the area.

Greg shrugged. "Got to get to work. Keep me posted."

Jim nodded. "Soon's I hear something."

It was forty five minutes later that Jim heard from Maria. "Jim, I just heard from Dom."

"What'd he say?"

"He's doing something to protect the property and he'll be staying close to me. Another guy will be keeping an eye on you."

"Okay. Thanks. Love you."

"Me too."

—

The next morning Ferrari received a call from DiCosta. "Tony, my guy, Dom, told me that McGregor is planning to take over my equipment yard. I don't know what the asshole expects to prove, but that's what I'm hearing."

"Oh for crisakes. Angelo, don't do anything. I have a guy runs a security firm, mainly for overseas work, that owes me a couple big ones."

"Who's this? I know him?"

"You never met him. He's an ex black-ops guy that runs his own crew. He's goddamn good at what he does."

"I think the asshole is really pissed that I'm selling the construction outfit to you and wants to create havoc."

"Who the hell cares what he wants. His clock is running out."

"Thanks, Tony."

"Stay out of the city for a while. Tell Dom to stay close to your daughter."

"I will."

Chapter 23

THE NEXT DAY, JIM, rummaging through his desk in the second floor comm room, discovered he had two bugs, he had previously found, still lying in his desk drawer, where he had tossed them weeks ago. Curious, he studied them for twenty minutes, forming an idea for their surreptitious use. He realized each had a small microphone embedded in the molded housing. By changing a jumper-wire, the module could be configured as a microphone or as a bug to monitor a phone or data line. Jim determined that changing one jumper-wire would make the microphone operational.

Going to the computer, he searched for unassigned telephone or data lines and found one in the basement as well as one at the terminal panel inside the second floor comm room.

A plan emerged where he would secrete a bug inside the rear basement door and place another bug just above the door frame inside the second floor comm room. He was sure the thin wire connections to a close-by cable panel would go unnoticed.

He would go down to the basement after the workday ended. If he worked rapidly, maybe no one would notice him. Jim hoped he would be able to record voices to give him some idea of what mischief the McGregor guys were up to. Also, anyone coming into the comm room on the second floor to give him a hard time could also be monitored and recorded onto a CD.

He smiled at the thought of the two FBI guys giving themselves away on a recording, and thought it might be helpful at some point if it turned out the two agents were involved with McGregor. Jim was sure the two agents were operating outside lawful boundaries in their collusion with McGregor, and he felt no guilt in entrapping them.

Jim grabbed some tools, locked the second floor comm room and took the back stairs to the basement. The outside door was locked, but he did a walk around the service equipment to assure himself that no one else was there.

Quickly he adhered the monitor to the top of the door frame with a glob of silicone, and then threaded the long thin wires into the nearby communications interconnect box. He found the numbered terminals he had identified on his computer and fastened the wires. When he closed and locked the box, he made a mental note to have the lock changed to a more sophisticated one.

He was upstairs in the second floor comm room a few minutes later. There he installed the second module behind an equipment bay, out of sight, but close to the interconnect panel, to which he ran the thin wires. He made a quick check with his computer to verify that the microphones were operating. He disabled the speaker and then turned off the monitor. He left the room and slammed the door closed, thus locking it.

"Put in a full day, did ya?" said Somers.

The two FBI men were standing just inside the main entrance as Jim approached. Each had a cup of coffee.

"This where my tax money's going?" asked Jim, then added, "Keeping the city safe, are you?"

Jack Reed scowled, turned to Wendell Somers. "This guy," he nodded toward Jim, "is keeping this place safe for the crooks."

Jim nodded unsmiling as he stepped closer toward the door. "Your surrogates been busy I hear."

Reed stared at Jim. "What the hell's that mean?"

"Scarsdale. New Rochelle. Saw it in the paper." After he voiced it, Jim wished he hadn't given in to bravado.

Somers looked at Reed. "What the hell's he talking about?"

Reed's stare turned into a scowl.

Jim felt a chill go up his back.

"You sure got a mouth on you," said Reed. "Where do you get this shit?"

Jim shrugged. "In the paper. Added two and two. Figured your stooges were up to their asses in it."

Somers stepped closer to Jim. "Talk like that sure to get you in the hospital, wrong people hear it."

Jim waved curtly and pushed open the glass door. Outside, he took a deep breath of the cool humid air, and then raised his hand for a taxi. When he looked out of the rear window, he saw Reed on his cell phone.

"Hey! I'm just tellin' you what this Randolph guy said." Agent Reed hadn't wanted to call McGregor; knowing his temper well.

"What else he tell ya?" growled McGregor.

"Just that he read it in the paper. He was being a wise-ass, pulling my chain."

"Yeah? Why's that?"

"He's seen your guys, seen us too, coming and going to the Empire Investments building. He's made a point of tellin' us that. Asshole likes to yank our crank."

Reed noted a change in McGregor' voice. "You two wanted distance, insulation, deniability."

"We agreed to that," said Reed.

"Well, if this jerk-off gets his nose in it and makes it so we can't do our end of it, then you don't get what you want either. I ain't allowin' this guy to screw things up. There's a lot at stake here."

"We're well aware of it," said Reed.

"Yeah, but it's my guys' asses in the sling here. Now ain't it?"

"What are you sayin'?"

"I ain't sayin' shit on the phone. But you can use your imagination."

Reed heard the click. He closed his phone.

"What's the deal?" said Somers.

"I think we either control this Jim asshole, or McGregor is gonna take him out. That's what I think."

Somers shrugged. "As long as we're not around when it happens."

Reed glared at Somers. "We can't let this guy screw things up."

"Yeah, if things get screwed up," said Somers, "the Bureau won't know us."

Reed nodded.

"So what're we gonna do?" said Somers. "We're not supposed to know the things they do, or we'd have to turn it all in."

"Ain't hard to figure out the bad shit they been doin'. Christ, it's in the papers," said Somers. He caught his breath and continued, "Lots of people would point at McGregor for these jobs."

"Yeah, it's their line of work," said Reed.

"Those guys must be using this Walker Building as a temporary hiding place," said Somers. "I think they got their shit hidden in the basement. We pretending we don't know? Aren't people moving in next week?"

"Yeah," said Reed. "Found out the city and insurance inspectors are visiting on Monday. Building engineering and management people will be moving in as soon as the inspectors let them."

"And what?" said Somers. "Those assholes gonna leave their stuff there? What about the inspectors? That's what they do – inspect."

"Calm down. Let me think," said Reed.

Somers hadn't finished yet. "These guys get nailed, they're gonna take us down with them."

"Yeah, I know," said Reed. "Look, right now this might be an opportunity for us."

"Like what?" Somers didn't sound convinced.

"Say these bozos have some shit in the basement, right?"

Somers nodded.

"If they're smart, they'll get it outa there before Monday," said Reed. "That gives us a few days."

Somers frowned. "To do what?"

"Well, we been hoping that those guys would set it up so we could give the prosecutor something to hang around DiCosta's neck. That was the plan; we get DiCosta and McGregor gets free of what's around *his* neck."

"I don't want to end up in prison just to get DiCosta," said Somers.

"Listen, we've been spending a lot of time on this. Boss ain't gonna approve much more. We gotta get this done."

Somers shook his head. "I ain't goin' to prison."

Reed scowled. "We do this right, we'll retire."

"Hopefully not in the dirt," replied Somers.

"Listen to me," said Reed. "Those bozos will never admit it to us, but they did those jewel robberies in Scarsdale and New Rochelle."

"You don't know that." Somers said. "And, you don't know that there's *anything* in the basement."

"Suppose we go down there and look?" said Reed.

"Someone will see us. What excuse we got to be down there?"

Reed scowled. "Look, goddamn it, you want to make a few bucks on the side? Well, then you gotta take a few risks."

"McGregor catches us snooping into his shit, he could make *us* disappear."

"Oh, for Christ's sake. He knows killing FBI agents would bring him all kinds of grief. His bosses wouldn't okay the hit."

Somers shook his head. "He's a psycho. You think he'll worry about permission?"

"Christ. Okay, we'll run downtown and get us a warrant to search the basement for drugs and contraband. But, I don't know if I'll be able to get one."

"I don't like it," said Somers. "One of McGregor's assholes sees us down there; they'll think we're there to rip them off, warrant or no warrant."

Reed smiled. "Now you're catching on."

Somers looked at Reed wide eyed. "You're crazy. Gonna rip them off? Holy shit."

"Yeah, why not? This thing with DiCosta ain't going anywhere. We might as well face it. Boss is gonna pull the plug soon. So what're we gonna do?"

"Pack it up, I guess. What the hell else?" said Somers.

Reed shook his head. "We been busting our humps here for too long. About time we got something out of it."

"You're crazy. They'll kill us," whined Somers.

"Not if we make it look like it was DiCosta's guys. Hell, maybe even that jerk, Jim Randolph."

Somers shook his head. "I don't like it. What are we gonna do, go around and fence stolen jewelry and securities?" His head was still shaking. "If the mob doesn't get us, goddamn FBI will."

“Yeah, maybe you’re right. Lets find out if there is any cash hidden down there. We’ll grab that. Let them try and figure it out.”

“I don’t like it,” said Somers. “I ain’t goin’ to jail, no goddamn way.”

“Christ, you’re such a pain-in-the-ass. Let’s go over there later and see what’s there.”

“Shit. I ain’t touchin’ the stuff.”

“Fine. Whatever,” said Reed. “I’m gonna see about a warrant.”

“Yeah. Good luck with that.”

Chapter 24

THE FOLLOWING MORNING, Jim looked at the computer screen and saw there had been time indicated and voice recorded on the audio-activated channel to the CD. Although access to the basement is through a combination-locked door, Jim knew that anyone could get in who knew someone on the DiCosta construction crew. He wouldn't be able to secure access to the basement until the construction crews had completed their contract and departed. Jim closed and locked the door to the comm room and proceeded to listen to the audio on the CD through the small speakers on the computer.

Jim heard a half minute of mumbling by two voices. He soon recognized the voices of the two FBI agents. Jim stopped the CD and plugged a headset into the unit. When he turned it back on, he could more clearly hear the discussion. He heard bumping noises and sounds of metal objects being moved. There was frequent cursing and mumbling. Then Jim heard the faint voice of Jack Reed seeming to come from a distance from the microphone hidden at the doorway.

"Wendell. Hey, come look at this."

There were sounds of footsteps and something being moved.

"Holy shit," said Wendell Somers. "Christ, put it back. We can't take any of this."

"I *knew* those assholes pulled those robberies," said Reed.

"Put it back. We can't take any of that stuff," said Somers.

"Okay. Christ, get a grip, will ya."

Jim heard the sound of a metal object sliding across a rough surface.

"Leave the jewelry here. Lets get out of here," said Somers.

"Don't piss yourself. I ain't done looking yet."

Jim heard more mumbling and cursing. Then Reed gave a yell. "Somers, look at this, will ya."

"What?"

"Come here. It's payday."

There were more footsteps and shuffling noises. The next voice was that of Somers. "Jesus!"

Then Reed's voice. "There's two boxes back here. Sitting right here on top of the pump controller, maybe more. I can't reach way back."

"How much you figure?" asked Somers. "This one box must have what, a couple hundred large?"

"Two hundred grand?"

"Yeah," said Reed. "Then there's this other box, too."

"Why the hell these guys stash all this down here? It's nuts. Somebody would find it."

"Its only been here a day or two. They're probably gonna fence the stuff real soon."

"Yeah, but there are inspectors coming in here in a few days."

"That means the stuff will be gone tomorrow. They can't flash it around and let Ferrari get wind of it."

"McGregor must be a little insane. This is real crazy."

"I'm thinking it's payday for us."

"We take it, they'll come looking for us," said Somers. "*Us*, goddamn it. We can't leave here with a box in our hands."

"What a candy-ass," exclaimed Reed. "You want to leave? Go on, leave."

"I'm stayin'. Hurry up and do what you're gonna do," said Somers.

"I ain't leaving all this cash here, that's for damn sure. Here, stuff these in your pockets."

Jim heard more mumbling and swearing, and after a minute the voices got louder.

"Okay, let's get outa here," said Reed.

"You put it back the way it was?" asked Somers.

"Yeah. A little lighter, but yeah." Jim heard the door lock operate and then the door opened, closed, and all was quiet.

Goosebumps went up Jim's arms. He wondered what the hell he had stepped into. He could hardly believe what he had heard. *The FBI stealing McGregor's money? There will be hell to pay.* Jim attached the CD to a page in a test equipment instruction manual, and installed a new CD into the recorder. He paused to wonder what he should do about what he had just heard. Without coming to a conclusion, he started the morning test routine. Once started, it would run by itself; allowing him to go to other floors and assess their communications readiness. He wanted to secure all the floors, but first he had to complete the required acceptance tests.

With the testing completed on the first and second floors, and the areas secured with his own lock combination, Jim went to the third floor. While he waited for the test routines to run, he worried about what he had heard on the recording. He was troubled by what his responsibility should be. An hour later, Jim changed the combination on the secure area doors and headed up to the fourth floor. He had neither seen nor heard from anyone.

The fourth floor was empty and had been cleaned. In the comm. Room, Jim set up the computer to perform diagnostic tests, and then sat down at the small desk. He wondered if he should talk to Greg about what he had heard. Should he advise Dom about it? He grew increasingly uncomfortable with the knowledge he now had. Did he have a responsibility here? It was nearing 11 o'clock when the diagnostic routine was completed. Satisfied, Jim closed the comm room door and started toward the back of the building to reset the combination on the lock. On the way back towards the front, he saw Greg coming towards him.

"Yo, Jim. You all finished with this floor?"

"Yep. I reset the back door lock. I'll be doing the same with the front. What's up?"

Greg shuffled his feet, looked behind him and in a lowered voice said, "Something happened in the basement."

"What do you mean? Something broke?" asked Jim.

Greg shook his head, and then rubbed his chin before replying. "There was this big argument going on when I went down there to do my usual checks. Marc and a couple of McGregor's guys were really getting into it."

"What was that about?" said Jim.

"Dunno. They clammed up when they saw me come in. What little I picked up sounded like something was missing. Don't know what, though."

“Equipment? Tools?”

“It sounded to me like it was something else, something personal. Maybe something they stole.” Greg again shuffled his feet. “I saw Marc take some metal boxes down there some days ago; I think I mentioned it to you. Don’t know what’s in them.”

Jim shook his head. “They know that you know. That can’t be healthy for you.”

Greg shook his head. “What the hell am I supposed to do? I didn’t take any of their shit. I don’t even know what’s in the boxes.”

“Those guys get to pointing fingers . . . shit, you can bet someone’s gonna have to pay.”

“I guess we can expect some stiff questions from some of McGregor’s guys.”

“Yeah. He won’t stand still for this.” Jim started moving toward the front door of the secure area. Greg followed.

“I’m going up to the sixth floor comm room and run the test routine,” said Jim.

“Okay. I’m going up, too. Got guys working on the twelfth.”

Jim reset the door lock combination to a new code and both went to the elevator.

Trouble with the test routine kept Jim working on the sixth floor for several hours. It was after noon by the time he realized the trouble was a faulty computer file and reloaded it from the master disks. Skipping lunch, he set the combination on the sixth floor doors and went to the seventh floor comm room to start the diagnostic tests. The seventh floor was empty and swept clean and ready for the carpet and office partitions. The dark and quiet vastness of the empty space gave him a chill. He turned on some of the lights, but couldn’t see into the distant corners. In the comm room, he made sure the door was locked before beginning the test routine.

Jim worried about having knowledge of the FBI break-in and theft of McGregor’s hidden loot. Greg’s men had access to the basement and all the floors not yet secured. Would McGregor make their lives miserable? Would they suspect *him*? Why not? He had easy access to everywhere in the building. Surely McGregor would remove everything before the inspectors came through. Jim stared at the screen and watched the test routine, but his mind was racing from one thought to another. It seemed strange to him that McGregor's guys would hide stolen loot in the basement of the building. Was it a temporary thing? Was it an attempt to compromise DiCosta Construction by staging a 'discovery' by the police? It all seemed so preposterous. Jim knew he and some of Greg's men would be in danger.

Jim wondered why a move hadn't been made yet by McGregor against the DiCosta equipment and warehouses. Was there something else going on to distract him?

Chapter 25

WHEN JIM CALLED MARIA, he was told she was at a customer site in the city and wouldn't return until morning. He had hoped to spend a quiet evening with her, but now turned his thoughts to where to go for supper.

When he stepped outside, he was accosted by two men, standing on either side of the doorway. They took Jim by the arms and walked him to the corner of the building. His complaints went unanswered. Around the corner stood a black Buick, idling with exhaust vapor rising from the tailpipe. Jim struggled to prevent the two men from forcing him into the car, but it was futile.

The rear door opened and he was shoved in, to find himself sitting next to McGregor. The two muscle men stood outside.

"I'm Mike McGregor," he said, staring at Jim.

"I know. What do want with me?" replied Jim.

McGregor scrunched up his face muscles, "You're that Randolph guy, right?"

"What do you want with me?" Jim said again.

"You're the guy that tests all the secure lines and stuff like that, right?"

Jim nodded, "Yep."

"So, you have access to all parts of the building, right?"

"Yep, me and everybody else in the crew, except for the secured areas. What's it to you? You're not part of the crew." Jim tried to control his irritation.

McGregor gave Jim a steely stare. "*You* can always get into any place in the building."

Jim nodded slowly and then repeated, "Any of the crew can get into any place in the building except those places I have locked off."

McGregor studied Jim's face.

Jim then added, "The tenants will change the combinations as the floors get occupied."

McGregor looked out the front window. "And who has access to the basement?" he asked.

"As I said, everyone in the construction crew. That area will be controlled by the engineering people who come in next week, if that's any of your business."

McGregor again ignored the taunt. "What's your relationship with those two FBI guys that haunt the place?"

"Relationship? They're a pain in the ass, always coming around asking me stupid questions."

"I heard you're working with them."

Jim laughed, "*I'm* working with them?"

"Yeah, and I see you keep bringing in non-union people to do your rigging and trucking."

"What about it?" Jim tried to keep a grip on his temper. He continued. "The way I see it, the FBI and some of *your* guys are pals, hanging out in the building over there." He pointed to the Empire Investment Trust building across the street.

McGregor's face tightened, his eyes narrowed.

Jim continued. "SCCI delivers the equipment for installation here with contract truckers and riggers. I don't have any control over that."

"You got a mouth on you," said McGregor, looking directly at Jim. "I don't like you. I find out you're getting into my business, it won't go well for you – not well at all. Now get the hell out of my car."

Jim stepped out of the car, slamming the door shut.

One of the muscle men grinned. "Have a nice day, asshole."

Jim flipped him off as he headed back to the building entrance. He stood at the doorway and watched the Buick drive away. He heard the door behind him open.

"Waiting for a cab?"

Jim turned to face Greg. "Just thinking. You headed home?"

"What's wrong?"

"McGregor. A couple of his goons forced me into his car. Seems like he probably suspects me of taking some of his stuff. He kept saying I had access to all parts of the building, et cetera."

"Did they hurt you?"

He shook his head. "No. I think McGregor is looking for the person that took some of his stuff, whatever it was, from the basement."

"He had his guys in the basement earlier and I think they removed everything they had down there," said Greg. "I never saw a construction guard down there, like maybe they were warned off. Didn't you say that fellow, Dom, had put some guards here to keep an eye on things?"

"They're around, just not when you need them."

"Yeah, well, I saw McGregor's guys taking out several metal boxes," said Greg. "Looked like the same ones they brought here is the SUV a few days ago."

"Why the heck they use this building to hide their stuff? Doesn't make sense."

"Yeah, you'd think they'd keep it in one of their cars or in a storage place somewhere."

Greg shrugged. "Who knows? Maybe some sort of expedient thing?"

Jim nodded. "There's going to be trouble."

"I'm worried that he'll be looking for a fall guy for anything that's missing," said Greg. "Don't know if it's drugs or money or jewelry."

"Yep," said Jim. "He'll be looking at you and me as primary suspects if anything is missing."

"Bastard will never let it slide. Someone will have to pay."

"You're right. Hope it ain't us."

"I can't figure who took his stuff from the basement," said Greg. "Just about anyone in his own crew could have done it."

"McGregor is looking hard at me as a suspect," said Jim. He was hesitant to tell Greg of the recording he had made. He would keep it to himself for now.

Jim got back to his hotel room late and found a phone message from Maria. She had gone to her parent's place. Dom had told her that her mother was ill. Maria called again before Jim left for work in the morning.

"How's your mother doing? I was worried."

"She's got an upper respiratory problem. Some kind of infection."

"Is she in the hospital?"

"No. She's pretty stubborn about that. Dad has the doctor over to medicate her."

"I'm sorry. I hope she gets well soon."

"I'll be staying here a few more days. I want to help my dad. He tires so easily."

"I understand. I sure miss you."

"I could use your arms around me. Maybe in a few days."

"I hope your mom gets well."

"The doctor thinks she'll pull through this. She's a strong woman. What about you? What mischief have you been up to?"

"More of the same. McGregor rousted me yesterday. He thinks I took something of his from the basement; some of his loot, no doubt."

"Is he serious? Shouldn't you tell Dom?"

"I'll give him a call later."

"You'll be careful?"

"I will. If he wanted to hurt me, he would have done it by now."

"Jim, you're crazy. Please take him seriously."

"Okay. Please give my best to your mom and dad."

"You make me nuts. But I love you. Bye."

Later, Dom called and they discussed the meeting with McGregor. Jim did not mention the recording he had made. He spent the weekend keeping busy documenting the test routines he used in setup and troubleshooting, documents that should prove helpful to whoever succeeded him. He was glad to stay busy. He missed Maria.

The building Engineering and Maintenance group moved into the basement on Monday and Tuesday. The Building Management group moved into the first floor on Tuesday and Wednesday. The basement and first floor were now secure with tenant locks. Ferrari Investments moved into the second floor at the end of the week. DiCosta Construction was integrated with Ferrari Investments in the same office area.

Jim saw an article in the NY Daily News; a short item on page four on the sale of DiCosta Construction to Ferrari Investments. DiCosta would be responsible to complete the contract on the building. Things would be different, Jim thought, but maybe not for him.

—

McGregor sat at the bar at Casey's lounge flipping through the Daily News. "Son-of-a-bitch!"

Casey, tending bar, turned and strode toward McGregor. "What's the matter?"

McGregor scowled and waved him off. He read the article again. Perspiration formed on his brow. He realized his best chance to form his own business group, separate from Ferrari, was vaporizing. He'd have to call off plans to physically take over the construction equipment. Now he was certain, Ferrari would have him killed.

McGregor muttered to himself. "I'm gonna get even with that old bastard, DiCosta, one way or another."

He dwelled again on the missing money; sure that Jim Randolph was somehow involved in its disappearance. "Is he involved with the FBI?" he asked himself. "Do I dare take him out?"

McGregor took a long pull on his beer, and then rubbed the cold bottle across his forehead. "I gotta find out about that prick," he said out loud. "Then I'll take care of him."

—

"Hey, Jim!"

Jim turned toward the guard desk where a guard he knew as Pete was waving energetically.

"Pete. What's up?"

"There's been some wireless cameras installed out back by the generators and some others in the stairwells."

Jim nodded. "Uh-huh. I know about those. There's a WiFi repeater on this floor for the ones out back."

Pete rolled his eyes. "What I want to show you is here on this screen. Come around and look at it."

Jim went into the guard kiosk and looked at the monitor Pete pointed to. "What am I looking at?"

"I was hoping you could tell me. It's supposed to be a picture of the fourth floor landing at the stairwell."

Jim stared at the screen. "Looks like a shot of a doorway. You sure the camera wasn't moved?"

"The camera is okay. I went up there earlier."

"The WiFi is picking up some other camera," said Jim.

"Yeah, but from where? Some other building? It can go that far?"

"Not very likely. How long has it been like that?"

"Since the other day when all those guys moved in."

"I'll tell my boss, keep him in the loop," said Jim.

"Let me know, 'cause this ain't right."

Jim waved and started toward the elevator.

Jim sat in the second floor comm room staring at the computer screen. The incident downstairs at the guard desk bothered him. He wondered if there could be a clandestine camera in the building. But why? And where? Certainly not inside the secure areas. The shielding would prevent any signal from getting to the guard desk. No, he thought, there had to be a camera somewhere on the first few floors. Later in the morning, Jim went downstairs and stood outside the main entrance while he called Art Wagner, his boss at SCCI.

"Hey Jim, how's it going down there? Are the tenants in there now?"

"Yeah. The first are in. No problems so far. But I do have a question."

"Okay."

"The guard station on the main floor has several monitor screens that can be switched to different remote cameras. These are wireless cameras in stairwells and out back by the generators."

"Yeah, I know. They're on the equipment list I have," said Art.

"Well, this morning the guard pointed out one of the monitors was receiving a picture from an unknown camera. The pictures from all the cameras we installed have identification info on them, this other one doesn't. I don't know where it is, but we should locate it."

"It has to be outside of any secure area – signal wouldn't make it through those walls."

"Yeah, it's what I figured. But where?"

"You think it is an illegal camera?"

"Well, *I* can't account for it," said Jim.

"I'll have someone bring down a new piece of equipment I got recently. It's pretty slick. It's a handheld receiver with a small screen. Lets you receive signals from the variety of wireless cameras sold these days."

"That'd be neat to try here."

"Yeah. I'll have it there tomorrow."

Jim marveled at the new piece of handheld equipment and spent an hour reading the manual and studying its operation. The unit had a 2.5 inch color display and would show an image from any wireless camera within a range of hundreds of feet.

Near the end of the work day, Jim made an inspection tour in the basement, but saw no image on his receiver. As he approached the rear of the first floor he received an image of the generators. "Well, the damn thing works, at least."

When he climbed the stairs to the second floor, he picked up another image; this time looking down the stairs from the landing. As he approached the heavy doors to the secured area, his receiver picked up another image. "I'll be damned," he muttered. It was the same image he had been shown the previous day at the guard station.

He stared at the screen, and then looked around him, then back at the screen, then at the big security doors. Almost in disbelief, he came to the realization that the clandestine picture was that of the area where he was standing, specifically aimed to capture the image of the combination lock and whoever entered or left through the doors. Jim felt a chill go through him.

He looked around, but it was several minutes before he spotted it. A very small wireless camera was mounted in the same ceiling hole that accommodated a sprinkler nozzle. It had a clear view of the doorway to the second floor secure area. Jim knew the entranceways to the secure areas were not directly monitored by design with only the hallways and stairs observed. This had been done to disallow purposeful or accidental observation of the keying sequence on the door lock.

Jim realized the combination push-buttons on the door lock could be readily observed by the rogue camera, and a clear view of the person entering or leaving would be shown on the intended receiver, just as Jim observed himself on his hand-held unit. The question that bothered Jim was who installed the camera, and where is the intended receiver unit?

Jim brought the handheld receiver to each floor of the building to test for hidden wireless cameras. However, the unit at the entrance to the second floor secure area was the only one found. Someone was very interested in the comings and going, or even the door lock combination, to Ferrari Investments.

Jim wondered if McGregor had installed it for the FBI. He wondered if this was a legal snoop operation or something off the books. He would call Maria later; let her pass the information on to Ferrari.

Jim found Steve Arnold from SCCI still at his hotel and asked him to examine the camera installation. Steve and Jim brought a large step ladder from the back of the building and climbed up to the ceiling. Steve carefully removed the ceiling tile.

"What do you see?" asked Jim.

"Well, there's a tiny camera clamped to the sprinkler pipe. It looks like there's a separate module that's the transmitter."

"Any writing on it?" asked Jim.

"Uh, yeah. There's a large 6-Volt battery taped to the sprinkler pipe. The unit is a 1-Watt output device, it says."

"Well, that's clearly illegal as it's ten times more power than allowed."

"It's what it says on it. What do you want me to do?"

"Just leave it there. Can you put a piece of electrical tape over the lens?" asked Jim.

Art chuckled. "No problem."

Chapter 26

ANTONIO MORETTI WAS muscle that McGregor kept busy. One evening he was seated in the back room of Casey's lounge with Marc Fontana when McGregor came in, letting the heavy door slam shut behind him. McGregor looked around the room and took a seat at the round table.

"Got your message boss," said Moretti.

McGregor turned instead to Fontana. "Well? You come up with something or what?"

Marc straightened his back in the chair and leaned forward onto the table. "There's nothing that says any of our guys knew what was in the basement, or would even think to rip us off."

McGregor slammed his fist on the table. "God damn it. Two hundred large is gone. GONE!" His eyes bored into Marc. "Where the hell is it?"

Marc shook his head. "Been thinking about it. Talked to the guys."

McGregor looked up, his eyes widening. "Yeah? What?"

"Only the Randolph guy and the two FBI pricks could have gotten down there after we brought the stuff in," said Marc. "All of the work crew was on the upper floors, no need for them to go in the basement. That's why we decided to temporarily keep it there." Marc shook his head and continued. "The Randolph guy has all the combinations to the doors, and the two FBI assholes can get in wherever they feel like it, with or without a warrant." Marc shrugged. "Shit. For all I know, maybe it was all of them."

McGregor leaned back in his chair as a young waiter brought their usual drinks. When he departed, McGregor sat up and glared at the two men.

"Someone's gonna pay for this," he growled. "I want that two hundred grand back in the till."

"Shit, you want us to roust the feds?" exclaimed Fontana. "Those pricks can bite back. You know that."

McGregor's fist came down on the table again. "God damn it! Find out what those two know. And that asshole Randolph, shake it outa him."

Fontana and Moretti glanced at each other.

"When I get my money back, I'll deal with whoever it is myself."

"Money's probably gone for good," grumbled Moretti.

"Well, then you bring me the guy who took it," McGregor rejoined, glaring back and forth between Fontana and Moretti.

McGregor turned when he heard the door open.

"Hey, Mike. Got a call for ya out here," yelled the bartender.

Mike shook his finger at his two cohorts. "Get me results," he said as he walked through the doorway.

Fontana shook his head and turned to Moretti. "I haven't seen those feds in a while. Shit, how the hell we gonna find 'em?"

"How 'bout the other guy? asked Moretti.

"Randolph? Yeah, he's still around," said Fontana. "We can start with him."

"We searched his hotel room last week," said Moretti.

"Yeah. So if he's got it, he stashed it somewhere. He's gonna tell us where."

"How you gonna get him to talk?"

"Don't know yet."

—

The next morning Jim was setting up a test routine in the twelfth floor comm room. He turned when he heard footsteps and saw Greg approaching.

"You got all the other floors working?" asked Greg.

Jim shook his head. "No. Boss wanted me to finish this floor. I guess there's a tenant that wants to move in," Jim replied. "What's new with you?"

"Same old shit." Greg shuffled his feet, pausing for a couple seconds. "Fontana approached me a few minutes ago. Said that he wants to sit with you and have a chat. When I asked him what about, he told me to mind my own business. So I came up to tell you he wants a sit-down out of this building. Imagine it has to do with McGregor. What the hell else?"

"Shit. What's he up to?" Jim said.

"Rumor has it, someone ripped off some stuff McGregor stashed in this building. Might be about that."

Jim shook his head. "What's he been hiding in here?" *As if I didn't know.*

Greg shrugged. "I heard Marc's been asking around about who has access in the building."

"So I'm the fall guy?" said Jim.

"Look, I'll go with you if you want. Where shall I tell him to meet?" said Greg.

Jim hesitated a moment, then suggested Angel's diner. "Greg, I don't think Fontana is gonna want anyone with me."

"Let him say so when we get there. Then I can take a seat at the counter. Least I'll be there. Bet your ass he'll have someone with *him.*"

Jim nodded, "Okay. I appreciate you doing this."

"Let's just see what those guys want. I'm sure Marc will be speaking for McGregor."

"Okay," said Jim, "set it up for tonight at six."

Greg nodded and turned to leave. A feeling of dread came over Jim. McGregor was likely in a foul frame of mind with DiCosta selling to Ferrari and some of his stash being stolen. He wondered if McGregor even suspected the two FBI guys. *By the way, where the hell are they? Haven't seen them since they stole that stuff from the basement.*

Jim pulled his cell phone from his pocket and called Dom's number.

"Hello."

"Dom, its Jim. Are you in town?"

"About twenty minutes away."

"Greg and I will be at Angel's Diner at six. One of McGregor's guys wants to talk to me."

"I know the place. I'll be outside in my car before you get there. Not to worry."

"Okay. Thanks."

Not to worry? Easy for him to say.

—

Reed and Somers sat at the conference table, each gripping a cup of coffee, while they waited for their boss to come in.

"We okay?" whispered Somers. "You heard anything?"

"Calm down," replied Reed. "It was a clean deal, no loose ends."

"What'd you do with the stuff?" said Somers.

Reed turned to him and smiled. "It's in a safe deposit box."

"Shit, mine's still in my garage," moaned Somers.

"Goddamn it," hissed Reed. "Get it outa there. Tonight."

Just then the conference room door opened and Leon Freedman, supervisor in the RICO branch, came in. He sat down and passed out a sheath of papers to each agent. "All right," he said. "The DiCosta project has ended." He looked up at the two agents. "I told you earlier the Director was shifting focus."

Reed nodded.

Freedman continued. "In front of you is our approach to putting an end to the Ferrari operation. It's estimated that they pulled in over 300 million last year, and most of it disappeared offshore somewhere. Now, they've fully absorbed the DiCosta operation so they'll be doing even more. These guys are a royal pain in my ass."

He looked at his agents. "Of course, I'm preaching to the choir here. So, we'll go over the plan and get the project rolling. Some things have already started. For instance, I had a wireless camera installed where we can see who comes and goes into their new headquarters in the Walker building." Freedman opened his folder. "Let's get started."

—

When Jim and Greg entered the diner they spotted Marc Fontana and Antonio Moretti in a booth at the back. No other customers sat near them. As Greg and Jim approached, Moretti got out of the booth.

Fontana looked at Jim. "Sorry, bear with me. I gotta be careful."

Then Moretti quickly patted down Jim and Greg. Moretti nodded at Fontana.

"What the hell? You think we're wired?" exclaimed Jim.

"Have a seat," said Fontana, looking at Jim. "You two take a seat at the counter," nodding to Antonio and Greg.

Greg looked at Jim, who nodded.

Jim sat opposite Fontana as the waitress appeared. Jim ordered a hamburger and coffee. Fontana, just coffee.

Jim scowled. "This little chat couldn't happen at work?"

"No," said Marc. "This is better."

"So, what's on your mind?" asked Jim. He was irritated by the brash attitude of the young man. He wondered if he was even twenty five.

"Listen, I ain't going to beat around the bush. There's been stuff belonging to McGregor stolen from the basement of the building." He paused and glanced at Jim. "I wanna know where it is, and who took it. You gonna help me out here?"

Jim let out a long breath. "McGregor. What's he got to do with that building? He isn't part of the authorized work crew."

"Let's not get bogged down on details. You know how things work; you've been around long enough."

"Someone hid some stuff in the basement for McGregor. That's what you're saying?" asked Jim.

Marc nodded and said, "A few days ago. They went to get it, but some of it was missing. What d'ya know about that?"

"You've got a crew in there of at least twenty-four men. They all have the access code to the whole building except for the secure areas where I have completed my tests." Jim shrugged. "What do you expect *me* to do?"

"I've talked to everyone in the work crew; each had a solid alibi."

Jim raised an eyebrow. "If you say so."

Marc grimaced then said, "So now we get to you."

"I'm the fall guy?" said Jim, "Because *you guys* lost something?"

"You gonna help us out here? Where should we be looking? You do have access. We can't ignore that."

The waitress arrived at the booth with Jim's hamburger, refilling the coffee cups. When she was out of earshot, Marc said, "Help us out here."

Jim bit into his burger, chewed and swallowed. "You're right. I have access all over the building until the tenants arrive. I'm probably in the basement at least once every week for some test or other. I didn't see any of your stuff, but then I wasn't looking for it. I certainly didn't steal any of it, whatever it was."

Marc looked directly at Jim. "Who did?"

"Odds are that it was someone in your crew."

Marc shook his head.

"It was not me. Some asshole searched my room recently, sure as hell didn't find anything, now did he?"

Marc glared at Jim. "Help me out here. Who else could get around that building?"

"Well, there's always the boss, Ed Marcello. But he goes to Greg to get the combination on the locks. They're changed by Greg every Monday morning early."

Marc nodded slowly. "Okay."

"There's the two FBI pricks that used to hang around. They'd come in and wander around wherever they please."

"Haven't seen them around since before the stuff went missing," said Marc.

"For Christ sakes, Marc," Jim scowled. "I understand I'd be the first suspect. Think I don't know that?"

Marc ignored the comment and asked, "When's the last time you saw those feds in the building?"

Jim took a few moments to finish his hamburger while he thought about a reply. "I don't recall the exact day. It was at least the week before anybody moved into the basement and first floor."

"Don't the feds need a warrant?" asked Marc.

Jim laughed. "They come in with all kinds of bullshit reasons and who's going to stop them? They were there once looking for illegal aliens, another time for contraband. It wouldn't take much to intimidate the guard."

"Did you see anyone down the basement that shouldn't be there?"

Jim shook his head. "The last few weeks everyone's been working the high floors. Didn't see anyone but the city inspectors."

The two men sipped their coffee. Jim hesitated at fingering the FBI. He thought of it as money in the bank that he could draw out if needed. But doubts clouded his thinking, the focus was probably still on him.

"What else?" asked Marc.

Jim shrugged. “Like I said, odds favor someone in the work crew. I don’t know who it would be. It sure as shit wasn’t me.”

Marc put his cup down and stared at Jim. “If I think you’re lying to me, Moretti over there, he’s going to pay you a visit, and he won’t be as nice as me.”

“You ought to do your homework first,” said Jim meeting his stare.

Marc slid out of the booth. “I will. Count on it.”

Greg slid back into the booth after Fontana and Moretti left. “What’d he want with you?” said Greg.

“He’s saying that someone stole some of McGregor’s stuff, whatever that was, from where it was hidden down in the basement.”

“Shit. Is he looking at me?”

Jim shook his head. “He said that he thinks the crew working in the building is clean, they all got good alibis.”

“Then what? Looking at you?”

Jim nodded. “Yeah, makes sense to him since I have access everywhere.”

“Well, hell. What about those feds, they’re always underfoot,” said Greg.

“Yeah, he knows about them. I think he’s gonna give it more thought before he turns his goons on me.”

Greg looked wide eyed at Jim. “You shittin’ me? You mean Moretti? He’s a mean prick.”

Jim looked at Greg. “You have any idea what the hell was stolen?”

Greg shook his head. “Remember, I told you I saw Marc and some other guy moving metal boxes into the basement?”

“Yeah. They didn’t see you,” said Jim.

“Right. That’s all I ever saw. I don’t know what’s in them.”

“But that happened right after those robberies up at New Rochelle and Scarsdale, right?” said Jim.

Greg nodded. “Yeah. Jewels, money, who knows.”

Jim grimaced. “I think one of his own guys ripped him off, that’s what I think.”

“Shit. Suppose he gets a burr up his ass and comes after you?”

"Guess I'll have to deal with it." Jim slid out of the booth. "Let's go. Been here long enough." He laid a ten dollar bill on the table.

Jim glanced around the immediate area when he left the diner but did not see Dom. He and Greg walked back to the Walker building from where they hailed a cab.

Jim kicked his shoes off, reclined on top of the bed, then reached for the phone and punched in Maria's home number. She picked up on the third ring.

"Jim. Glad you called. I just got home."

"Just got home myself. How's your mom?"

"She's up and around but still pretty weak. The doctor comes over every day."

He told her about the meeting with Fontana and Moretti and of his worry about retribution by McGregor if the stolen items from the building basement weren't recovered since McGregor had it in mind that he, Jim, was somehow responsible.

"But that's ridiculous. Isn't it?"

"From his point of view, it makes sense. He claims all the work crew has an alibi."

"How can he be so sure?"

"Well, I don't think he can. It's true that I have access to every part of the building before the tenants arrive. He's basing his judgment on that," Jim said.

"But there are so many workers there. How can he so sure?"

"There's something else I need to tell you, but not on the phone," said Jim.

She paused for a moment before replying. "I think Dom is still in town. I could call him. He could pick us up. Could we talk about it in front of him? Would that be all right?"

Jim hesitated. "Okay."

"Why don't I put you on hold while I call his cell phone? I'll come right back to you."

"Sure. I'll hold."

He heard a click and he was on 'hold.' It was almost two minutes before he heard Maria again.

"Jim? Still there?"

"Hi. What did he say?"

"We'll pick you up at your hotel in thirty minutes."

“That’d be great,” said Jim.
“See you then.”

Chapter 27

JIM GOT IN THE BACK of the limo and it started to move.

Maria hugged and kissed him. "I've missed you."

Jim wrapped his arms around her. "Missed you, too. Hope your mom's doing okay."

"The doctor is happy with her progress."

"How about your business? You've been away from it . . ."

"I'm seriously looking for another salesperson. It's getting to be too much." She kissed his ear. "Besides, I don't get to see enough of you."

Dom turned his head slightly toward them as he drove. "Hold off on what you want to talk about until I park. It's just a little ways."

"Okay, sure," said Jim.

Maria put her arm around Jim as Dom pulled into the parking lot of the Red Coach Inn, a tavern just off the Henry Hudson Parkway. Dom threaded his way through the crowded parking lot until he reached a high concrete retaining wall cut into a hillside that marked the edge of the property. Dom backed the car to the wall and stopped the engine. The nearest car was fifty feet away.

Jim looked about, curious. "I've never been here. Looks upscale."

"It is," said Dom. "I'm part owner and we've always catered to a higher class crowd. We set the prices to discourage the young rowdies. The food is good, though."

"I've never been here either," said Maria. "I heard about it from clients though. I didn't know you were part owner, Dom. How long?"

"Oh, over five years. Fellow owed me, and we settled accounts by my taking his share of the place. It's just me and two friends now. We bought everyone else out." He turned in his seat to face them. "So, Jim, what's going on?"

"McGregor doesn't like me and thinks I'm sticking my nose in his business. He thinks I'm working with the FBI or maybe I'm actually an agent. As you know, I've had run-ins with McGregor and some of his guys. The other day, my hotel room was searched."

"I didn't know," said Maria.

"You were out of town. Anyway, I managed to tick McGregor off even more when he rousted me one day, and I told him I knew he was helping the FBI install snooping hardware in the building." Jim shook his head. "That meeting didn't end well."

Jim looked at Dom, whose face didn't give away his thoughts. Jim continued. "Following the robberies in Scarsdale and New Rochelle, I was told by Greg that he witnessed Fontana and some other guy bringing metal boxes into the basement of the building. Correct or not, I assumed these boxes held money and jewels from their robberies."

"Did they?" asked Maria.

Jim raised a hand and continued. "I haven't been down in the basement since that happened except once. I had confiscated two tiny microphones that someone had installed on the second floor. Well, just for the hell of it, I put one in the basement near the back door. I didn't search the basement. I just wanted to install the microphone. A few days later, I recorded an interesting event onto a CD. That's what I want to tell you about."

He looked at Maria and then at Dom.

"What's on the CD?" asked Maria, sitting up straight.

"I'm not sure of the legality of this recording," Jim mused aloud. "But anyway, what happened was that one evening I was in that comm room when I heard two men come into the basement through the rear door. No one's supposed to be there after six. So I started recording as I listened to them."

"Get to it! What happened?" said Maria.

Dom didn't say anything.

"The two men that entered the basement were the FBI guys that come around a lot and annoy me. It seems they suspected, or maybe knew, that there were valuables stored down there. They also knew that, in a few days, the basement would be taken over by the new tenant. So before McGregor could retrieve his loot, these two guys went down there and apparently lifted at least 200 grand in cash, maybe more, if I understood what's on the CD correctly."

Dom spoke. "McGregor doesn't suspect the FBI?"

"I don't think he puts a lot of weight on it because he figures the FBI only comes into the building with a warrant. Maybe they had one. Who knows?"

Maria looked at Jim wide eyed. "He blames you? Thinks you took his money?"

Jim nodded. "Tonight, as you know, I was asked to meet with Marc Fontana and this muscle guy, Antonio Moretti at a local diner. Marc informed me that McGregor wanted his money back and wanted to nail someone for it. He said I looked like the best candidate. Marc said, if I knew anything about it, I should tell him; otherwise it might not go well for me."

Jim felt Maria punch his arm. "You never said *all* this to me."

He sensed that she was a bit hurt. "I wanted to." He looked at Dom. "I guess; now we have to decide what's best to do."

"You're saying no one knows about this?" said Dom.

"I haven't told anyone."

"Where are these two feds now?" asked Dom.

"I haven't seen them in about two weeks. Very odd," replied Jim.

"Lawyers tell me that the FBI has increased their demands for information from Ferrari's operation," said Dom. "It's like they're no longer interested in the construction company."

"Maybe since Ferrari bought it?" asked Jim.

"Yeah, could be. They weren't getting anywhere with it. They've always had a spotlight on Ferrari. The RICO guys have been snooping around often. Maybe now, things are heating up."

"Is there a grand jury seated?" asked Jim.

"I haven't heard. Maybe," said Dom.

"What should we do?" asked Maria.

"The money they stole is gone, if they're smart about it. Untraceable," said Dom.

"If we turn them in, what'll we get out of it?" said Jim.

"Prosecutor probably can't use the CD; legally it's iffy, and I can't positively ID the voices.

"Dom, there's got to be something we can do. Isn't there?" pleaded Maria.

Jim felt Dom's eyes staring at him. "What do *you* want to do?" asked Dom.

Maria turned to look at Jim.

He slowly exhaled. "I don't much care that those two FBI jerks made off with the money. I just don't want McGregor thinking I took it."

"And what?" asked Dom. "You don't want McGregor to know the feds took his money?"

Jim grimaced. "I was wondering if it's something we can use. You know, like money in the bank."

Dom shook his head. "Where's the payoff? We keep this secret. Those two get away free. McGregor thinks you did it, comes after you."

"Could the CD be useful in the likely upcoming grand jury thing?" asked Jim.

Dom shrugged. "How?"

"Blackmail the two FBI jerks to get info on what the prosecutor is presenting to the jury?"

Dom looked at Jim, and then turned to Maria with a smile. "You got a smart one here."

Jim felt her snuggle up to him. "He's cute, too," she said before kissing his cheek.

Dom chewed on his lip for a few seconds. "I'm not saying I would, but if I did do as you suggest, this wouldn't help *you* at all. McGregor would still think that you stole his money or know who did."

Jim grimaced, nodded.

Dom continued, "If we let it leak to McGregor that the feds made off with his money, he'd probably have them tortured and killed. That'd take the pressure off you, but would make the CD useless for your grand jury idea."

"He's going to keep coming after Jim, isn't he?" said Maria.

Dom didn't reply, but stared out of the window for a few seconds.

Jim looked at him, suddenly feeling discouraged. "I hate the idea of those FBI pricks getting off with it and leaving *me* in the lurch."

"If we rat them out to their bosses, they'll go to prison," said Dom, then added, "That should get you off the hook with McGregor."

Jim shrugged, "That could take a couple years before it's resolved. He'll be coming after me soon; that's the feeling I get." Jim saw the scared look from Maria.

Maria turned to Dom. "What can he do?"

Dom let out his breath slowly. "I'll have to think about this. How about you two come inside with me. Get a bite to eat and a drink."

Jim looked at Maria, she nodded. "Okay. Lead the way," said Jim.

As they entered just off the main dining room, Jim heard a small band. He admired the rich leather and wood interior and the nattily-dressed waitstaff. The rich odor of roast beef wafted to his nostrils. The host greeted Dom warmly and guided them to a large booth near the fireplace. Jim noticed that it was a real wood fire, not the modern gas burner and fake logs popular in many places. He noticed, too, that Dom took a seat that allowed him to see nearly everyone in the dining room.

After the waiter brought their drinks, Dom made a dinner suggestion. "You can't find better roast beef anywhere, but if you want something lighter, I can recommend the lamb or salmon. The beef is like nothing you have ever tasted. It's my treat so get what you like."

The waiter came back and took their orders. Jim noticed Dom scanning the crowd.

"What kind of folks do you usually get here? Different on weekends?" asked Jim.

Dom shrugged. "Weekdays we get a lot of salespeople, do a heck of a lunch trade. Evening is like this, couples, some small groups." Dom raised an eyebrow. "Tie and jacket required after five."

"No happy hour?" teased Maria.

"Not hardly," Dom replied. "All the salesmen and riffraff head to other places, come 5 o'clock."

Jim noticed Dom gazing often in one particular direction. Facing the fireplace, he couldn't see the crowd. Finally he asked. "Something wrong?"

Dom shook his head. "No. Ferrari came in with his wife and another couple. I don't think they've seen me."

"Is he part-owner, too?" asked Jim.

"No. I'm not into him for anything. Got this place with money I borrowed from Maria's dad." Dom started to slide out of the booth. "I'll be back in a few minutes," he said and started toward the front of the dining room.

Jim looked at Maria. "Can you see where he went? I don't want to turn around." Maria twisted on the seat.

"See him?" Jim asked.

"Uh-huh. He stopped at Ferrari's table. They're both heading to the back, to the kitchen door." A second later, "I can't see them now." Maria sat straight in her seat, reaching for Jim's hand.

"What do you think he's up to?" asked Jim. "Maybe he's talking to him about the two feds and McGregor."

"Wow. I guess that would get things moving, one direction or other."

Twenty minutes later Dom returned.

"Starting to worry about you," said Maria.

"Everything okay?" asked Jim as he searched Dom's face.

Dom scowled. "Didn't go the way I had hoped."

"What?" said Maria.

"He appreciates Jim's willingness to challenge those two feds," said Dom, "But he's worried about what would happen if the two jerks were caught. No doubt they'd point the finger at Ferrari and Jim. Tampering with the jury or the prosecutor's office is punishable with heavy jail time. He's not willing to take that risk. He said he'll keep relying on his contact network to hopefully keep him out of serious trouble."

Jim started to say something, but Maria spoke first. "The heck with the two jerks. What about Jim? What about McGregor?" Her face was reddening.

Jim reached for her hand.

Dom looked at Jim and then back to Maria. "He repeated what he had said once before. That McGregor would get his cord cut, but it wasn't the time, yet."

"How about leaking to McGregor that it was the FBI that took his money?" asked Jim.

Dom nodded. "I mentioned that. He didn't seem to have a problem with it, except that McGregor might not believe it."

"Wonderful," exclaimed Maria, folding her arms across her chest. "Just marvelous."

"He said McGregor is a sociopath," said Dom, "Also mentally unstable."

Maria looked at Jim, leaned her head against his arm.

He looked at Dom. "Guess I'll be tip-toeing around this guy."

Dom signed the slip and slid several bills into the check folder. As they started to slide out of the booth, a well dressed man of middle age appeared and motioned for Dom to slide farther into the booth. The man took a seat next to him.

"I thought I should explain in person," he said turning to look at Maria. "Maria, nice to see you again."

She smiled and nodded.

"This is Mike Ferrari," said Dom. "Mike this young man is Jim Randolph, a good friend of Maria. He works for SCCI at the Walker building."

Ferrari extended his arm and the two shook hands. Jim studied Ferrari when he could without being obvious. He guessed the pin-striped blue suit had set Ferrari back more than Jim made in a month. His eyes were something that gave Jim pause. They softened when he spoke to Maria, but otherwise appeared stern and without life. His gaze swept the dining area often. Jim noticed Ferrari tilt his hand up off the table momentarily, and out of the corner of his eye Jim caught movement, but then it was gone. Bodyguard?

Ferrari turned to look at Jim with a slight smile. "I'm sure Dom told you about our conversation, but I wanted to come by, meet you, and *personally* tell you what I think you should know about all this."

Jim nodded.

Ferrari glanced around and lowered his voice. "In my organization there's a guy I am forced by circumstances to keep on. This man follows no rules and is unmanageable. Until something changes, I'm stuck with him. He is dangerous to me, as his behavior could reflect badly on what otherwise is a business I've managed to keep pretty clean and very profitable. That the government would like to get inside my business is a given, and this person could give them probable cause with his undisciplined behavior." Ferrari paused, glancing at Jim and Maria. "I understand that you have had some difficulties with him and with some of his people."

"I have," said Jim.

“I understand you’ve also come into some information that could compromise some government people in regards to property this man had squirreled away.”

Again, Jim nodded.

“I have no doubt how this property was obtained, no doubt whatsoever. This situation could have disastrous consequences. How long can secrets be kept?” He shrugged. “It could turn out to be dangerous for me as well.”

Jim started to speak, but Ferrari silenced him with a raised hand. “I personally don’t care that two sleazy characters have some of this fellow’s property. However, I don’t think there is anything to be gained for you or for me by disclosing this information. Your gesture in regards to squeezing those two is appreciated. However, it will increase the danger for you, and the information obtainable is something I can deal with using my own resources. And,” Ferrari paused, “I’ll deal with this guy in due time.”

Jim felt Ferrari’s eyes on him. They had softened from what he had seen before. “I think I understand,” said Jim. “It was nice to meet you. Thanks for the suggestions.”

Ferrari slid out of the booth, turned to Dom. “Come by my new office.”

Dom smiled, “I will.”

No one spoke for almost a minute.

“Interesting fellow,” said Jim.

Dom raised an eyebrow. “He’s smart and ruthless; not someone to mess with.”

Chapter 28

MCGREGOR SLAMMED THROUGH the door, his foul mood obvious to the two men at the table in the back room of Casey's lounge.

"Shit," mumbled Antonio Moretti as he and Marc Fontana looked up from their card game.

McGregor dropped into a chair and glared at his two associates.

"What's biting you?" said Marc.

"What's biting me?" McGregor yelled. "I just got braced by goddamn Ferrari. That's what's biting me!"

"Ferrari?" Marc's eyes widened. "What the hell?"

They quieted as the night bartender brought in a tray of drinks. When he left, McGregor's fist slammed down on the table. "Goddamn him!"

"Mike, what the hell's going on?" asked Marc.

"You two haven't helped me at all," said McGregor. "I still don't know who grabbed the stuff."

"Boss, we –," started Moretti.

"Shut up," yelled McGregor. "You two are goddamn useless. Someone whispered to Ferrari that the feds took the money. The goddamn FBI."

Marc's mouth hung open. "FBI? Who told them about it? How'd they know?"

McGregor leaned back in his chair. "Now that's the question, ain't it?"

—

"Here he comes," said Fontana, looking out the windshield. "He just left the building. Go get him."

"Yeah, I see him," said Moretti, opening the car door.

Fontana watched as Moretti approached Jim and nudged him with the pistol in his jacket pocket.

Moretti opened the rear door and pushed Jim into the back seat.

"Hey Marc, what the hell is going on?" said Jim.

"Relax. McGregor wants to see you."

"So he sends you two? Who the hell is this clown?" Jim nods toward Moretti.

"Antonio Moretti. Now just relax. We'll be there in no time," said Fontana as he started the car.

Several minutes later, Fontana stopped in front of Casey's Lounge. Moretti and Fontana escorted Jim into the bar and then to the back room. Jim stood between the two men as McGregor turned on his seat to look at him.

"So, you had some time to think about what I told you the other day. Now, I want some answers. Who has my stuff?"

"I don't have anything of yours."

"Wrong answer." He looked at Moretti and nodded.

Moretti's fist sank into Jim's side. Fontana held him upright as Jim gasped in pain.

"Let's do this again," said McGregor. "Who has my money?"

Jim shook his head. "I don't know," he gasped.

"You're a slow learner." He nodded to Moretti.

Again, a fist slammed into Jim's side. Fontana's tight grip kept Jim from falling to the floor. McGregor got out of his chair and moved to stand in front of Jim.

"Let's try this again. Where's my stuff? Who has my money?"

Jim shook his head.

McGregor landed a blow on the side of Jim's face. Jim's head drooped. Blood trickled out of his mouth. He moaned. Moretti helped Fontana hold him up. McGregor landed another vicious blow on Jim's face. This time, Jim's head drooped and stayed that way.

"Hold his head up," yelled McGregor.

Moretti pulled Jim's head up by the hair. McGregor pulled a semi-automatic pistol from his waistband, and with his other hand pried open Jim's bleeding mouth, and then pushed the pistol into it. Spit and blood splattered out as Jim fought the intrusion.

"Now, asshole. One more time. Where is my stuff?" yelled McGregor. He pulled the pistol away from Jim's mouth, but held it close to his face. "Do you want to die, asshole?"

Jim shook his head and sputtered, "No."

McGregor pulled the slide back on the pistol, and pressed the gun to Jim's neck. "Tell me or I'll kill you." McGregor's voice was almost a shriek.

Fontana reached a hand out to McGregor and gently pushed him away from Jim. Moretti struggled to keep Jim on his feet. "Enough, Mike. He doesn't know anything."

McGregor shrugged off Fontana's hand. "Keep out of it."

Marc again pushed against McGregor. "It's enough." He looked over at Moretti. "Get Mike out of here."

Moretti let go of Jim, who crumbled to the floor, moaning. He took Mike's arm and started toward the door. "C'mon Mike. Tomorrow's another day. Let's get the hell outa here."

Fontana watched them leave the room and the door close behind them as they passed into the bar area.

Marc grabbed Jim under his arms and dragged him to a chair. Then he went through a small door into the kitchen and returned with wet towels. Casey, the bartender, pushed through the lounge door bringing a bottle of antiseptic solution.

"Is he gone?" asked Fontana.

"Yeah. Him and Moretti left," said Casey. "What the hell happened?"

Fontana shook his head. "He lost it. He was ready to kill this guy."

"Who's he?"

"Some dude works with me."

"Well, you better get him the hell outa here." Casey turned and went back to the lounge.

Marc cleaned Jim's wounds with the antiseptic and wet towels. Jim moaned loudly.

"I'm sorry, Jim. I didn't know this was gonna happen. Had no idea. Said he wanted to talk to you."

Jim moaned. "Fuckin' bastard."

Marc finished cleaning Jim's face and tossed the towel aside.

Jim opened his eyes and stared at him. He wet his swollen lips. "Thanks." He licked his lips again. "I'm gonna call the cops on that asshole."

Fontana looked hard at Jim. "Damn little they'll do."

Jim shook his head, silent for a moment. "Enough of this shit." He tried to pull his phone from his pocket.

"You call the cops, you'll be dead. You know that . . ."

Jim shook his head slowly. "Get me back to my hotel."

"Yeah. Sure."

When Marc helped Jim into the hotel lobby, the night desk clerk looked up. "Hey, you guys need a doctor?"

Fontana smiled. "No. Rough night. Gotta get him to bed." He helped Jim to the elevator.

As they walked to the elevator, the desk clerk pulled a yellow Post-it note from the top of his desk, looked at it, and picked up the telephone.

Dom and Maria arrived twenty minutes later and the desk clerk described what he witnessed, saying the man with Jim had left a couple of minutes after bringing Jim to his room. They thanked the desk clerk and went to the elevator. At Jim's room, Maria knocked. A few seconds later, she knocked again. The door opened to a badly beaten face. Maria cried out. Dom pressed Jim into a chair, and checked the seriousness of his wounds. Maria got a wet towel and wiped his face, occasionally pushing away her tears with the back of her hand.

Dom pulled off Jim's shirt and checked the dark bruises on his torso. Satisfied that there were no cracked ribs, Dom sat down and asked Jim to describe the incident. Then, he asked Jim to give him the CD of the voice recordings. Afterward, he left and Maria stayed.

The next morning, Jim called Art Wagner at SCCI, and briefly described the incident, saying he was ill and would not be at work. Maria stayed with him until mid morning. Jim spent most of the day sleeping.

Maria called her father and told him of Jim's beating. He said that Dom had already told him and to let him and Dom work things out.

—

Ferrari listened to the voices on the CD for the fourth time while sitting in his new office in the secure area of the second floor of the Walker building. Afterward he sat for a few minutes quietly in thought. Suddenly he slipped the CD into his jacket pocket and reached for the phone.

"Mr. Salerno, please." A pause. "Yes, Tony Ferrari."

There was a longer pause before Ferrari heard a reply.

"Tony. How ya doin'? It's been a while."

"Yes, sir. I hesitate to bother you, know you've been ill."

"Forget about it. What's up?"

"I have a CD with a voice recording that I would appreciate your advice on."

"What's it about, Tony?"

"I don't think I should talk about it on the phone."

"Okay. Come on over. We'll have us a drink."

"I can be there in an hour," said Ferrari.

"See you then."

Carmine Salerno, 70 years old and ailing, insisted they sit down with a drink before entertaining any business. He glanced at a waiting maid who then brought a silver tray with glasses and a decanter of what Tony knew would be premium whiskey.

"Neat, sir?"

Tony nodded and the maid poured two fingers into each glass, put down the tray, and left the room and closed the heavy double doors.

"If you don't mind, Tony, I'd appreciate it if you play the CD on the machine over there." Carmine pointed to a stack of entertainment electronics on a book shelf. "This body is pretty worn out, gotta keep nursing it along."

"Of course." Tony took the CD and went to the electronic equipment. There, he spent a minute figuring out how to play it. Finally, the sound came out of the speakers. Tony stood by the equipment as the CD played.

Salerno listened intently. "Play it again, Tony." He asked to have it replayed three times before signaling Tony back to the sofa. "Tell me what I just heard – what it means."

"This CD was made by an engineer working in the Walker building for the communications security people. He did not witness what happened, only heard it as it was recorded. As he is a friend of Maria, Angelo's daughter, the CD came to me through Dominic."

Carmine looked steadily at Tony, and Tony continued.

"This friend of Maria, Jim, and Dominic convinced me of what I'm about to tell you. I ask your indulgence, sir, to let me say what I have to say."

Carmine waved his hand. "Tony, give me the truth, or as close as you think you have it."

"Sir, I realize that Mike McGregor is your sister's son, and it pains me to say what I have to say."

Carmine scowled and nodded. "Go on."

Tony carefully stated his suspicion of McGregor's activities in New Rochelle and Scarsdale, activities that were highlighted in the newspaper. Carmine sat quietly and listened. Tony described how they came to suspect that McGregor had hidden his stolen treasure, temporarily, in the basement of the Walker building. He stated the CD recording is likely that of two FBI agents who frequented the building and that they somehow found out about the stash and helped themselves to quite a bit of the cash, maybe a hundred grand. He described how McGregor suspected everyone in his own team of robbing him, but then focused his attention on Jim Randolph, since he has access to all of the building. "Now," Tony said, "Jim is being threatened and has been beaten seriously by McGregor and his pals."

Carmine shook his head. "Goddamn FBI has been looking for any way to break open the organization with criminal indictments. I've been trying to keep the crews away from drugs and violence, mainly due to the risks involved. I'm sure there is freelance work going on that I would not approve of, and it puts us all at risk."

"Sir, McGregor's behavior, his insubordination, and his recklessness involve my crew and subjects the organization to danger, especially if police or FBI catch him in some act. I'm at a loss how to handle him and would appreciate any advice."

Carmine looked away for a minute without speaking.

Then Tony spoke again. "Sir, it's highly probable that McGregor would fold under police interrogation and try to slide out from under by pointing his finger at others."

Carmine turned to look at Tony. "There's no crew boss that wants McGregor around them. Although my sister denies it, I'm convinced the guy is not wired right."

Carmine looked directly at Ferrari. "I can't sanction anything on the guy. It's not something I can do, given my circumstances."

Ferrari nodded. "I understand."

Carmine stared at Ferrari. "Do you?"

Ferrari didn't respond.

Carmine continued. "All the crews have to protect themselves. You'll have to do what you have to do."

Ferrari nodded slowly.

Carmine put his hand on Ferrari's shoulder as they walked to the door. After a second or two, he added, "I don't want it on *me*."

Chapter 29

JIM COULD NO LONGER access the second floor comm room at will. It was now inside the secure area of Ferrari Investments. Jim pressed the doorbell and waited. In a few seconds, a young woman opened the door, smiled and asked his business. Jim showed her his credentials and requested he be allowed access to the comm room. She picked up a phone from the wall inside the door and after a few seconds of conversation she hung up.

"Come in. You're already on the list." At her desk she asked him to sign in. Please wear this badge and sign out when you leave."

Jim unlocked the comm room and closed the door behind him. The room smelled of warm electronics. He turned on the computer monitor and sat down to run tests. He was still sore from where he had been kicked, luckily no cracked ribs. He thought about when he would finish the job in the building. He wanted to get away from McGregor and his cronies. He had talked with his supervisor and there was a job soon to start at a shipping company off 23rd Street near the West Side Expressway. It was farther from Maria, but hopefully he wouldn't ever hear of McGregor again.

He left the comm room at noon and waved to the woman at the desk. She wrote something down and smiled at him. The area looked like any other office area he'd been in. Cubicles were the main furniture. Permanent walled offices stood along one side. It sure didn't look like a mob organization, at least not what he pictured. Jim went downstairs and walked by the guard station. A new guard service had been employed by the building management team. On seeing Jim, the guard called out. He handed Jim a telephone message. Jim glanced at it and left the building.

He looked at the message again. Ben Lansky of the Philadelphia DA's office. He opened his cell phone and dialed the number. "Ben. Jim Randolph here."

"Hey, how're things in the big city?"

"Crazy. Really crazy."

"Well, I might have something here that'll interest you."

"Really? In Philly?"

"Yep. We got this dude in lockup that wants a deal. We nailed him trying to fence a $35,000 necklace to this guy that we know who breaks them down and sells off the gold and ice. This guy saw what it was and called us. I guess he wanted to get on our good side."

"You know where it's from?"

"You bet. We squeezed it outa him."

"Where? Up this way?"

"Yep, part of that Scarsdale robbery."

"Wow. There's the New Rochelle robbery, too."

"This is the first piece we could trace to either robbery."

"This guy is a fence?"

"Yeah, but he knows the actors. That's why I called."

"What?"

"We talked about Ferrari, remember?"

"Uh-huh."

"Well, this dude says that he got the ice from McGregor, guy who works for Ferrari."

"No shit? He said that?" said Jim.

"Yeah, gave up other names, too."

A chill went through Jim. "Can you tell me?"

"Listen, pal, I'm telling you a lot more than I should already. That's all you get. Just wanted to give a heads up on the guys you're working with. Watch yourself."

"Ben, I appreciate your calling."

"Yeah, well. I *didn't* call, okay?" He hung up.

.

Jim walked to a small corner eatery a few blocks away. It was jammed with lunch patrons hoping for a quick take-out. Jim took a stool at the window counter and ordered a hamburger and coffee. He thought about what he had heard and what it meant. The FBI would have to get involved, he was sure. What would happen to Marc Fontana? Was there any way to save him? Would Greg be drawn into this mess? He wished he could finish the job soon and rid himself of these troubles. He thought of Maria. Being away from her would be torture. Hopefully, he'd get an assignment in the city.

He pulled out his cell phone and dialed Maria.

"Where are you," she asked.

"Sitting in a little corner joint a couple blocks away. You in your office?"

"Yep. I just finished a presentation to a potential new client – a brokerage office out in Great Neck."

"Sounds awesome. Business is really picking up."

"It really is. I have to make sure we can service all these people." She paused. "What's happening at the Walker Building?"

Jim told her about the conversation he had with his friend in Philadelphia. "I was wondering if maybe you wanted to tell your dad."

"Boy, this guy is a real pain in the butt," she said.

"McGregor? Yeah. Literally."

"What about the other connection – the two guys?"

"This keeps getting more complicated."

"I know. Let me call you back later," she said.

"Okay. I'd like that." He closed his phone.

Outside, Jim leaned against the wall of the eatery, near the doorway. The warm sun felt good. He watched hundreds of people walking by. It was then that he saw someone in the corner of his vision. A man approached and stood next to him. He recognized him when he pushed his hat back, Jack Reed, FBI.

"Thought I recognized you," said Reed.

Jim scowled. "You tailing me?"

"Now why would I do that?"

Jim didn't offer a reply.

"Say, what do you hear from our old pal, McGregor?"

"*Your* old pal. Just an asshole to me."

"Well, you got a point there, not a solid citizen."

"Yeah."

"Ferrari move in, did he?"

"Yeah, as if you didn't know. You hounding *him* these days?"

"He's not one of your good guys."

"And what? You and your buddy are? Not what I heard."

Reed moved away from the wall to face Jim. "What? What'd you hear, smartass?"

"Hear things. You know how it is."

Reed's face reddened. "No, I don't know how it is. Suppose you tell me, smart guy."

Jim shrugged. "Word is that you and your buddy ripped off some stuff from McGregor. Heard he's really pissed."

"You're full of shit. Where'd you hear that fairy tale?"

"It's not true?"

"Don't be such an ass."

"Well, some folks are taking that information to the bank."

Reed stared at Jim, a nervous twitch in his right eye. "Who's believing such nonsense?"

"McGregor, for one."

"Bullshit."

"Bullshit? He beat the hell outa me, just to make sure I understood him. He thought I was in cahoots with you. Dumb asshole."

"He did that? Holy shit. Who's spreading these rumors?"

"Beats me. You can bet your ass Ferrari knows about it by now."

Reed turned to look away. "This is insane."

"So you say."

Reed walked away, pulling his hat down closer to his eyes and turned back. "Like I told you before, better keep your nose clean."

Jim started back to the Walker Building.

Jim got off the front elevator on the sixth floor. His supervisor had told him that a client would be taking occupancy within a week, and Jim had to make sure the comm room equipment was functioning properly. When he got off the elevator, he saw Marc Fontana walking toward him. Jim looked around, but saw no one else.

"Greg wanted these power strips tested," Marc said as he approached.

Jim nodded and stopped in front of him.

Marc shuffled his feet. "I'm sorry. I didn't think he'd hurt you. Said he wanted to talk to you. Maybe, I should have known better."

"Yeah, maybe so. Anyway, thanks for getting him outa there."

"You okay now?" he asked.

Jim shrugged. "Gotta tell you, though. Heard the FBI is looking into some jewelry that showed up in Philadelphia. Makes sense they'll be looking at McGregor, soon as they squeeze the fence. You may want to rethink your involvement."

Marc stared at Jim for a couple seconds. "Philly?"

Jim nodded and started toward the comm room. He heard Marc walk away. He would have a rough afternoon.

Jim started the automated test routine on the comm room computer. As the data streamed by on the screen, he leaned back in the chair wondering what was going to happen next. With the news from Philadelphia, he realized that pressure would be mounting on McGregor. Would the guy come unglued, he wondered, and turn on him for revenge? What about the two FBI agents? What would they do to cover their tracks? He needed a long vacation, but that wouldn't happen any time soon.

Ferrari arrived at Casey's Lounge just after 5 p.m. It had taken him over an hour for someone to locate McGregor. It seemed that McGregor had been trying to avoid him. Ferrari didn't knock, just burst through the back room door with two of his men. The two men stood on each side of the door and slammed it shut. Ferrari looked at McGregor, sitting and drinking with Antonio Moretti. Antonio got up from the table and slowly moved away and toward the door. McGregor didn't move, only stared at Ferrari as he approached. Ferrari pulled out a chair and sat facing McGregor.

The bartender came in the side door. Ferrari cursed and waved his hand, sending him scurrying away. He stared at McGregor, but got only a sullen look in response. Ferrari swept his hand swiftly across the space in front of him and sent McGregor's whiskey glass flying across the room.

McGregor sighed, seemingly bored with the performance. "What brings you out here? Slumming?"

Ferrari resisted the urge to punch the insolence from the unshaven face. "We've got a big problem here. A problem you're going to fix. That don't happen, your future prospects will be seriously diminished."

McGregor looked off to the far wall.

Ferrari didn't see any recognition that he had been heard. He slammed his fist down on the table. "Asshole," he roared, "I'm talking here."

McGregor flinched, turning slowly to look at who was, organizationally, his boss. "Yeah. I heard you."

"Word on the street is you're trying to unload some stones down in Philly. Well, that's gone to hell. Guy's singing like a canary."

McGregor didn't flinch.

"This shit you're in, gets back to me, to the family, you'll have a lot to answer for. The feds will have all this linked up with New Rochelle and Scarsdale before you know it."

"Nobody can prove anything."

"Proof? Proof? I don't need no goddamn proof! I feel heat and you're going to be looking for a new line of work, and far away."

"Ain't going anywhere. Don't have to worry much what you think."

Ferrari saw the insolent stare again and he resisted smashing his fist into McGregor's face. "I didn't see any of that haul, now did I?"

McGregor shrugged.

"Well, asshole. You're gonna need it for a good lawyer."

"I ain't sayin' shit. Don't know what the hell you're getting at," said McGregor.

"Now I'm hearing there's two feds walking around with some of the money you hauled. I heard about it, you can bet your ass their bosses heard about it. Now what? Don't think they'll be pointing the finger at you?"

Ferrari shook his head. He knew that McGregor was a hard case. Stupid and arrogant and feeling invincible with his aunt married to Carmine Salerno. Ferrari knew eventually Salerno would demand action despite his wife's ranting.

Ferrari pushed his chair back and stood up. "You don't have long to get this fixed." He walked swiftly to the door. His two men followed him out.

"What the hell?" Moretti took the chair vacated by Ferrari.

McGregor shrugged. "He thinks he owns me. He don't."

"Yeah, but what the hell was that about? FBI? Shit, man."

McGregor waved him away. “Go get us a couple drinks. Let me think.”

Moretti scraped back his chair, got up, and left the room. A couple of minutes later he returned with two whiskeys. “What you think happened?” he asked.

McGregor scowled. “Supposed to be broken down. Ice goes one way, metal the other.”

“So, what’d he do?” asked Moretti.

“Bastard got caught with the whole piece, still in the case,” said McGregor. “I dunno. Maybe he thought he had a buyer.”

“Shit, coulda been a sting,” said Moretti.

“I dunno,” said McGregor. “He was to get it disassembled before he did anything.”

“We got a lot of stuff out in the field. Is he gonna point fingers – make a deal?” said Moretti.

McGregor stood up. “Come by my place later tonight.”

“Want I should take care of it?” Moretti asked.

McGregor nodded. “The dumb shit should be out on bail by now. Play it safe. Take your time. You’re gonna visit somebody down there – make sure you do. Drop the piece. Maybe visit someone else before coming back, huh?”

Moretti nodded. “Yeah, got friends there.”

“See you when you get back.” McGregor motioned with his thumb for Moretti to leave.

McGregor had set up for a weekly electronic sweep at Casey’s Lounge. He called to make sure it was happening. What was he gonna do about the two feds? They’d talk for sure to save their asses. The money – where the hell was the money? That creep Randolph; he had something to do with it. Maybe he and the feds were together in this. Was it too late to take care of him? McGregor kicked a chair out of his way. “Son of a bitch,” he roared.

McGregor sat in the car looking at the main entrance to the Empire Investment Trust building, across the side-street from the Walker Building. He raised binoculars to his eyes every few minutes as the day shift people left the building. He knew the FBI had leased the entire sixth floor after shutting down their DiCosta investigation. McGregor had heard that a dozen new agents had been moved in with primary focus on the Ferrari organization. He kept staring at the people leaving the building, not sure the two FBI jerks were still working there. Reed and Somers, yeah, he'd catch up to them, find out what they knew about his money. Then he'd go after that asshole Randolph.

McGregor spotted Agent Reed leaving the building. He started the engine and waited. Reed chatted with an attractive woman, but she soon broke off and joined two other women. "Better luck next time dip-shit," he said. McGregor watched as Reed walked to the front of the Walker Building and hailed a cab. As the cab pulled away, McGregor was two cars behind him. He let two more cars slip between them as they headed north. In another minute they had turned west. Another six minutes and the cab stopped in front of the Barclay Arms, a residential hotel that had seen better days. Two blocks west he found a parking lot and walked back to the hotel. The marquee suggested that a dining room and lounge was part of the establishment. He decided to try his luck in the lounge.

McGregor ordered a whiskey on ice. The reflection in the mirror behind the bar showed him that there were only a few couples at tables and no one in the booths along the far wall. Would Reed come in the lounge for supper or go to the dining room? Well, he'd finish his drink and then check out the dining area.

He didn't have long to wait. Reed had changed his clothes, and he came into the lounge in a sport coat, polo shirt and khaki pants. He took a seat in a booth and a waitress went to him immediately. McGregor waited until Reed had a drink in front of him, then he picked up his glass and walked over to Reed. He slid into the booth facing Reed.

"What the hell you doing here?"

McGregor saw tenseness in his face. Was it fear? "It's been a while. Can't really say I missed you, though."

"You followed me here?" asked Reed.

"Yeah, piece a cake."

"So, what do you want? The DiCosta investigation is closed."

McGregor scowled. "Yeah. No shit. Guess our agreement is terminated as well, huh?"

Reed shrugged. "That's between you and my boss."

"Yeah, right. Well, I'll tell you; got something else on my mind."

Reed looked at his drink, toyed with the glass. "What's that?" he said.

"I'm hearing some shit on the street that is really upsetting."

Reed looked up.

"Heard it from a couple of sources." McGregor shook his head. "Really disappointing."

"What hell are you talking about?" said Reed, taking a long sip.

"Word is that you and your buddy made off with over a hundred large of my money," said McGregor.

Reed frowned. "How'd we do that?"

"You ripped off the stash I had in the basement of the Walker Building. That's how."

Reed shook his head. "I have no idea what you're getting at."

"Well, here's how I got it figured. You and your buddy stole 100 Gs that belong to me. I don't care which one of you pricks got it, I want it back."

Reed shook his head again. "Where'd you get this shit?"

McGregor ignored him and continued. "Since I'm a reasonable guy, tell you what we'll do. You pay me the vig every week until you bring me what you stole. You don't do that; I will have to make other arrangements. You following me so far, or am I talking too fast."

"You're outa your fuckin' mind. I don't know who's telling you all this crap. This got to do with the trouble up in Scarsdale and New Rochelle?"

McGregor ignored him. "The vig is 2500 bucks. That's every goddamn week. First week you miss, we go to plan B."

Reed scowled and looked at McGregor. "Are you threatening a federal agent? You can shove plan B up your ass."

McGregor slid out of his seat, tossed down the remainder of his drink and looked at Reed. "You *don't* want me to have to come looking for you."

Agent Reed watched McGregor leave the lounge. Plan B? What the hell is plan B? Break my bones? Crazy son of a bitch. Who told him about it? Who the hell would have known? Had they been spotted? He sure as hell wasn't going to give the money back. What if the FBI found out? No, paying that asshole anything was out of the question. He'd have to have a serious talk with Somers, couldn't let him be giving away the game. Someone knew, but who, and how? He'd have to find out, couldn't keep going with Damocles' sword hanging over his head.

There was only one person that had free rein in that building: Jim Randolph. He came and went at his own hours, and he had access to all the areas. Reed thought about it, but couldn't reconcile the disparate threads. Randolph hated McGregor, so why would he be the source. Maybe Randolph told someone else, he thought. He frowned. "Yeah, sure. He woulda told that DiCosta woman." He shook his head. "Son of a bitch . . ."

Chapter 30

JIM COMPLETED THE test routine and closed the comm room door. He glanced at his watch, 4:06 p.m. He'd give Maria a call when he got outside the building. When the elevator door opened, he almost ran into Greg.

"Just coming up to see you."

"I'm going down. Come on."

As they rode the elevator to the lobby, Jim asked, "What's going on?"

Greg seemed ill at ease, shuffled his feet. "Marc talked to me. He's kinda scared."

"He keeps some bad company. I told him that," said Jim.

Greg nodded. "He mentioned it."

"So, what's he want?" asked Jim.

"I think he realizes now he's in shit up to his eyeballs."

"He looking for a way out?"

Greg nodded. "Yeah. He's afraid if he makes a move to distance himself, he'll be seen as a high risk to McGregor. On the other hand, he's afraid of doing prison time or having to kill someone. He's never been arrested."

Jim sighed. "What's his involvement in McGregor's business? Has he told you?" asked Jim.

"He said he's been the driver on several robberies, but that he's never killed anyone and never entered anyone's property. I guess he's afraid that McGregor will get him more involved next time."

Jim scowled, shook his head and started across the lobby. He waved at the guard, and then they went through the door to the sidewalk. Jim turned to Greg. "He's a young guy, but he's got to know that under the law he's as guilty as the rest of them in robbery or murder."

"Yeah, he knows that. He's at the point where he sees nothing but trouble whichever way he turns. He wanted to know what I though he should do."

"What did you tell him?" asked Jim.

"Said to him not to get in any deeper. But he worries about how McGregor will react to that. He said he's got folks living upstate and doesn't want to move far away."

"Tell him that for sure he can't get in any deeper. Right now, if he got hauled in, he could maybe get charges dismissed if he turned state's evidence. It'd be risky though. Guess he's thought of that."

Greg nodded. "I don't know how clear he's thinking. He's just a scared kid. What, twenty years old? Got an early sniff of easy money. Having second thoughts, now."

"Glad we talked about this. Let me think on it some." Jim pulled out his cell phone.

Maria asked Jim to come to *Maria's Interiors*, and wait while she completed a cost estimate for a new customer. The cab dropped Jim off in front of the building. Jim nodded at the guard and announced himself to the receptionist who smiled and said that he was expected. She escorted him up a flight of stairs to Maria's expansive office. Jim thanked her and met Maria with a warm hug. He heard the door close behind him. Maria put her hands to his face and kissed him. He sat in a comfortable chair as she went back to completing her cost estimate. A few minutes later, a young woman entered with a coffee service tray. Maria thanked her, got up and poured coffee for Jim and herself. Walking back to her desk, she asked him about his day. He told her of his conversations with Marc and Greg. Then he described his exchange with Agent Reed.

Maria put down her pen and placed her elbows on the desk. "What's going to happen? Marc will be eliminated if McGregor gets suspicious, won't he?"

Jim nodded slowly. "Marc thinks he will be required to get more involved in whatever McGregor has planned, eventually killing someone. If he refuses, knowing what he's already seen, I can't imagine McGregor will let him walk away."

Maria turned in her chair and stared out of the window for a minute.

"What're you thinking?"

She slowly turned back to face him.

"You think he's worth saving, that he's got a chance?"

"Yes. He helped me when McGregor worked me over the other night. That probably didn't endear him too well with McGregor."

"I imagine, Ferrari would look on him as a threat, too; unless, of course, he were to testify against McGregor," she mused.

Jim nodded. "Marc fingering McGregor might be the way in the feds are hoping for. The feds figure this out; he'll have a lot of pressure on him."

"He's between a rock and a hard place," said Maria. "Maybe he should just disappear until McGregor burns out. And he will."

"That makes sense to me, but then I don't think he's of a mind to hear advice from me, maybe from Greg."

"I can't ask Dom about it," said Maria. "If he sees Marc as a threat to Ferrari, he'd be obligated to do something about it – maybe even ordered to."

"Jesus, there's no way out for Marc," said Jim. "Maybe best if he did go into hiding."

"Jim, I could call Dom before we leave. He put a scrambler on my phone some time ago. He has one in his car. Ask him a hypothetical, see what he says."

"He'd figure it out."

"But he might not act on it if I pose it right," said Maria. "I'll let him know it's important to me. His first allegiance is to my father."

"Is that going to get you in hot water?" asked Jim.

Maria smiled. "Maybe. A little."

Jim left her office and sat at the end of the hallway in a small alcove for informal meetings. It was ten minutes later that Maria joined him.

"We had a little chat. He was driving back to my parents' place."

"How'd it go?" asked Jim.

"He listened to what I had to say. Then there was this long pause. I had to ask if he was still there."

Jim looked at her, frowned.

"I guess he was thinking. Anyway, he said that whoever I was talking about was walking on thin ice." She glanced at Jim. "Of course, we knew that."

Jim nodded.

"He insisted that no one deserves a free ride. And that this person, can't pick and choose what he wants to participate in. He wanted the big bucks, and there were risks that he had to assume."

"That doesn't sound encouraging," said Jim.

"No. At least not at first. I guess he had to give me the lecture before he let me have some wiggle room."

Jim's eyes widened.

"I told him this guy helped you when McGregor worked you over, and had been otherwise a decent person as far as you were concerned. That this guy really regretted getting involved with McGregor and he didn't want to have to end up killing someone for him."

"He accepted that?" asked Jim.

"Maybe. He said he knows people in Albany and Syracuse, and would be willing to see if he could get him a job there. Marc would have to keep his nose clean. But, there's always the risk that he'd be found out by one of McGregor's guys."

"It would be great if Dom would do that," said Jim.

"He will." She stood up. "Why don't I finish the proposal tomorrow morning?" She smiled. "That way you can take me to dinner."

He flipped his eyebrows.

"Uh-huh," she smiled. "*After* dinner."

The waiter refilled their coffee and left.

"I think I ate too much," said Maria.

"Me too. It's so darn good," replied Jim. He felt the phone vibrate in his pocket. He scowled, "Sorry," and he reached for it. When he flipped it open, he saw that it was from Art Wagner, his supervisor at SCCI. Jim looked at Maria. "My boss."

"Kinda late for a call, isn't it?" she asked.

"I'll call him back when we get outside. It'll wait."

Jim called his boss when they were seated in the taxi headed for Maria's apartment.

"Art. What's up?"

"Sorry about the late call. I just wanted to get you before you started on the test routine tomorrow," said Art. "I received a call from Ferrari Investments. Some woman called – forgot her name – said she had been asked to get you to come in and look at a real fancy copy and printing machine."

"What do I know about copiers?" asked Jim.

"This is an important client," said Art. "Please take a look at their problem and it may well be they have to call the copy machine repairman. The woman that called said something about computer interface. I didn't really understand what she was getting at."

"Must be a hell of a copier."

"Please. Just check it out. They asked for you specifically."

Jim sighed, "Okay. First thing tomorrow. Bye."

The night was one he wouldn't soon forget. It seemed like he still had some of Maria's scent on him as got to the Walker Building the next morning. Jim climbed the stairs to the second floor and stood before Ferrari Investments and pressed the button for the door bell. A few seconds later the door opened, and he was greeted by the same young woman he had met before.

"Good morning Mr. Randolph, I'm Jeanie. Please come in and sign our visitor's book."

Jeanie wrote out a name tag and placed it on Jim's lapel. She smiled, "There, that'll do it. Let me find Randy. He'll show you around."

Jim thanked her and took a seat. A couple of minutes later, a middle aged man appeared and introduced himself. "We've got this new fancy-shmancy copy and print machine out back. Not something *I* woulda bought, not for the $6,800 it cost."

"Must be a whizzbang of a copier," said Jim.

Randy nodded, pointed to a doorway, and then they were in a small room taken up mostly by the behemoth copy and print machine.

"We've had this thing a couple of weeks," said Randy, "And it worked okay up until yesterday morning. This thing does regular copying, but it's also a remote printer. We have it hooked up to a server so anyone here can access it. That worked fine too, until yesterday."

"What happened yesterday?" asked Jim, walking around the machine.

"When we tried to run a print job here, or request something from the server, we'd get this warning on the display," he pointed to the glowing blue screen at the control panel. "It said that software updates were ready for download and that we had to be connected to the Internet."

"Did you do that?" asked Jim.

"Yeah, I . . . shouldn't I have done that?"

"You shouldn't have touched it. Calling the vendor would have been the right move. So, anyway, what did you do?"

Randy grimaced. "See the two cables in back? One goes to the server port, the other goes to the Internet port."

"Uh-huh, you connected the Internet cable. What then?" said Jim.

"Well, we then got a READY TO UPLOAD message. We pressed that on the panel there, and about 20 seconds later the UPLOADING sign went out."

"So what then? The machine was ready to use?" asked Jim.

Randy nodded. "We started a print job. It was about thirty pages. It took the first page inside, did its thing, and then waited to eject the print copy for about five seconds."

"Sounds weird. It didn't do that before? Before you uploaded it?"

"No. It was super fast before."

"So, what did you do?"

Randy shook his head. "I was desperate so I took off the server cable and tried it. Still that same problem. Then I took off the Internet cable, and the damn thing quit altogether."

"You put the Internet cable back in and tried it?" asked Jim.

"Yep. It worked, but still had the problem."

"Weird. You call the vendor or what?" said Jim.

"Mr. Ferrari has to approve any visitors to this operation. When I told him what was happening, he said to call you. That you would advise us what to do."

Jim nodded slowly. "Okay. I'd like to do a simple test on the machine."

He reached for his briefcase that he had placed by the door, opened it, and retrieved a handheld data line tester.

"What's that do?" Randy stared at the instrument.

Jim walked to the back of the copier. “I’m going to insert this tester in series with the Internet cable.” When he had the connections completed, he turned to Randy. “Okay. Put in something to copy. Just a single sheet.”

Jim watched Randy pull a paper from the trash bin and place it on the glass copy surface. He lowered the paper handler and looked at Jim. Jim nodded.

Randy pressed the COPY button and the machine scanned the paper. Jim watched the tester he held in his hand as the operation proceeded. As Randy had said, seconds passed before the copier delivered the copy. Jim looked at Randy. “The machine is sending something onto the Internet, probably a file of what you just copied.”

“You gotta be shittin’ me? I gotta call Mr. Ferrari.”

Randy paced nervously until Ferrari came into the small room. He looked at Jim, holding his gaze for a moment before speaking. “Glad you could come. What do we have here?”

“I connected my data line tester between the machine and the Internet port. What I see is that during the period that the machine pauses, just before it spits out the printed sheet, it is sending data out onto the Internet.”

Ferrari’s eye widened. “You gotta be kidding me.”

Jim shook his head. “It seems to me, when you connected the Internet cable to the machine in order to do the requested update of its software, the computer inside was hijacked and a malicious file inserted. This file probably sends a copy of everything that you do on this machine to an Internet address somewhere.”

Ferrari smashed his fist on top of the machine. “Son of a bitch!” He turned to Randy, who had backed into the doorway. “Get this piece of shit outa here. You get them to haul it out now. Have ‘em replace it with a regular machine, like we have all over the place.”

Randy’s head bobbed up and down. “Y . . . Yes sir. I’ll do it right away.”

Ferrari looked at Jim. “Stop at my office before you leave.”

Jim nodded.

Ferrari left the room mumbling.

Jeanie brought him to Ferrari’s office. He had expected a large opulent office, but it wasn’t. Ferrari waved him in and asked him to take a seat in front of his desk. Jim admired the furnishings.

Ferrari smiled. “Maria set this up for me. I kinda like it.”

“Tastefully done,” said Jim.

Ferrari leaned back in his chair. “I appreciate you coming out this morning. I was thinking about that machine yesterday and got more suspicious as the afternoon wore on.”

Jim nodded. “Your instincts were right.”

“Well, I can guess where the malware originated,” said Ferrari, “But that’s not your problem.”

Jim sat quietly as Ferrari stared at him for a few seconds.

“I’m going to say this once, and then I’m going to forget I said it.”

Jim nodded. He guessed what was coming.

“There’s this guy in your building. . . . Let’s say he could become a problem for me. If he chose to take a job in Albany or Syracuse, I wouldn’t have an issue with that . . . as long he kept his mouth shut.”

Jim nodded, “Okay.”

“If he stays here, he lives by my rules,” said Ferrari.

Jim looked at Ferrari, knew that there was nothing else, and he stood up.

“Thanks for your help on this,” said Ferrari. “I owe you one.” He pushed a button on his phone. “Jeanie. Mr. Randolph is ready to leave.”

Jim advised his boss, Art Wagner, of what he found in troubleshooting the copy machine at Ferrari Investments. Jim was told SCCI responsibility does not include making-safe the client’s equipment, but what Jim did can be considered as good will. Jim reiterated that the clients have to be made aware they are susceptible to malware if they connect to the Internet. Art agreed to send a memo to all clients of the Walker Building with a warning about Internet susceptibility and cautioning that access to their secure private network could be compromised by a computer on the network operating with malware and connected to the Internet. He thanked Jim for taking care of the client.

Later, Jim talked to Greg and suggested the safest thing for Marc was for him to take a job in Albany, and the sooner the better. And, to keep his mouth shut. He didn't mention his conversation with Ferrari.

Chapter 31

MCGREGOR LEANED INSIDE the doorway of a shop across from the corner hamburger stand. He had been following Reed and Somers, trying to learn their routines. He took notes of places, streets and times, and pondered how he would get rid of them. He knew it had to happen soon, before the FBI got wind of what those two were involved in and opened an investigation. Any investigation was certain to sweep him up in it. The agents had to be eliminated, but how to do it and lay the blame for their demise on Ferrari's doorstep?

—

The FBI team on the sixth floor of the Empire Investment Trust building, across the narrow street from the Walker Building, was headed by Leon Freedman. The RICO group included agents Reed and Somers. Freedman discussed with Reed and Somers a new warrant to glean information from a computer at Ferrari Investments as they accessed the Internet. Although they had been successful several times, and most recently had intercepted what had passed through a copy machine, all the information gathered had produced little useful intelligence.

Freedman closed the folder and looked up at Reed and Somers. "My boss is bitching about the expense of this operation. He wants to see results."

Reed grimaced. “We’re doing everything we can think of to get eyes and ears into that place. Those guys aren’t totally stupid, either.”

“I know,” nodded Freedman. “The intercepts on that copy machine went well for a while, but I think we’ve been discovered. They disconnected it.”

Reed replied. “Someone discovered our little camera by their door. So, I don’t know who’s been going in there. I suspect that security dude might have helped them discover the Internet connection. He probably took care of the camera, too. He’s a real pain in the ass.”

“So this guy still works there?”

“Far as we know,” said Somers.

“What’s the connection between him and the Ferrari business?” asked Freedman.

Reed sighed. “There shouldn’t be any. SCCI is contracted to DiCosta. The SCCI contract does not cover internal business equipment or services, only the building networks.”

“But didn’t you tell me DiCosta’s daughter is this guy’s squeeze.”

Somers grinned. “Yeah.”

“Could be the pipeline to Ferrari,” said Reed.

Freedman looked at Reed. “I want to talk to him again. Bring him in.”

Reed nodded. “Done.”

Reed escorted Jim into a conference room on the sixth floor of the Empire Investment Trust building. Reed hadn’t told Jim what the meeting was about, only that Freedman was interested in getting his point of view on some things.

Jim was pleased to see a coffee service in the middle of the large conference table. Jim nodded to Somers sitting across the table with Freedman. Freedman rose and shook hands with Jim.

“Nice to see you. I’m glad you could make it.” He offered Jim coffee, which he accepted.

“Let me start with my boilerplate speech.” Freedman outlined the FBI’s efforts in reducing the impact of organized crime in New York and elsewhere by using the powers given them in the RICO laws. He talked about there being a long running effort to bring down the Salerno mob, but they had only been able to prosecute a few low level members. His particular group, he said, was focused primarily on the workings of the Ferrari crew and their relationship with the local boss, Salerno. Freedman said this was all common knowledge. But what he wished to talk to Jim about was what he knew of the Ferrari organization.

"I don't see where I can help you," said Jim. "I don't work for them. The SCCI contract ends at their door. Once I have the building networks running properly, the tenants are on their own."

Freedman toyed with his coffee cup. "You hear things. You see people coming and going. You put two and two together. We need to know what you're coming up with. We're not asking for trade secrets."

"All I know is that I'm being hassled by these two guys," Jim pointed to Reed and Somers. "And, I'm getting trouble from this McGregor guy. He thinks I'm helping you guys at his expense. What McGregor is involved in is not something I care to know about."

Freedman nodded. "We know about him."

"Marvelous. Makes me feel better already," said Jim.

Somers grinned, but didn't say anything.

Freedman paused and looked into his folder, then closed it again. He looked at Jim. "Ferrari Investments is the tenant on the second floor, right?'

Jim nodded. "Yep."

"We could use your help in investigating this well known criminal."

"I have nothing to do with him."

Freedman nodded. "Right. However, what we need are any clues you can offer from time to time regarding their investments, off-shore banks they use, how they launder their cash, loan sharking and their protection racket."

Jim shook his head and laughed. "You guys don't want much. How the heck am I going to find out anything about their business?"

Somers looked up and grinned. "How about your girl friend? She's got to be telling you stuff."

Freedman scowled at Somers. "Knock it off," he cautioned.

Jim directed his response to Freedman. "As you know, DiCosta sold his construction company to Ferrari. Neither the old man nor his daughter have an interest in Ferrari's business."

"Can we count on you to help us put away a serious criminal in our city?" asked Freedman.

"My responsibility is to honor the contract with DiCosta Construction. I have to turn over to the tenants on each floor a clean communications system. What they do with it is not my business, nor do I care."

"Don't you do consulting to the tenants? Don't they need help with the communications system?" asked Freedman.

"When they need help, they contact my employer and I get a work order number to put my time against."

"So you do get into their locked area," said Freedman.

"I would ask permission to enter, if I was given a work authorization number."

"You can make certain observations that could aid our investigations," said Freedman.

Jim scowled. "If I was witness to obvious criminal activity, I would report it. Otherwise, I am not a spy for the FBI or anyone else."

"You hear things," suggested Freedman.

Jim shook his head. "I do not ask, nor am I told anything about criminal activity by anyone in the DiCosta family. At work, the tenants aren't about to confide in me."

Freedman went on undaunted. "Ferrari makes a big effort to appear as Mister Clean and member in good standing of the BBB. But the fact is Ferrari is the best money maker Salerno has. The New York dons leave Salerno pretty much alone as he and Ferrari serve a very useful service for all the bosses in the area by cleanly and efficiently laundering vast sums of money."

Jim grinned. "This is all very interesting. You guys have more info than I'd ever get."

"You have the run of the building. You are on the inside. What about all the common equipment?"

Jim shook his head. "When I need to service any of the common equipment inside a tenants' secure area, I have to request access and become a "guest" of that business while I service the equipment. Each communications room is locked and only I have access to them."

Freedman looked at Jim. "What do you know of the IT capability of Ferrari's organization?"

"There is a secure server in the locked comm. room that provides a portal to a wideband service provider set up by SCCI. Each tenant takes the risk and responsibility for the hazards in using the Internet, not SCCI," said Jim. "We don't know what they do, and we don't care unless they request assistance."

"So each tenant has to establish their own network?" asked Freedman.

Jim nodded. "Each tenant is independent from any other. They have to establish their own closed network. SCCI designed the systems in the building so there is no way to get into their network - unless they get careless with their Internet connection, for instance."

"That's the only portal?"

"The only one I know of," said Jim. He put his hands on the table and stood up. "I have to get back to work."

Freedman escorted Jim to the elevator and wished him a 'good day.'

—

When the conference room emptied, Agents Reed and Somers stood by the window and talked quietly.

"Does he know anything?" asked Somers. "He ain't letting on if he does."

"Well, how else would anybody figure it out. There was no one down there. I'm certain of that." Reed said.

"I agree with you. No one was down there or even outside." Somers glared at Reed. "So isn't it possible that he has some sort of camera or sensor or some goddamn thing down in the basement? Maybe he's more than what he says."

"Anything is possible. What you say makes sense, but the prick ain't on the FBI payroll. We'd know about it."

"How 'bout Internal Affairs?" said Somers.

"Shit." Reed glared at Somers. "We're dead if that's the case." Then he shook his head. "There's no sign of that - is there?"

"How the hell is McGregor coming up with this shit?" said Somers. "Who's talking to him?"

"Don't think it's that Randolph prick," said Reed. "Those two don't get along at all."

Somers shook his head, looked down at the floor. "Somebody figured it out. What'll we do?"

"We're not going to panic, that's what," said Reed. "If somebody has something, how come they haven't come forward?"

"Maybe they will," said Somers.

—

McGregor sat in the Toyota Camry he had borrowed and watched the people coming and going from the Empire Investment Trust building. He felt nearly invisible as nobody even glanced his way. When Jim Randolph left the building, McGregor looked at his watch.

"Over an hour," he mumbled to himself. "Son of a bitch has to be working with the FBI."

McGregor wondered if the recent events were part of a conspiracy. Was Randolph actually an agent of the FBI? "Goddamn. That would explain it."

He watched as Randolph crossed the street at the end of the block and disappeared from view. *Was it him all along? Did he somehow found out about the stash, and maybe told the two FBI assholes about it? It made sense. How the hell else would the rumor have been started?*

He shook his head. What to do about Fontana, he wondered. Could he really trust the guy? His cell phone buzzed and he reached for it.

"That you?" the voice asked.

"Yeah," McGregor said.

"I'm on my way back."

McGregor recognized Moretti's voice. "Take care of business?"

"Yeah."

"Good. See you later." McGregor closed the phone and hoped that the job had been done before the fence had a chance to roll on him.

—

Jim kept walking. His fleeting glimpse of the man in the Camry looked like McGregor. What the hell was he doing hanging around? Keeping an eye on him or maybe the FBI guys? Jim had planned to catch a cab, go back to the hotel and change clothes. Instead, he walked past the Walker

Building to the next side street. Walking rapidly, he went to the back of the building and turned toward Enterprise Investment Trust. Approaching the end of the Walker Building, he stopped and peered around the corner. He saw the Camry parked opposite the Enterprise building nearly at the end of the block. Other cars blocked his view of the driver, but Jim clearly saw who left the Enterprise building. He waited a half hour but the Camry stayed parked. Jim wondered whether McGregor was still in the car. Just as he made up his mind to give up, he saw Reed and Somers leave the building. They stood together talking for a minute and then entered a cab that just pulled up. When the cab reached the end of the block, Jim saw the Camry leave the parking spot. The cab turned right and the Camry followed at a distance.

Chapter 32

SOMERS ARRIVED AT his office in the Enterprise building at 8:30. The trip from his home in Brooklyn had gone well, unlike most days. He passed Reed's office, the lights still off. Somers wondered; Reed was almost always in before him and on his second coffee by now. Somers had arrived at work and turned on his computer. When he looked up he saw Leon Freedman, his supervisor and head of the local RICO unit, standing in the doorway. His dour expression gave Somers a chill. Freeman stepped inside and closed the door.

"Jack won't be in today. There was a bit of trouble at his house."

Somers stared at Freedman for some seconds. "What happened? Is he . . . ?"

Freedman nodded. "Jack's okay. Around 2:45 this morning, a bomb placed under his car exploded. Car was outside. Nothing left of it. Some damage to the garage."

"His family?"

"They're fine. Everyone was asleep at the time."

"Who's out there? " Somers got up from his chair. "Anyone out there?"

Freedman raised his hands, palm out. "Local and state cops are there. We sent a team out. Maybe we'll learn something."

"Why Jack? I . . . I mean what the hell?" said Somers. "Some kind of warning?"

Freedman shrugged. "I was hoping *you* could shed some light on this. You two have been working this Ferrari thing together. Right?"

Somers nodded slowly.

"So what can you tell me?" asked Freedman. He stared at Somers.

"Lately, we've been working here in this building most of the time. Working with our IT guys. Seeing how we can get into their computers. We did that copy machine, but I think they discovered it. I don't know who would have done this." Somers shook his head. "Maybe McGregor."

"McGregor?" said Freedman. "Why? I thought he was a minor player since we closed down the DiCosta project."

"Well, yeah. But remember, we cut him off from any further consideration when the project ended. I think he was banking on getting *all* charges reduced or eliminated."

"Well, that's tough shit, isn't it?" said Freedman, and then added, "He would do this?"

Somers shrugged. "Can't think of anyone in the last couple months would be that pissed at us."

"What about the Ferrari bunch across the street? Was this some kind of message?"

Somers shook his head. "Doesn't seem his style." He felt his stomach lurch. It was McGregor, of that he was sure. "We haven't really leaned on anyone. We've just been doing the IT thing," said Somers.

Freedman scowled. "People don't set off bombs for no reason. You and Jack are into something. I need to know what it is." Freedman stood up and headed for the door.

"*Could be* McGregor, I guess," said Somers

"We can bring him in, have a sit-down," said Freedman.

"If there's no evidence, he'll just sit there and smile," replied Somers

Freedman shook his head. "We'll go over this tomorrow when Reed gets in." He opened the office door and left.

Somers put his hands on his knees, trying to stop the trembling.

Somers called Reed later that day. Reed assured him he was okay and the only damage beside the car was to the garage door. When Somers pressed him to discuss his suspicions, Reed abruptly told him they'd talk about when he saw him the next day. Somers felt even more ill at ease after the call.

—

Somers was first to arrive the next morning at the meeting Freedman had called. What was Freedman thinking? Somers felt nauseous. Freedman and Reed walked in together. Reed took a seat next to his partner. Freedman opened the meeting with casual conversation about Reed's welfare and that of his family. Reed said that the police in Great Neck had placed a surveillance unit in his neighborhood. Freedman said that State Police forensics people had removed the vehicle remains. The explosive material had been identified as C-4 detonated remotely by a cell phone, a simple but effective method.

Freedman went next to explore what lay behind this assault. What did these two agents know about McGregor or anyone else that would suggest this type of response? The two agents expressed confusion to the reason for the attack. Freedman said that forensics had yet to find any clue to the maker of the bomb or to the person who had placed it under Reed's car. He also said, they had no cause at this time to bring anyone in for questioning, but he would have an interview with McGregor just to see what he could learn. While Reed and Somers nodded in agreement, Freedman stared at them, saying that a detailed investigation would take place by Internal Affairs and State Police. The two agents nodded again, but their faces gave away nothing. Freedman left and the door to the conference room swung shut.

Somers turned to Reed and whispered. "I got something in the mail at home. Gotta show it to you."

"So, show it to me."

"Not here. Can't risk Freeman barging in."

Reed nodded. "Meet me at the corner joint down the street at 12:30." They got up and left the room.

Somers was seated on a stool at the window counter when he saw Reed approaching the small hamburger joint. He took a stool next to Somers. "You got it with you?" he asked.

Somers reached into his vest pocket and pulled out the envelope.

Reed looked at the writing. "Ink jet printer."

"Yeah," said Somers. "Same on the inside."

Reed slid the paper from inside the envelope and unfolded it. There was but one sentence. *You are 3 weeks behind on vig.*

Reed looked at Somers as he refolded the note. "I guess we now know what his Plan-B is."

Somers took the note and put it back in his pocket. "What're we going to do?" said Somers. "I can't pay it and I can't get my hands on the money anytime soon. Too risky."

"Get hold of yourself," said Reed sternly, his hand covering most of his mouth. "Neither one of us is paying that asshole a damn thing. He has no proof we have his stuff – no proof at all."

"He believes we do," complained Somers.

"What? Third or fourth hand rumors?" said Reed.

"He believes it. You know he does," said Somers.

Reed nodded. "Yeah, I got the message the other night."

"It's not going to stop, is it?" Somers whined. "It'll be me next. What'll we do?"

"Nothing, just yet. I'm sure Freedman has guys watching your place," said Reed. "You get a grip. We ain't caving in to that shitbag. And what, go to prison for it?" When Somers started to speak, Reed raised his hand. "I'll come up with a permanent solution. Just hang tight."

Chapter 33

JIM STOOD JUST INSIDE the doorway of the Walker building. He had called a cab, but in late afternoon, knew there might be a wait. The last two days had been boring with no sign of trouble at the work site and Maria out of town. When he phoned Maria that morning, her secretary told him she was in Long Island and wasn't sure what time she would return. So he decided to go for a nice dinner by himself. Greg had mentioned the Black Hat on the Upper West Side as a quiet place with excellent food. He called Dom as he waited for the cab.

"You should stay close to your hotel. I'm just getting into town from the Palisades."

"I'm getting really tired of that hotel. I heard the Black Hat had good food."

"I've been there a couple times. But I think you should stay closer to home."

"Thanks. I should be okay."

"You have my number." The phone went dead.

Jim was sure Dom was annoyed. "Hell with it. I'm going."

As he stood there, he thought about the rumors that one of the FBI agents working in the Enterprise building had been targeted with a bomb at his home. Probably something to do with McGregor, he mused.

Jim looked out the glass doors nervously. Maybe he had said too much already, he thought. He was increasingly uncomfortable with the possibility of two FBI agents being hurt or killed from something he had said. And, what was that the other night, the night of the bombing? Had he seen McGregor start to follow Reed home? He looked through the glass doors at the traffic flow and wondered if McGregor was eyeing him. Then the cab appeared at the curb.

—

Mike McGregor flipped the pages of the newspaper. He saw nothing new on the bombing of Agent Reed's car. The door open behind him, and the bartender's brought a beer and a shot of whiskey. McGregor put several bills on the tray and the footsteps receded. He heard the door close. McGregor studied the whiskey in the glass, swirling it close to the rim. He went over the bomb event again. There was no direct connection to him. The bomber had been paid by someone else, the money not traceable to him. It'd been a couple of days, why hadn't he heard something from those two asshole agents, he wondered? He smiled; he had those two in a tough spot. If their boss found out about it, they'd go to prison for taking a bribe – that'd be what *he'd* call it if he had to. Or they could admit to stealing it from him – but without reporting the existence of the stash to their boss? Yep, he thought, the only way for those two is for them to quietly return the money. Of course, there was the issue of the vig. The whiskey went down in one gulp.

He was still bothered by how the two agents had known about the stash. Had they seen something, he wondered, or had that SCCI prick discovered it and told them? Was that Randolph guy actually FBI? The thought infuriated him. He took a long pull on the beer. He didn't know why the thought of Randolph sent his blood pressure skyward, but he had never liked the security guy. He had been key in the undoing of everything he had done in the Walker Building for the FBI. And now, they had shut the DiCosta project down. Where did that leave him? He knew where: back on the FBI's shit list.

Those guys were obsessed now with Ferrari. Hell, he thought, Ferrari was too smart for them. He grudgingly had to give Ferrari his respect. The man was the most talented money laundering machine he'd ever heard of. Hell, every family in New York funneled their income through his organization. There were no family disputes that touched him; his machine just kept going. His respect for Ferrari was countered by resentment, for he hated being treated like some junior flunky. After all, he was a Salerno.

—

The Black Hat was laid out like many small restaurants in the city. A bar ran along one wall as one entered. Beyond the bar, a dining area opened to the full width of the room with booths and tables. A small kitchen was stuffed into a narrow room behind the bar. This place was self-seating, so Jim walked to the dining area, passing the crowded bar. All the tables were occupied with couples or people gathering after work. Jim saw an empty booth and sat down. A middle-aged waiter approached with a menu; a laminated card with the daily special taped to it. Jim asked for a glass of wine and looked at the menu. He saw the printing, but he thought again of the times he had been with McGregor, of the threats and beating. He came out of the cloud when the waiter placed a glass of wine on the table.

"Sir? Have you decided?"

Jim flushed, quickly scanning the menu.

"If I could suggest the roast beef, sir. You won't be disappointed."

Jim smiled and handed the menu to the waiter. "Sounds perfect."

"Very good, sir."

—

McGregor turned to the classified advertisements and scanned the Personal ads. He was reading the third column when he saw it. He had placed the ad days ago, but still no response. *Return what's mine. No questions asked. Meet me at hamburger joint.* He had made sure that someone had been there before work, at lunch time, and after work; but the two FBI agents had not shown. He saw no reply ad. Would he have to raise the ante? He'd have to be careful, he thought. Carelessness and the FBI would link him with the doings in New Rochelle and Scarsdale. They already were on first base, having caught his fence in Philadelphia. Well, he thought, that guy wouldn't have any more to say.

The door closed loudly and McGregor recognized Antonio Moretti. He sat down opposite McGregor, placing his long-neck beer on a napkin. He looked at McGregor, shook his head, and scowled. "Neither one showed. What do you want to do?"

McGregor let out his breath slowly. “Been sitting here thinking about it. I’m sure those two dicks have my money. I’m getting more sure that asshole Randolph was in on it.”

“Really?”

“Yeah. A strong gut feel.”

“You think he has some of it?” asked Moretti.

“Dunno. It may be that he found out about it and just told the two dicks. I hate that guy.”

“Think them Fed pricks are gonna want a piece of you?” asked Moretti.

McGregor looked at Moretti for a few seconds. “I guess I should think about that, huh?”

Moretti shrugged. “If they took your stuff, then they might want you quiet about it.” Moretti drained half the bottle in one swig, belched, leaned back and waited.

“Okay,” said McGregor. “We’ll hit them again, but not at their house. That was kinda dumb.”

Moretti nodded. “Had ‘em checked out like you wanted. Both those guys park their cars at a garage just off the F.D.R.”

“Just south of the tunnel?” asked McGregor.

“Yeah. Sometimes they get a ride downtown. But lately, they’ve driven right up to the Enterprise building.”

McGregor nodded slowly. “We’ll do the other guy’s car; see if they get the message. Tomorrow, get some street punk to trash it while it’s in the garage.”

“What’d you want to do about that Randolph guy?”

McGregor scowled. “I don’t think he has any of my stuff.” Then he grinned. “But I personally would like to break some of his bones.”

Moretti started for the door, and then turned toward McGregor. “I’ll get the car taken care of in the morning. Want I should see where that Randolph asshole is?”

McGregor nodded. “Yeah. Call me.”

—

Agent Reed stared absently out the cab window as he went over the Queensboro Bridge. He still hadn’t rented a car, the bombing had shaken him. His wife still had the Subaru and local cops inspected it every morning. There wasn’t any doubt in his mind; McGregor believed that he and Somers had his money. He worried about Somers; knew that he would cave in if the threats got close to home. He was vulnerable, what with a sick wife, huge medical bills, and living in a dumpy apartment in Brooklyn off of Flatbush Avenue. Reed worried too, that Somers would cave in if Internal Affairs leaned on him. That would be the end of their careers, and probably their families. He couldn't let that happen. No, he thought, better if McGregor was whacked and the sooner the better.

—

The waiter refilled his coffee cup, and then stood there. Jim looked up; saw the wrinkled brow on the old face.

"Sir," the waiter began, "there was a man in here a few minutes ago. I guess you didn't notice him." He glanced toward the bar area. "Fellow walked in and looked at everybody. Walked back and looked in the dining room. Then he asked me if the man in the back booth was Mr. Randolph. Is that you?"

Jim stared at the waiter.

"I . . . I told him I didn't know."

"Where is he? Say who he was?"

The waiter shook his head. "No. Looked like he was up to no good. Not someone I saw before. Anyway, he's outside. Last I looked he was leaning against the building out past the door."

Jim thanked the waiter. He sipped his coffee while he worried about what he'd heard. A few minutes later, he felt his cell phone vibrating in his pocket. He looked at the display: Maria. He smiled and looked around. There was no one within earshot that he thought would be disturbed by the call, especially if he kept his voice low. "Maria."

"Hi. Just got back to the office. Heard you called."

"I did. Your trip go well?"

"Oh, yes. Where are you? Can't you talk louder?"

"I'm in a restaurant, got to keep it down. Maybe call you when I go outside."

"Well, okay. Sorry I couldn't be with you. You okay?"

"I'm not sure. Waiter told me that someone came in looking for me. The guy is still hanging around outside."

"Who? I mean . . . you think its trouble?"

"It might be. Things have been happening . . ."

Maria interrupted him. "Please. Stay there. Let me call Dom. He's driving into town. Will you stay there until he calls?"

"Okay."

"Where are you by the way?"

"At the Black Hat."

"Okay. Please stay there. Love you." She hung up.

—

Antonio Moretti leaned against the wall of the Black Hat, to one side of the doorway. He opened his cell phone and pushed the speed dial button for McGregor. "I found him," he said. "He's in the Black Hat."

"The what? Where's that?" asked McGregor.

"Up on the west side. Little place. He's in there by himself eating supper."

"Okay. I'm on my way. Don't lose him." McGregor hung up.

Moretti pocketed the phone. What was he supposed to do if the dude came out? Grab him? Follow him? He decided to intercept him before he got into a cab, hold him in the shadows of the nearby side street until McGregor showed up. He would need fifteen minutes to get here, he thought, maybe more. He fingered the gun in his jacket pocket. He had his car parked in the narrow side street, a place little used except for dumpsters and delivery trucks.

—

Dom received Maria's worried call and he mentioned that Jim had been determined to not stay in his hotel. She asked him to please check on him. Dom made a quick stop to pick up two friends, and then continued to the Black Hat. When he drove past the restaurant, he saw a man leaning idly against the wall near the entrance, and circled the block to the opposite end of the alley. He stopped the car and turned to the two men in the back seat. "The restaurant is at the end of the alley at the next street and just to the right."

The two men nodded. "Got it," said Vinnie, the bigger of the two.

Dom continued. "You saw his car down there?"

"Yeah, I saw it," said Alfredo.

Vinnie nodded.

"You can bet he's packing," said Dom. "Vinnie, you'll have to disarm him right away. Alf, you take your cue from Vinnie. Everybody straight on this?"

Vinnie smiled. "No problem."

Alfredo nodded. He looked at Vinnie. "Ready when you are."

"Okay. I'll drive down the alley after I see you guys turn the corner. Get going."

The two men got out of the car and headed down the alley, keeping close to the wall of the building. They crept to the far corner, moving carefully from dumpster to dumpster. A cigarette arced into the street. Vinnie turned the corner, toward the man near the restaurant doorway. Alfredo moved up to the edge of the building.

Vinnie nodded to Moretti as he approached, feigning intention to go into the restaurant. The man returned a nod, but moved slightly away from the wall to stand erect. Vinnie, reaching the restaurant door, saw the man turn to face him. Vinnie stopped, smiled. "You don't know if Randolph's in there, do you?"

Alfredo moved fast and jammed a pistol into the man's back.

Vinnie, still smiling, pulled his jacket open, showing the man the pistol in his waistband.

"What the hell is this?" stammered the man as Vinnie pushed him toward the alley. "Who the hell are you two shit-birds? You want my wallet? That it?"

"No man, we don't want your wallet," said Vinnie as his fist slammed into Moretti's kidney.

Alfredo landed a hard fist into the man's stomach.

The man was doubled over, gasping. "What . . . what . . . you guys want?" he moaned.

Vinnie brought a fist up to connect with the man's jaw as he tried to straighten. "You're in the wrong neighborhood. You tell your boss that."

Alfredo slammed his fist into the man's midriff again.

Vinnie hit him with a solid punch to the side of his face. The man dropped to his knees. Blood and spittle dripped from his mouth. Blood ran from his nose.

Just then Dom brought the car down the alley. Vinnie signaled Alfredo, who grabbed the man's arms. Vinnie grabbed the ankles. The man twisted in a vain attempt to free himself.

In seconds, however, he was propelled through the air. He disappeared into the dumpster. Vinnie and Alfredo got in the car.

Dom hurried into the restaurant and moved quickly toward the dining area. When he spotted Jim Randolph, he went to him. "Let's go. Right now."

Jim got up, dropped some bills on the table, and followed quickly behind Dom. At the door, Dom stopped. He opened the door and peered out, then tugged Jim's arm to hasten his movement to the car.

"Where'd the guy go? Did you see him?" asked Jim.

"Let's go." Dom pushed Jim to the car.

No one spoke as the car moved out into the street, turned, and headed south. Then Dom turned to Jim and grinned. "Meet Vinnie and Alfredo. You can thank them anytime."

—

McGregor had borrowed a friend's Camry for the drive uptown. Nearing the Black Hat, he speed dialed Moretti's phone. His call went immediately to voice mail. "Goddamn it," he mumbled and stuffed the phone back into his pocket. He drove slowly past the restaurant, but saw no one. On a hunch, he stopped and backed up to the alley nearby. He saw Moretti's car parked by the dumpster and pulled in next to it, blocking the driveway. McGregor walked around Moretti's car and looked inside. Nothing seemed amiss. He then went into the restaurant, walked slowly past the bar patrons and looked in the dining room. When a waiter approached, he waved, turned, and went outside.

"Where the hell is he?" he mumbled.

He stepped back into the alley and peered into the dimness toward the far end. Nothing moved. He heard a metallic thump, then a muffled moan. He put his hand in his pocket, gripping the gun. He heard another moan, seeming to come from the dumpster.

"Moretti! Moretti!" he shouted, and listened for a response. A few seconds later he heard two hard thumps; this time he was sure it came from the dumpster.

"Hey, Moretti! You in there?"

He heard garbled speech, then another thud.

"Hang on. Let me find something to climb on."

McGregor looked around, but saw nothing that would support his weight and raise him the several feet he needed to look inside the large container, its lid tilted back against the building. Swearing, he got into his car and positioned it so he could climb on the trunk lid to gain the height he needed. He mumbled a continuous string of invectives as he hoisted his overweight body onto the trunk. He found a stable perch and peered into the dim interior of the dumpster.

"Holy shit, Moretti! What the hell happened?"

McGregor saw him lying on his back on a pile of trash, his face bloody. "Christ, Moretti, come on, stand up. You gotta stand up so I can reach you." He watched as Moretti turned onto his side, and then sat up holding his face in his hands, moaning. "Come on, pal," said McGregor. "You gotta stand up. Lean on this wall so I can reach you."

At first Moretti just sat there moaning, holding his head. Then he made efforts to stand. When he was able to stand, he leaned face-forward against the wall. McGregor now saw clearly the damage to Moretti's face. Rage boiled up in him.

"Who did this to you?" Moretti didn't respond. He reached up along the wall and McGregor bent over as far as he could, enough to grab the man's wrists.

"Walk over to where the shit is piled up." He kept his grip on Moretti's wrists as Moretti stumbled for footing on the loose trash.

"Yeah, that's it." They were now able to grip each other's wrists, and McGregor could use brute strength to pull the skinny Moretti to the top of the dumpster. Cursing in exhaustion, McGregor finally had Moretti over the edge of the dumpster. Moretti lost his footing and tumbled from the trunk of the car to the ground. McGregor jumped down and helped him into the car. As McGregor walked around to the driver's side, he phoned a friend to come and pick up Moretti's car.

Moretti couldn't tell him who had attacked him. There had been two guys working him over while a third came with a car. He didn't get a look at the driver. McGregor drove south for half an hour, and finally reached a doctor that he knew would keep his mouth shut.

Chapter 34

SCCI HAD SENT A YOUNG technician to take over the more mundane maintenance duties. Soon, all the tenants would be installed in the building and Jim would be reassigned. *That can't happen too soon*, Jim thought. The new fellow, Randy Fisher, seemed knowledgeable, although hardly a year out of technical school.

The night before, Dom had dropped Jim off at Maria's apartment. They spent half the night talking about the seemingly increased danger facing him. Jim brought up his hoped-for reassignment: a project on the west side, about midtown. Tension and trepidation seemed to melt away as they explored each other's body, finally falling asleep in the early morning darkness.

The next morning Jim escorted Randy to all floors of the building, showing him the communications rooms that would require his attention. He didn't ask for admittance to Ferrari Enterprises, leaving that for another day. At the end of the day Jim and Randy went downstairs to the lobby.

As they walked to the front doors, Agent Reed got up from a sofa, where he had been hiding behind a newspaper. Jim bid goodnight to Randy and turned to face the agent.

"Let's sit for a few minutes," said Reed.

Jim sat on the couch with Reed at the opposite end.

"So, what's new?" said Jim, not hiding the total boredom he felt.

"Don't get so excited," said Reed, a smirk playing at the corners of his mouth. "I wanted to ask you a couple things. No big deal."

Jim nodded, "So ask."

"You see much of McGregor?" asked Reed.

"Now why would I want to do that?" Jim shook his head. "He doesn't come in here."

"Word has it, he's been making threats."

"Yeah, heard your car got bombed," said Jim. "Was that him?"

"We don't know. Someone trashed Agent Somers car this morning."

"You guys pissed off *someone*. Think it was McGregor?" said Jim.

Reed looked at Jim for a few seconds. "Have you had trouble with him?" he asked.

Jim shook his head. "Haven't seen him lately. Don't want to either."

"One of *his* guys got the shit beat outa him last night. You know about that?" said Reed.

"I haven't heard anything. Been in here all day."

"Where were you last night?" asked Reed.

"Went out to eat, then went to Maria's place."

"Where'd you go?"

"A little place uptown. Friend said to try it out."

"The Black Hat?" asked Reed.

"How'd you know? You following me?" Jim was surprised that Reed knew this.

"No, didn't follow you. But I hear things. That's what I do – I'm a detective." Reed grinned.

"Yeah, I was there. So what?"

"Nothing," said Reed, "Except it's where one of McGregor's guys got beat up."

"No kiddin'?" said Jim. "I'm not going to get all choked up about it."

"Look," said Reed. "I'm trying to see which dots connect here. Like you to help me out."

"What can I do?"

"Be a little more forthcoming," Reed replied.

"Like what?" said Jim.

"What do you know about McGregor's activities?"

Jim shrugged. "He's heads that union local, but I don't know what he actually does to make a living. Well, I guess being the head of a union pays pretty well."

"He's a mob low-life. There's a long list of things the locals suspect him for."

"He doesn't share that with me. We never hit it off," said Jim.

"Yeah, noticed that. Didn't he rough you up a couple times?" Reed asked. "What was that about?"

Jim shrugged. "One time he accused me of working with you guys. Another time he accused me of helping you guys steal stuff he had in this building." Jim took a breath.

"What stuff?" asked Reed.

"Money, I think he said."

Reed shook his head.

Jim continued. "Then, he thinks I had something to do with nixing the arrangement he had with you guys – whatever that means."

"He's roughed you up," said Reed.

Jim nodded. "Yeah, he's not wired right."

"Who did the punching? Him?"

"Yeah, him and some punk," said Jim.

"Was it Alfredo Moretti? We've been keeping an eye on him."

"Coulda been. Sounds like it."

"So," said Reed, "You don't know why he would be blowing up my car?"

Jim shook his head. "You sure *he* did it?"

"We're working on that." Reed stood up. "Anything comes to mind, you know my number."

Jim nodded. "Yeah. Got it."

Chapter 35

MIKE MCGREGOR SAT in the back room of Casey's lounge with Antonio Moretti planning a robbery in Scarsdale at the home of Ricardo Santos, a Ferrari lieutenant. A large amount of cash was known to be in a safe. McGregor had been told that Ferrari would hold a big party that very night and that Santos would be attending. The Santos house was expected to be empty for several hours starting around nine.

The coded radio signal to open the gate was captured by an electronic technician McGregor knew, who then constructed a simple opening device. The device was satisfactorily tested late the previous night at the Santos gate. McGregor was told three guard dogs have free reign within the gated property. He gave Antonio Moretti permission to shoot them. Months earlier McGregor had paid a Santos lieutenant a large amount of money to find out the combination to the safe. The man had come through the previous day.

McGregor turned to Moretti. "Get Fontana to drive. Have him stay with the car as you guys go inside."

"I was gonna tell him to stick around after work," said Moretti, "but no one's seen him since noon."

"Send a couple guys to find him," said McGregor. "I'm gonna be here tonight. Watch what you say when you call me."

"Yeah, no problem," replied Moretti. "Where do you want us to drop off the goods?"

"You have the key I gave you?"

Moretti pulled a key ring out of his pocket and shook it. "Got it."

"Drop everything in unit 212 at Uptown Warehouse and Storage. I already checked for cameras. There's only the one at the entrance."

McGregor pulled two padlocks from his jacket pocket and handed them to Moretti. "Secure the unit with these two locks, then all you guys return here."

Moretti nodded. "Got it."

-

Agent Reed was parked around the corner from Casey's Lounge. Ever since the DiCosta project ended and the eavesdropping warrants expired, he had parked near Casey's almost every evening hoping for a good lead on Ferrari's activities. He had never bothered to have the listening device removed. It was illegal to be listening, but Reed didn't care. He would use the information for his own purposes. He listened as McGregor planned a robbery. Best he could tell from the pieces of conversation was that another Scarsdale job was planned for that night.

Reed didn't much care and wasn't going to do anything with the information; that is until he heard them planning to store the stash at Uptown Warehouse and Storage. He pulled a beat up phone book from the back seat and found the location of the storage unit. *Piece a cake.*

-

McGregor pulled out his buzzing cell phone.

"Hey Mike. No one knows where he is."

He recognized Antonio's voice. "What the hell you talking about?"

"The guy you wanted us to find, remember?" said Antonio.

"He's gotta be somewhere. Look at the job?"

"We looked *everywhere* and called all around. One of the guys saw him earlier this morning talking to that security guy, what's his name?"

"I know who you mean," said McGregor.

"Looks like he might have skipped. Bet that security guy knows."

McGregor didn't want to say what he was thinking, not on the chance his phone was being tapped. "Pick up the guy we used last time. I'll look into this."

"Okay, no problem."

McGregor closed the phone. "Goddamn Fontana," he mumbled. "Asshole's runnin', sure'n shit. Bastard's made some kinda deal."

—

"Reed here. Where are you, Somers?"

"Still at my desk. Wife's on the warpath. No use in going home 'till it blows over."

"Christ, Somers. You piss her off every other week."

"Yeah, seems that way. So, what's up?"

"How 'bout meeting me at that pizza place we go to sometimes, over at Garrity and Fourth."

"Okay. I can be there in thirty minutes," said Somers.

"See ya there." Reed had many hours to kill before McGregor's guys would return to Casey's lounge. He was thinking to involve Somers in his plan to stick it to McGregor yet again. Reed needed Somers to eavesdrop on McGregor while he positioned himself close to Uptown Warehouse and Storage. Reed wasn't sure Somers would go along, as it wasn't exactly a sanctioned operation. He started the car.

Reed had given the monitoring receiver to Somers and instructed him where to park while listening to McGregor at Casey's. They dragged out the pizza supper as long as they could, then both drove along the East River to pass the time. At 9:30, they headed back uptown. Reed continued north to Uptown Warehouse and Storage, while Somers found a parking place for eavesdropping of Casey's lounge. At 10 p.m., Somers called Reed.

"Reed."

"Just checking in," said Somers. "It's been quiet. Heard a door banging open and closed, heard a phone ring, not much else."

"If it goes according to plan, those guys ought to be back there before 11:30."

"Why 11:30?" said Somers.

"If anyone comes home early they'll be trapped. They gotta get outa there as soon as possible. Wouldn't be surprised if they're back by eleven. Stay awake."

"I'm okay," said Somers. "Drank so much coffee, I had to take a whiz right here by the car."

"You're a class act, always said that about you."

"Yeah, yeah" said Somers. "I'll call you soon's I hear 'em. Bye."

—

It was a few minutes before 11 o'clock when Antonio Moretti went into the back room at Casey's. He closed the door and took a seat across the small table from McGregor. Antonio smiled. "Went like clockwork."

"Start at the beginning," said McGregor.

"Okay. We got there early, had to drive around a bit until they left. It was 9:20 when we opened the gate, drove through, and closed it."

"Yeah, good. The dogs?"

"Soon's we got up by the house, they came at the car. Joey took 'em out, pop, pop, pop."

McGregor nodded, smiled.

"We pulled into the side yard, the kitchen entrance. We knew the whole place was rigged with ADT sensors, so Ralphie went to the telephone junction box on the side of the house and used his *borrowed* phone tester thingie and tied up the line. Then he disconnected the wideband cable. The ADT box couldn't send out a signal."

"Good work," said McGregor. "Where are your guys?"

"Sittin' at the bar," said Antonio. "Bought them a round."

"Any problem with anyone?" McGregor looked intently at Antonio.

Antonio shook his head. "Nope. Everyone did what they were supposed to. It's a good crew."

"The safe?"

"Piece 'o cake." said Antonio. "I took the camera outa there."

McGregor nodded. "Good."

"Six hundred large. Almost all random 50s and 100's. . . . Beautiful."

"The old lady's jewels?"

"I guess tonight she's wearing the best stuff. We got about 20 grand, though, in various necklaces and rings."

McGregor stood up. "Great. Tell Casey to buy a few more rounds. You and I are going to look at the stuff."

"Let's go." Antonio stood up. "I locked it up like you said." He pulled the padlock keys from his pocket and handed them to McGregor.

—

Agent Reed felt his phone buzzing in his shirt pocket. He looked at his watch, 11:08. "Reed."

"They're back. The two main guys are about to leave and probably going up to the storage place. I bet the man wants to see it for himself."

"Okay. That gives me another fifteen minutes," said Reed.

"What are you doing?" asked Somers.

"Not on the phone. Can you meet me at Uptown Warehouse and Storage?"

"Yeah. I'll find it."

"You sure?"

"Yeah. Starting down that way right now. I'll wait in my car until you get there."

"See you soon," said Reed. He closed his phone and started his car.

Reed stopped a block before reaching the storage unit and Somers pulled in behind him at the curb. Reed opened his trunk and removed a spray can and shook it as Somers got out of his car.

"Why are we stopping here? What do you have there?"

"It's a silicone spray. I'm putting some on our license plates so the video cameras can't read the numbers. We can just peel it off later."

"You're smarter than you look."

"Yeah. I been tryin' to tell you that."

A minute later Reed drove up to the storage unit numbered 212 and stopped with the engine running. Somers parked about 100 feet away, backed up his car to the front of Reed's and got out.

"We better hurry. Christ, I'm gonna piss myself," said Somers.

Reed pulled bolt cutters out of the trunk of his car. "Get a grip. This'll only take a few minutes."

Reed easily removed the two padlocks with the bolt cutters. Somers helped him pull open the steel door.

"Hold the flashlight." Reed handed the light to Somers.

Cardboard boxes were stacked against the back wall, but it was the travel bags in the middle of the room that got Reed's attention.

"This is it – the jackpot," exclaimed Reed as he opened the three bags.

"Jack! Look at these jewels," gasped Somers.

"Leave it. Forget it. Look in *these* bags."

Somers bent over to shine the light into the other bags. "Holy shit! Look at it."

"Come on. Let's get the hell outa here."

"Leave the jewels?" asked Somers.

"Leave it. Come on, grab that other bag."

"But the jewels . . ."

"Forget it. We can't deal with that. Let's go. Hurry."

Reed's hands trembled. He could hardly believe how easy it had been - pop the two padlocks and enter. Three minutes later he had two travel bags with cash in the trunk of the car. When he closed the door, he looped the locks back through the hasp, and from a few yards they looked undisturbed. He glanced at his watch and sped out of the storage area and onto the street. There would be holy hell to pay when McGregor got there.

Chapter 36

ANTONIO MORETTI TURNED into the warehouse and then farther, past stacks of crates and shipping containers, to the storage units at the back of the building. "We're on row 2," said Antonio. In front of number 212 he stopped and they got out of the car.

McGregor squatted to open the padlocks. He stared, and then turned to face Antonio, his face darkening. "What the fuck . . . ?"

Antonio came up to him. "What?" Then he saw what McGregor had seen; the broken padlocks. "What the hell . . . ?" He stared at McGregor. "Christ, I don't know what's going on."

McGregor stood up and pulled his gun from his shoulder holster. "Is there a back way to this unit?" he asked.

Antonio shook his head. "Just this door."

"Open it."

Antonio hesitated.

"Pull up the goddamn door," he bellowed.

Antonio took the locks from the hasps, pocketed them, and pulled the overhead door open. He stared at the one bag in the middle of the floor. "Holy shit." He looked at McGregor. "We had three bags. Ask any of the boys . . . three bags."

"Yeah. I believe you," said McGregor. He walked to the one bag, knelt and opened it. Then he stood up and kicked it viciously. "Goddamn ice. All we got is goddamn ice!"

"I don't know what happened. It was all here," stammered Antonio. "I swear."

McGregor stared at Antonio. "I can't fuckin' believe this." He kicked the bag with the jewels sending it skidding across the floor. "Who knew what we were doing? Who the hell you guys talk to?" McGregor's voice rose in pitch and volume.

Antonio shook his head. "Mike, listen. We all left Casey's in the borrowed car. We were all together."

"Someone made a call," roared McGregor. "*Someone* knew."

"No! . . . No one. We left there together and came right to Casey's." Antonio was sweating. He wiped his brow with the back of his hand.

McGregor paced around the small room then stopped. "I'm gonna kill somebody. Goddamn it, somebody's gonna die for this." Again he kicked the bag of jewels.

"I don't know how this coulda happened. It wasn't any of us. Mike, I swear . . ."

"Yeah-yeah. Put the goddamn bag in the car. We're going back to Casey's."

"What are you thinking?" said Antonio his eyes darting back and forth and back again to McGregor. He picked up the bag as they left the unit and then pulled the roll-up door down. "What do you wanna do?"

"I'm going to think," said McGregor. He opened the car door. "You drive."

When McGregor and Moretti stormed into Casey's, his crew standing at the bar froze. They stared with mouths open as the two men went into the back room and slammed the door shut. McGregor's crew looked at each other, shaking their heads and muttering. Suddenly Moretti came out of the back room and told Casey to give his guys another round, then went back to the room.

McGregor paced around the room, cursing and kicking the chairs. Antonio stopped a chair as it skidded toward him. "Mike, what the hell we gonna do?"

McGregor stopped pacing, turned to look at Antonio. "Bring the boys in here. We're taking this room apart."

Antonio looked at McGregor in confusion. "What?"

"Get 'em in here, goddamn it!"

Antonio hurried into the bar and returned in a few seconds, the crew trailing behind him. They stood in a bunch near the door. "What you want us to do?" asked Antonio.

"All right, one guy to each wall. We're looking for listening devices. Look at every square inch." He pointed to Antonio.

"Get up on the tables, look at those lamps. Check everything. There's got to be something in here." He turned to the others. "Find it," he roared.

McGregor told Casey to bring his tool box into the back room and informed him what he suspected. Casey shook his head. "Tell your guys to put it all back like it was."

"Yeah. Don't worry about it," replied McGregor. He went around the room looking at every light switch and power outlet. He had Antonio loosen the lamp fixtures on the ceiling. But they found nothing that looked out of place.

McGregor turned when he heard Joey yell. He was waving and pointing. McGregor and Moretti went to him. Joey had the phone box off the wall and dangling by its wires. But his attention was on the nearby alarm system by the door to the bar. The plastic housing had buttons and lights and when McGregor looked, he saw that it was inactive. Casey had turned it off when he came in, he thought. McGregor looked at Joey and put his fingers to his lips.

Joey beamed with self importance and whispered close to McGregor's ear. "Look at the pry marks underneath. Also, the special screws that are used aren't in there. Cover's just held on with some kind of glue. Bet when I pull on it, it'll pop right the hell off."

"Shit," McGregor looked at Joey, and then whispered to Moretti. "Pry it off. Be careful, we got to get it back together."

Joey slid a penknife around the base of the alarm unit cutting through what looked like a bead of silicone glue. He pried the cover carefully with his fingernails. Finally, he used the knife again and in a few seconds the cover to the alarm unit was in his hand. McGregor and Moretti leaned over him to examine the inside of the unit. Off to one side of the assembly was a small black module. Wires ran from it into the back of the alarm unit. The black module had numerous holes and perforations on the top surface.

"What the hell is that?" pointed Moretti speaking in a whisper.

Joey looked at it closely. "It's glued in place."

"What's it do?" asked Moretti.

"Shit if I know."

McGregor pointed. "Take those screws out. Let's see what's behind it."

"Don't want the alarm to go off."

"Just don't hit any of the buttons and don't disconnect any wires," whispered Moretti. "Right now it's deactivated." He handed Joey a small screwdriver. "Be careful."

With the mounting screws removed, the alarm unit hung by the wires going into the wall. When Joey turned the unit over, they saw where the black module was connected. That it was an afterthought was evident by the extra solder joints.

"Son-of-a-bitch," hissed McGregor. "That's gotta be it. Gotta be."

"All these wires," said Joey, "they must go to the phone line."

"Cut the wires to that black thing, only the black thing," said McGregor. "Take it outa there. I want to see what it is."

"Okay, I'll bring it to ya."

"Yeah," whispered McGregor, "and put everything back together." He looked at Moretti. "You help him."

McGregor, Moretti and Joey sat at a small table. Joey had borrowed a serrated knife from Casey and was sawing through the sides of the module. Moretti left and brought back three beers. After a half-hour Joey put down the knife. He gripped the upper part of the small black module and removed it. The three of them examined the opened assembly.

"I ain't no electronic whiz, but that looks like a fuckin' microphone." Joey pointed to the round object, which took up most of the top surface nearest the perforated cover.

"Sure 'n shit is," said Moretti. He stared at McGregor. "Who the hell did this? FBI?"

Joey looked at McGregor wide eyed. "Just thought of something."

McGregor and Moretti stared at him. "It was a couple nights ago. I saw that FBI prick going into the Walker building. I crossed over to that side and saw him and that security jerk talking serious in the lobby."

"You talkin' about Reed? The big guy?" said McGregor.

"Yeah. Yeah, Reed. It was him and the security asshole."

McGregor rubbed his chin then shook his head. He looked at Moretti. "Put this stuff in a bag and hang on to it. Have the boys get this room ship-shape." He started toward the bar door.

Moretti frowned. "Where you goin'?"

"Buy the boys another round. I'll call you in a while."

—

Reed turned off FDR Drive onto a side street. Two blocks later, he turned again to stop at a dilapidated old building that served as a FBI safe house. Reed stopped the car, nose toward the heavy wooden doors, got out, and then removed a heavy-duty padlock. He drove in and closed the big doors. Inside, he checked the alarm system and deactivated it. He had expected Somers to be there, and just as he was reaching for his phone he heard a tap of a horn. Reed swung the doors open and Somers drove in.

"Bolt the door," Reed said as Somers got out of the car.

Somers threw the bolt and turned to Reed. "What the hell's going on? What're we doing way down here?"

Reed smiled. "Don't get your shorts in a knot." He walked to the back of his car and opened the trunk.

Somers stared at the two large black bags then turned to Reed. "How much is in there?"

"Open it up. Take a look."

Somers bent over the trunk and pulled back the zipper on one of the bags. He jumped back so suddenly that he banged his head on the trunk lid. Reed laughed.

"Jesus, Reed," gasped Somers. "How much is this?"

Reed was still smiling. "I'm thinking almost six hundred grand all together. McGregor's grand haul."

Somers shook his head again. "We're fuckin' dead meat. He figures it out - we're dead."

Reed shrugged. "I left one bag for him, full of jewelry. Let him try and hock that."

"Are you crazy? Proceeds of a major robbery?" said Somers. "They'll put us away for twenty years." He shook his head some more. "McGregor will figure it out. He'll come for us."

"I'm *sure* he'll figure it out," said Reed. "Might take him a while. Sooner, if he finds the bug at Casey's. If it quits working, we'll know he found it."

Somers stared at Reed. "Christ, they're gonna kill us . . . our families. Reed – what the hell?"

"Calm down. I'm going to get him before he comes for us."

"What?" Somers looked at Reed in shock. "Kill him?"

Reed shrugged.

Chapter 37

JIM STEPPED OUT OF the Walker building into the afternoon sunshine. He touched the speed-dial for Maria, hoping she'd be in her office.

"Hi Jim. Just getting out of work?"

"Uh-huh. I'm standing in front of the building. The sun feels good after being locked up in there all day."

"A quiet day, I hope," she said.

"The two FBI guys squeezed me again. Still trying to get me to work with them. They're suggesting that I could be caught up in whatever McGregor is involved in."

"Why'd they say that? You don't have anything to do with that rat."

"It's their way of putting pressure on me. They know McGregor is really angry with someone stealing his stuff and I think they're looking for a way of taking McGregor's attention away from *them.*"

"And you're the fall guy?"

"Could be. McGregor already suspects I'm involved in some way. He's said as much."

"This scares me, Jim."

He responded with a shrug. "I think if he really thought I had his stuff, he would have come after me already. He may suspect I know who did it, though."

"I'm worried."

"I'm sorry for that."

"Are you up for buying me supper?"

"I'd like to see you," said Jim. "Supper would be great."

"Sounds good to me," she replied. "Then what, back to my place?"

Jim chuckled. "If you insist."

"I insist."

"Seven o'clock?"

"I'll be in the lobby."

Jim grinned as he closed the cell phone and slipped it back into his pocket.

-

"Maria, something wrong?" asked Dom. He held the phone to his ear as he walked down the hall to his hotel room.

"I was just talking with Jim. We're going to supper at seven. I don't know where. But, I'm getting increasingly worried about Jim at the Walker building. Today the feds were there again leaning hard on him."

"They're still trying to get him to snoop for them?"

"Uh-huh. There's the issue with the stuff those two took from the basement. Between the two FBI men and McGregor, I'm worried that Jim is going to take the heat for this. McGregor won't stand still until he gets his stuff back. I think he's going to keep at Jim hoping he'll tell him where it is and who took it."

"You're probably right. Jim's in a bad position. McGregor can't go against the FBI directly, but with Jim, he may get really tough. He probably thinks that Jim either took his stuff or told the FBI about it, and he intends to find out.

"What'll we do?"

"Let me make a couple calls," said Dom, "see what my options are."

"Okay. I don't want him hurt anymore."

"I'll get back to you." Dom closed the phone and entered his apartment.

Standing by the sliding glass door to the small ledge, he hit the speed-dial for Angelo DiCosta. The conversation was short and cryptic, both knowing that either or both phones might be monitored.

"Hello. DiCosta."

"Dom here. I just had a worrisome call from Maria about the situation with her friend at the building that we talked about before."

"Was there more trouble?"

"This guy is getting very threatening and scary. It sounds like he may be coming unglued over the loot that is missing."

"I want you to keep a close eye on Maria and her friend. I'm going to have a talk with family members, get their advice."

"He's been pretty well protected so far," said Dom.

"Yeah. So far," replied Angelo. "I'm going to push for immediate action."

Dom said he understood and closed the phone.

—

McGregor slammed the bottle of beer on the table top. "Where the hell is he?" he roared at Moretti.

Moretti shook his head. "No one's seen or heard from him. I checked with everybody I know."

"That son-of-a-bitch. Fontana's got to be working with those FBI pricks, maybe getting a payoff," said McGregor.

"Think he took your stuff?" asked Moretti.

McGregor looked at Moretti, and then shook his head. "Naw. It's got to be that asshole Randolph or one of the fed pricks."

"Could they have worked it together?"

"FBI and Randolph?"

"Makes sense, doesn't it?" asked Moretti.

McGregor glared at Moretti. "Get him. Bring that Randolph asshole here," he yelled. "He'll tell me what I want to know, or we'll put what's left of him in a dumpster." He waved his hand in dismissal. "Go get him."

—

Ferrari made a call to Ricardo Santos. "Rick, I heard. I'm sorry about what happened."

"They killed my goddamn dogs; . . . my beautiful dogs."

"We'll find out who did this," said Ferrari.

"They were in my home, opened my safe and . . . and killed my dogs. They were special to me."

"I understand," said Ferrari., "and I am very sorry. What have you heard so far?"

"Heard that McGregor was in Casey's that night with some of his crew. But something must have happened as he and another guy left and drove away."

"Who was the other guy?" asked Ferrari.

"I don't know. Tony, someone has to pay for this. My dogs, the money, the jewels, and violating my home. Someone has to pay!"

"I hear you, and we'll figure out who did this. They'll pay."

"Thanks, Tony."

Ferrari closed his phone, but hesitated only a few seconds before calling Carmine Salerno.

"Hello, Tony. Careful on this phone."

"I understand. I just talked with Santos. He's really upset."

"I can imagine. It's a terrible thing. What are you thinking?"

"I don't have any proof yet, but I'm thinking it's what we talked about before."

"I'm hearing that also from some of the guys. People upset that one of our own is responsible for this," said Salerno. "We can't tolerate it, not anymore."

"I wanted to get some proof before coming to you," said Ferrari.

"Enough with the proof. *You* need to stop this outrage."

"It can be done," said Ferrari hesitantly.

"Yeah, then do it. Now!"

—

When Dom approached the doorman at Jim's hotel he was told that two men had just snatched Jim and forced him into the back seat of a gray Toyota. The doorman gave Dom a scrap of paper with the license number. Dom made a call and fifteen minutes later had the name of the person that had rented the car, Antonio Moretti. Two more calls and twenty minutes later, he found out the car was at Casey's Lounge, the bar where McGregor usually held court. Dom rounded up Alfredo, Vinnie and Angelo, men he used before, and they headed to Casey's Lounge.

—

Jack Reed drove north from the old warehouse. Somers, agitated by Reed's idea to rid themselves of McGregor, had decided to go home. Reed realized he and Somers were now in much more danger; not just from McGregor directly, but what would happen if they were exposed by him? They would surely die in prison. He wasn't going to let that happen. Reed would have to silence McGregor permanently. He would have to think of something before he got to Casey's.

Suddenly he stopped and turned the car around. He remembered a man at the Russell House demolition site that owed him a big favor. When his boss had been arrested for fraudulent billing to the project, Reed had agreed to let this Ralph guy off if he told Reed where to find the man's records. He had led Reed to an explosives store in a locked metal building where the records had been secretly placed. This guy, Reed thought, stayed in a trailer on the demolition site and guarded the equipment and explosives. Reed found the fenced site and pulled up to the chain link gate. He called the phone number on the sign and reached Ralph.

"Hello."

"Ralph. This is Jack Reed. Remember me? We did a piece of business some months back."

"Uh, yeah. What's up? It's kinda late. How'd you get this number?"

"It's on the sign out here. I'm looking right at it."

"Shit."

"You sober, Ralph?"

"Two beers. Why?"

"If you let me in, maybe we can do some business."

"What kind of business? I haven't done anything."

"I'm thinking we can help each other, maybe you make a couple bucks."

There was a long pause. "I'll be there in a couple minutes."

Reed looked around. There wasn't any sign of life, not a person or a car. The rundown section was a ghost town shrouded in light fog. Most of the ancient buildings would be torn down in the next couple of years to make way for high-rise offices and parking garages. Ralph had impressed him with his technical capabilities when he had been here to arrest the manager of the operation. Reed had come away convinced that Ralph was a demolition expert, just what he needed tonight.

—

Jim was tied up in a chair. Moretti had found duct tape in the store room behind the bar. McGregor tossed the remainder of his cocktail in Jim's face.

Jim shook his head. "Needs more vermouth."

"Wise ass. Couldn't keep your nose clean, could you? You're working with the FBI."

Jim shook his head.

"What'd you do to Fontana? Did you turn him? He working with those guys?"

"I don't know about Fontana."

"You're a goddamn liar," yelled McGregor. "Tell me where that bastard went."

"I don't know that he went anywhere. All I know is he stopped coming to work. Didn't even call."

Moretti got up and stood behind Jim. "Asshole ain't gonna tell you squat."

"McGregor came closer. "If you don't, that Maria babe is gonna be the worst for it."

"Leave her out of this."

McGregor's fist came at Jim quickly, smashing into the side of his face. "What're doing with the FBI? I want to know!"

Jim shook his head, now reeling with pain. "They just come in and harass me. Looking for stuff on DiCosta."

McGregor raised his voice. "What do you know about them ripping me off?"

"Nothing. Nothing at all."

McGregor slammed his fist into Jim's face again.

Moretti moved up next to Jim. "Want me to make him talk, boss?"

McGregor didn't answer him. "Was it Fontana? He rip me off?"

Jim shook his head.

McGregor looked at Moretti and nodded. Moretti swung a powerful blow into Jim's waist. "Speak up asshole. Man asked you a question."

Jim couldn't breath. The pain was overwhelming. He fought for some air.

McGregor swung his fist against Jim's face, almost knocking him and the chair over.

Jim realized he might not survive the night.

"Who took my stuff?" McGregor roared.

Chapter 38

TONY FERRARI STOPPED in front of Delmonico, an upscale place on the Upper East-Side. He smiled as he entered the noisy lounge, crowded with merrymakers dancing to a three piece band. This place is a gold mine, he thought, a steady income producer for the last four years. He waved to several friends and started down a long hallway. At the end, he made sure to face the video camera and knocked on the heavy door.

The door opened and he entered. The two men he had called on the way to Delmonico were seated around a large table. A uniformed waiter stood ready. Tony greeted them but spent little time on small talk. Gene was an explosives expert who served eight years in Iraq and Afghanistan. Larry and Gene were a team and Tony appreciated their value. Larry was a marksman and knew weapons. The job was simple enough, but had to be done right. They were to watch the front of Casey's from the foyer of a dilapidated apartment building located across the street at an angle from the lounge. When McGregor leaves Casey's, Ferrari directed, he is to be executed with a shot to the head.

—

Dominic rounded up Alfredo, Vinnie and Angelo and drove to Casey's Lounge, a few blocks north of the Walker building. Casey's had been there a couple of decades, always an Irish bar, and a favorite with construction workers. Dom parked across the street and just around the corner from the lounge, studying it with night vision binoculars. Alfredo looked through a regular set checking on the patrons entering and leaving.

"Looks kinda quiet," said Alfredo. "Are we gonna rush the place?"

Dom shook his head. "That must be McGregor's car, the gray one he rented." He turned in his seat. "Angelo, take a quick walk to the end of the block and come back on their side. Check the plates on that car; see if it's the one I gave you."

"I'm on it." Angelo left by the curbside door and started toward the end of the block. There was hardly anyone on the sidewalk to notice him.

"Hasn't that blue Ford come by here before?" asked Vinnie. "Going pretty slow."

"I see only one guy," said Dom.

"Let's see if he comes around the block again. There are parking spaces just up the street," said Alfredo. "Must be looking for something."

A few minutes later, the blue Ford reappeared, this time stopping and backing into a parking spot several businesses before reaching Casey's. Dom pulled the phone from his pocket, pushing the speed-dial for Angelo.

"Hello."

"Where are ya?"

"Just crossed the street. Be coming down the other side in a minute."

"Okay. Did you see that blue Ford parked up from the lounge?"

"Yeah. Nobody got out of it, yet," said Angelo.

"Get the number when you go by. Take a quick look; see if you recognize the guy."

"No problem."

"Thanks."

"Plain-ass car," said Vinnie. "Think it's a cop?"

"We'll have to find out," Dom replied. "Something else might be going on."

Alfredo, looking through binoculars, "Here comes Angelo. Almost up to that Ford."

Dom swung his night vision to watch Angelo. "He's moved up to the curb to catch the plate number, I guess."

"Yeah, he just went past it," said Alfredo. "The guy in the car has got to be suspicious."

Dom's phone buzzed. "What've you got?"

Angelo read off the plate number and Dom wrote it on the palm of his hand.

"I couldn't get a look at the guy, but the car has radio gear at the dashboard," said Angelo.

"Some kind of cop?"

"I wouldn't be surprised," said Angelo. "Say, this other car, it's a Camry. It's got a rental sticker on the bumper. I'm checking the plate . . . aah, yep. It's the number you gave me."

"Yeah, rented to McGregor," said Dom. "Okay, circle around and stake out the back entrance."

"Will do."

Dom closed the phone and glanced at Vinnie and Alfredo. "We'll wait. There's something about to happen."

Reed had carefully prepared the two bags. The flat plates of plastic explosive were inserted in the bottom of each bag wired to a disposable cell phone, both set to the same number. He then placed plastic wrapped bundles of paper in the bags, and on top he placed bundles of 50 dollar bills. Reed hated to part with the money, but he had to make the bags look authentic. If McGregor was suspicious and took the back apart, Reed knew he'd have to kill him on the spot.

With the bags on the curb next to McGregor's rented Camry, Reed leaned against the wall of the lounge and punched in the number for Casey's.

"Casey's Lounge."

"Yeah. I'd like to speak to McGregor."

"Who's callin'?"

"Just tell him I have what he wants. I'll be outside for a few minutes."

Reed heard the phone placed on the counter with a thump. He waited.

"Yeah, who's this?"

"I got your stuff outside," said Reed.

There was a pause before McGregor replied. "What stuff?"

"The stuff you been looking for. What else?"

"I'm coming out. Better not be a trick."

Reed heard the phone hang up. He put his hand in his pocket and slipped the safety off the gun. The door pushed open and McGregor and Moretti stepped outside.

"You alone," said Reed.

McGregor looked around and then nodded his head toward Moretti. Moretti said something and McGregor repeated his gesture. Moretti went inside the lounge.

McGregor smirked. "So, you two assholes had it all along?"

Reed shrugged and pointed to the bags. "Count it later. I gotta run." He started for his car.

As Reed got into his car, he saw McGregor place the two bags in the trunk of the Camry. He looked around and then slammed the trunk lid closed.

—

Ferrari's men saw McGregor put bags in his car given to him by a man who then drove away. Larry feigned drunkenness as he stumbled across the street as McGregor got back onto the pavement. Larry stumbled onto McGregor's car, cursing and trying to open the driver's door. McGregor, incensed, came around the back of the car only to receive two gun shots in the head from Larry who dragged him and dropped him between the parked cars. Larry then withdrew into the shadows of a nearby narrow service alley.

—

Reed stopped his car a few hundred feet beyond the lounge, and turned to look back. He didn't hear the silenced pistol shots and couldn't see that McGregor had been shot. He did see an apparent drunk stumble toward the car and then some seconds later appear on the pavement stumbling away, but no sight of McGregor.

Reed was confused. He watched for a few more seconds and then assumed McGregor had got in his car. Reed grabbed a disposable phone and punched in the number for the cell phone detonators in the two bags. He immediately saw a fireball beyond the half dozen vehicles parked in front of the Camry. Debris was flying across the street. Reed pulled out of his parking spot, made a u-turn, and drove by the wreckage of the car. The Camry and the car behind it were burning violently. He saw a body on the ground and it too was on fire. "Good riddance, asshole," he shouted.

—

Larry hurried to the car parked just around the corner and across the street from Casey's.

"What the hell happened?" asked Gene as Larry got into the car.

"Exploded," gasped Larry. "Musta been a goddamn bomb in it. Christ, I thought I was dead."

"*He's* dead though, right?" asked Gene.

"Dead and cooked," said Larry. "Let's get the hell outa hear."

"This is fuckin' unbelievable," exclaimed Alfredo.

"Yeah," said Dom. "Guy comes along and gives our shit-head two bags. Then some other dude comes along and offs our shithead. Then the damn car blows up." Dom looked at his associates. "What the hell's gonna happen next?"

Dom's phone was buzzing. "Yeah," said Dom.

"What the hell happened. I heard this explosion," said Angelo.

"You at the back entrance?" asked Dom.

"Yeah, lookin' right at it."

"Stay awake," said Dom. "We're going in the front in sixty seconds." He closed the phone.

"Hey. Guys are coming out of the joint," said Vinnie.

Dom looked at his men. "Let's go. In the front and take Jim Randolph out the back. Then go up the alley to the end of the block. Anybody gets in the way, do what you gotta do."

The car doors opened and the men left. They moved swiftly across the street as sirens were beginning to be heard.

Chapter 39

DOM AND HIS COMPANIONS approached Casey's as a police cruiser screeched to a stop well behind the two burning cars. The bar patrons had all come outside at the sound of the explosion and stood against the wall of the building pointing and gawking at the burning hulks of the two cars, and the obviously dead McGregor between them.

Dom and his men rushed into the bar without interference. Casey, still behind the bar, yelled and reached under the bar. When he looked up he was facing Vinnie's pistol only inches from his head. "Not a good idea."

Casey laid the gun on the counter. Vinnie picked it up and forced Casey into the back room.

Dom threw the bolt on the door to the bar area, then looked at Vinnie and nodded toward Casey. Casey didn't have a chance to utter a cry before Vinnie landed the butt of his pistol on his head.

Angelo entered when Dom pushed open the back door. Angelo quickly cut the tape binding Jim's ankles and wrists. Dom and Vinnie picked up the unconscious Jim and went out the back door. Angelo and Alfredo joined the struggle to get Jim up the narrow alley to the end of the block. Fire engine air horns and sirens were heard and they quickened their steps. At the end of the alley they sat down next to a dumpster. Dom sent Vinnie to get the car, and then pushed a speed dial on his cell phone.

"Werner, Dom here."

"Yeah, can't be good news," said the doctor. "I'm just closing up here."

"It's important. Keep your nurse over. I'll make it worth your while. Be over in less than thirty minutes."

"Gun shot? You know the problem I have with that."

"Relax, not a gunshot." Dom closed his phone. He looked at Angelo. "How's he doin'?"

"He's gonna be hurtin' for quite a while," said Angelo. He looked at the seemingly unconscious figure then shrugged. "Poor bastard. Don't know if anything's broke."

Dom punched in another speed dial. It was picked up on the first ring.

"Dom?" said Maria.

"We got him. He's beat up, but he'll be okay. Taking him to my doc. Call you later."

"Thank God. Dom?"

But he was gone.

It was after-hours at the Duggan Walk-in Medical Office. Dom and his three associates alternately sat and paced in the waiting room. Jim had been in the treatment area for over an hour. When Dom poked his nose into the hallway, a stout nurse ordered him back to the waiting room. When he objected, she glared and informed him that the patient was doing well and the doctor would be out to see him shortly.

He turned to his men. "You guys go get something to eat, getting late."

Vinnie asked, "What can we bring you? You gotta eat."

"Where you going?" asked Dom.

"Louigi's ain't too far," said Angelo.

"Bring me an Italian. Grab a Pepsi, too."

"Got it. Be back in a little while," said Vinnie.

No sooner had his men left than the doctor came into the waiting room. Dom looked at his unsmiling face and felt uneasy. "What's the story, Doc?"

The doctor leafed through his notes. "His face has some serious contusions; his left eye is swollen shut." He hurriedly added, "But he's okay otherwise." He took a breath and continued. "His kidneys took a pounding, but I don't think there's any bleeding. His upper body is severely bruised. Thighs are bruised. We did some X-rays and found two cracked ribs, adjacent, on his right side. There are no other broken bones."

"Christ, Doc, what do you think?" said Dom. "We take him to a hospital? You know how important this is to my boss."

The doctor shook his head. "He's gonna be all right, but it'll take time. I can put him in a hospital if you like for a few days."

"What are we lookin' at Doc?" asked Dom, sweat forming on his brow.

"He's got to stay immobile, lots of bed rest; he'll be in a lot of pain for a week or more. It'll take a month, maybe longer, before he can even do light work."

"Can he be transported up to the DiCosta place? We can get a nurse to come in, can't we?"

The doctor nodded. "Sure. I could stop by. We can do that. I'd like him to be transported in an ambulance though. Not sitting up in a car squeezed between you guys."

"You can do that, right?"

The doctor hesitated.

Dom reached into his pocket and pulled out a roll of bills. He looked at the doctor. "For your care, for the nurse, for your coffee fund, and for an ambulance and driver – what?"

The doctor shrugged, "How about three large."

Dom didn't hesitate and pulled out the bills. "Is he conscious, Doc?" he asked.

"He was but I put him under. He's hurting pretty bad."

"How about medicine, Doc. What'll we have to get?"

"I'll give you some to start with and a couple prescriptions."

He stood up and straightened his white coat. "All right, I have a bit more work to do and then I'll order the ambulance."

Dom thanked him and sat down to wait for the return of his associates.

When the ambulance came to the back of the medical office, Dom called a cab for his men, and then reached for his phone. It buzzed as he picked it up.

"Dom! Talk to me!"

Dom moved the phone away from his ear. This was the third time she had called and hadn't gotten any calmer. "Maria, he's going to be okay."

"Okay? What okay? Is he in the hospital? Where?"

"Maria, I just talked to Angelo – to your father. Jim is being taken to your family place. The ambulance just left. Be there in less than an hour."

"Dom, I'm leaving now. I'm going up there."

"Okay. I'll be driving up there, too. Drive careful."

"Dom?"

"Uh-huh."

"Thank you."

—

Reed talked to Somers in his car and told him what happened. Somers was worried about somehow getting caught by the police or even their own FBI. Reed said there is only one loose end to tie off.

Somers looked at Reed, his brow knitted. "What're you talking about?"

"This Randolph guy," said Reed.

Somers shook his head. "You can't be thinking of that. No."

"Listen, he's the only one that could have known we grabbed the loot outa the basement. McGregor was focused on us. How the hell did he come to that conclusion if he didn't beat it outa Randolph?"

Somers shook his head again. "No. No. Don't want any part of that."

Reed sighed. "I don't know any other way. I get rid of him and there's no one else to point fingers at us."

"I can't," said Somers. "I just can't do that."

Reed looked at Somers in disgust. "You oughta put in for early retirement." His thoughts, however, were taking a darker tone.

—

Tony Ferrari and Angelo DiCosta met with Carmine Salerno at his home to bring him up to date on the recent events. Salerno straightened his posture in the wing chair and looked at Ferrari and then DiCosta.

"You're telling me there was some kinda altercation outside some bar and McGregor got whacked?" Salerno shook his head. "And then what, bomb went off in his car? This is what you're telling me?"

Ferrari leaned forward. "I was in my car with some of my boys, saw everything."

Salerno glared at Ferrari. “What the hell were you doing there?”

“I’d gone there to rescue Randolph, a friend of Maria, from the McGregor gang in the back of Casey’s Lounge. We got word he was snatched and taken there.”

“Why was McGregor outside? Who put the bomb in his car?” Salerno shook his head and grimaced. “I don’t understand what happened.”

Ferrari spoke in a calm voice. “He was outside talking to some guy who gave him two bags. He put them in the trunk of his car. I saw this. Then some guy comes down the sidewalk acting kinda drunk. Next thing, McGregor is down and this guy disappears around the corner.”

“Who’s this guy with the bags?” asked Salerno. “And a different guy shot him?”

“Guy that brought the bags drove off. That’s when this other guy shows up and does McGregor.”

“Who the hell are these guys, the Keystone Cops? Are they all working together?”

Ferrari shook his head. “We didn’t get to find out. The next thing, the car blows up and all hell breaks loose. People come out of the bar and nearby stores. A few minutes later, cops show up.”

Salerno stared at DiCosta, then at Ferrari. “Any of this coming back to me – or you?”

“No. Nothing,” said Ferrari.

“You’re sayin’ there’s no loose ends.”

Ferrari nodded. “That’s what I’m saying.”

Salerno turned his attention to DiCosta. “Your daughter’s friend, Randolph. What about *him*?”

“Randolph knows virtually nothing about our business,” said DiCosta, “but for what he learned on the job. Maria won’t discuss our business with him, or anyone.”

Salerno kept his stare on DiCosta. “This Randolph guy is your responsibility.”

DiCosta nodded.

Chapter 40

MARIA STOOD BY JIM'S bedside. "I was so afraid when Dom told me they had grabbed you. It made me crazy, not knowing, waiting for Dom to call back."

"I'll admit, I was really scared," said Jim. "McGregor was wild with rage. I thought he would kill me."

"I can't believe it's finally over," said Maria, and then added. "Is it?"

"McGregor is dead, shot by a gunman and finished off by a car bomb." Jim shook his head. "How it all happened is a mystery to me, but I'm not sorry he's dead."

"I asked Dom about it."

"What'd he say?"

"He just shrugged," said Maria.

Jim smiled. "Probably best not to ask."

"Uh-huh."

It was three weeks before Jim was able to walk unaided, although still in pain from the fractured ribs. During his recovery, he was well cared for by Maria's mother and her housekeeper. Maria's father stopped in to see him every day, sometimes staying to talk. Jim spent most evenings in Maria's company. A hired nurse visited Jim every day during the first two weeks, checking his vital signs, and medication usage.

Dom had insisted on escorting Maria daily to and from her business. However, there had been no threats to her safety.

Jim's employer, SCCI, told him the Walker building was now functioning with a new engineer and technician. Jim was instructed to report to the Walker building next week to review operations with the new engineer. He was informed his hotel room and rental car were still under lease. He was further told, when his work was completed at the Walker building, Jim was to report at SCCI in Schenectady to be trained in a new secure communications system to be installed at a securities brokerage in Albany.

-

Agent Reed smiled as he thought about Agent Somers. He had been gone for over a week and no one had seen him. A mystery indeed and he smiled again. Reed scouted the areas around the Walker building and the Clarion Arms Hotel as part of his regular surveillance of Ferrari's people. Not seeing Jim Randolph in two weeks, he asked at the Clarion Arms if he still was a resident. He learned Jim still had a reserved room at the hotel and was expected to return in a week or two. Reed now prepared to tie up another loose-end. He again visited the explosives expert at the eastside building site.

-

Jim walked to his car from the hotel on the morning of his first day to report back at the Walker building. As he went up the ramp in the parking garage to the second level, he got a brief glimpse of a man as he disappeared behind a concrete bulwark two vehicles away from where his car was parked. Jim hesitated, staring in that direction, but saw no other movement. Where had the man gone? There was no place to go but to hide behind the concrete structure. Was it a car thief?

Walking up the ramp might have been a mistake, he thought. He had wanted the exercise, but now his side pained him. He stood a moment to catch his breath and stared at where he had seen the man disappear. Was he still there? Hiding? Why? Jim knew he wasn't in any shape to confront a desperate car thief. The elevator and the door to the stairwell were directly in front of Jim as he stepped slowly the final few feet to the second level. He could see his car, the fifth vehicle to his right. Should he go to his car and pretend he hadn't seen the man? No, the man had probably seen him hesitate; the man knew.

While glancing frequently to where he had seen the man hide, Jim went to the elevator door where a small fire extinguisher was mounted in a smashed housing on the wall. The red enclosure was bent as if having been hit by an object while getting into the elevator. He lifted the extinguisher from the hook and yanked it out of the crumpled housing. He pulled the safety pin out and then pulled the spray horn up to make it point in front of him. He held the extinguisher in his left hand as he fumbled in his pocket for the car key fob. He saw that he would have to approach his car from the rear as the fronts of the cars were almost against the wall.

As Jim approached his car, his feeling of paranoia suddenly left him. A man stepped away from the concrete bulwark and approached him quickly. Jim saw the gun in the man's right hand, further alarmed on realizing a silencer was attached. The baseball cap cast a shadow on the man's face, but as soon as he spoke, Jim recognized him.

"Reed! What the hell . . .?"

"Get in . . . the passenger side."

Jim didn't move. "What're you doing? What the hell is this?"

"Get in the car. . . . Do it."

"Screw you. Everybody is catching on to what you and Somers did, aren't they? Is that why you had McGregor killed? Is that what this is about?"

"He was a pain in my ass . . . same as you. Drop that goddamn thing and get in the car."

"What happened to your buddy, Somers? Haven't seen him around. Was he a pain in the ass too?"

Reed looked around quickly. "Get in the car or I'll shoot you right here."

"No you won't. There are two cameras looking right at you."

Reed reached into his left pocket and pulled out a DVD and waved it in the air smiling. "Took care of that. Now get in the car."

Jim let his key fob drop to the floor but still held onto the fire extinguisher. He saw Reed move the pistol toward him and fire. There was a loud pop and glass shattered in his rented car.

"Pick it up." Reed came closer to him, the pistol now inches from Jim's head. "Pick it up, asshole. We're going for a ride. I want to take my time - with you."

Jim fought back the grip of fear; he looked for a way out. He felt the pistol against his head and slowly let the fire extinguisher down to the floor. As he straightened up, the key fob still lay on the floor.

"Pick it up, asshole!" Reed brought the gun down hard on Jim's head.

Jim staggered from the shock and pain; his hand reached out to the car for support. He bent over and with his left hand gripped the key fob. His foot bumped against the fire extinguisher and his head cleared. Reed yanked the key fob out of Jim's hand and moved behind him to open the passenger door. Jim saw that he had moved the gun to his left hand while he struggled to open the door wide.

"Get in there. Don't make me hit you again," Reed growled.

In a frantic move with all his energy focused, Jim suddenly had the fire extinguisher by the handle in his right hand, and with all the strength he had, he swung it over his head to smash down on the Reed's forehead as he was bringing the gun up to shoot. It was a glancing blow, sufficient to stagger the man. A gun shot sent a bullet to ricochet off the concrete ceiling as Jim swung the fire extinguisher over his head again to smack down on Reed's head. This time Reed fell to his knees. In a fit of rage and fear, Jim swung the heavy extinguisher again to bring it down solidly on Reed's left temple. Blood ran down from his scalp onto the pavement. Jim staggered to his feet, gasping for breath. After a few seconds he was able to focus, and reached into his jacket for his cell phone. He punched in 9-1-1.

"What is your emergency?"

"Uh . . . I was assaulted. There is a man down, hurt pretty bad."

"Where are you?"

"I'm on the second level of the Clarion Arms Parking Garage."

"What's your name?"

"Jim Randolph."

"Are you injured?"

"Pistol whipped."

"Stay on the line with me until an officer arrives."

"Okay."

Within three minutes a police cruiser roared up the incline to stop behind Jim's car. One officer worked his radio as he examined the immediate scene and the fallen man between the cars. The driver began questioning Jim, interrupted by curt messages to and from his lapel radio. Jim could hear sirens approaching at the street level.

Jim looked at his phone, and then pushed the speed dial for Dom's phone.

"Jim? Dom here."

"Dom - I'm in trouble. I'm going to need a lawyer."

"I've just been monitoring the police radio. I'm on my way. What the hell happened?"

"I was assaulted by Reed. I might have killed him."

"Jesus. . . . Don't say any more. I'll be there soon."

"Okay."

Within five minutes another patrol car arrived followed by an ambulance and the medical examiner. Behind them came an unmarked car with two suits. The detectives examined the scene and one sat down with Jim on a concrete barrier. He opened his small notebook and looked at Jim.

"I'm Detective Jack Morgan. Jim Randolph is it?"

"Yes."

"Can you show me some I.D.?

Jim reached for his wallet.

"What happened here?"

"I wanted to get my car. Saw someone stalking me, hiding behind the concrete bulwark over there." Jim pointed. "The guy assaulted me with a gun; told me to get in the car; that we were going for a ride. I resisted and he hit me with his gun. When he opened the car door I saw an opportunity and I hit with a fire extinguisher. Then I called 9-1-1."

"Where did the fire extinguisher come from?"

"I grabbed it when I first saw the stalker and kept it with me. He hit me, made me put it down. But I grabbed it when he went to open the car door and I swung it at him."

"Looks like you hit him more than once."

"I had to stop him."

"You had to use a fire extinguisher?"

Jim nodded. “I’ve got some cracked ribs and didn’t want to get into an altercation.”

The officer shook his head as he wrote in his notebook. “So what was this, some irate husband trying to get even with you?”

Jim shrugged.

“What are your injuries?”

“Got hit twice with a pistol.”

The detective called to an EMT who was talking idly with an officer. The EMT came over and examined Jim’s head and looked for symptoms of concussion. Jim was told that there wasn’t any sign of damage, but to seek medical help if he started to feel out of sorts.

Finally, Reed was loaded into an ambulance and driven away. The police and detectives stood around talking in a group. The detective came up to Jim, gave him a card and told him he’d have to go with them to the precinct shortly.

Jim sat on a concrete ledge of the garage and phoned Maria, but was only able to leave a message. Then he called his boss and related the event to him. A police captain arrived and went over Jim’s statement. The captain asked about the troubles he was having at the Walker building and they discussed some of the past events.

“Seems to me, you are familiar with the man that assaulted you.”

“Yep. FBI Agent Reed.”

“He’s in bad shape. EMT’s weren’t hopeful.”

“He came at me with a gun.”

“Yeah, we have it. It was fired.”

“He fired twice.”

“I heard from your friend, Dom. He speaks well of you.”

“He’ll be here soon.”

The captain nodded. “We’ll go to the precinct soon.”

“Uh huh.”

Jim heard Maria’s excited voice and he turned to see her and Dom hurrying up the ramp. Maria rushed toward him throwing her arms around his neck.

“I tried calling you,” he said between kisses.

“I was in the office when you called. Then Dom called me.”

Dom stepped closer to Jim. "A lawyer will meet you at the station."

"My god, Jim, what happened?"

Jim shook his head. "Unbelievable."

"What?" Maria shook his arm. "Tell me."

Jim told her what he had experienced on arriving at the second level of the garage.

Her eyes widened. "Who . . . who was it? Do you know?"

Jim glanced at the police captain and saw that he was in conversation with some of his patrolmen. "It was Jack Reed, the FBI agent."

"Reed? Really?" Maria shook her head. "But why?"

"I've been sitting here thinking about that. It might have been him cleaning up loose ends."

"You mean McGregor? Now you?"

"It's what I was thinking."

"I don't understand why he'd do that?" said Maria.

"He must have figured out I had somehow gotten evidence that he and Somers stole the money McGregor hid in the basement. If he was tying up loose ends by killing McGregor, then he sure couldn't leave me around to threaten him."

"He had McGregor killed?" asked Maria.

Jim shrugged. "He might have been the one to plant the bomb in McGregor's car."

"But someone else shot him. Right?"

Jim looked around and saw Dom talking to the detectives.

"Someone," said Jim.

"You mean . . . ?"

Jim shrugged.

"What became of the other agent, . . . Somers?"

"I heard at work that they only saw Reed lately, not Somers."

"Maybe he was promoted or retired," said Maria.

Jim shrugged. "Maybe he was another loose end."

"Jesus, what a nightmare." Maria hugged him. "You going to be arrested?"

"I have to go with them in a few minutes down to the precinct for an interview. Dom said he has a lawyer coming to the station."

"It was self defense . . ."

"Yes. But they have to do their investigation."

Maria put her arm through his and smiled. “Yeah, but then you start a new job in Albany, away from this madness.”

Jim pulled her tight against him. “A new beginning.”

Keep reading

For an advance look at

Bushwhacked

The next exciting novel by

Bernie Ziegner

Coming soon from Rosstrum Publishing

Bushwhacked

By

Bernie Ziegner

Chapter 1

Erica Stewart, Sheriff's Deputy from the small town of Bradshaw, kept the accelerator pressed down as she responded to the 9-1-1 call made to the main Sheriff's Office in Camden, the county seat twelve miles southwest of Bradshaw. The driver of a pickup had requested assistance claiming to have struck a deer on Sawmill Road. The road ran along the bottom of a narrow valley ending at a long abandoned sawmill. She saw the pickup as she rounded a bend on the narrow road. It was stopped facing her on her side of the road. It's bright headlights blinded her momentarily, and she braked her vehicle hard.

She had already stopped a few yards in front of the pickup when recognition dawned on her. She stepped out of her vehicle straining to see past the bright halo of the truck's lights, but didn't see the driver. Erica took a few steps forward and called, "Greg?"

She recognized the truck, the off-red faded color of the decade old Ford-150. Where was the deer, she wondered, as she walked toward the passenger side of the truck, where the door was wide open. Just as she passed the flood of light, she saw movement off her left shoulder and a man rushing toward her from the darkness off the side of the road. She was slammed against the fender of the truck.

"Greg," she screamed, as she fought to regain her footing.

"You bitch!"

She felt a pistol under her chin.

"Get in the goddamn truck. Gonna teach you about messing with me."

"Greg! Get away from me!"

His fist slammed into her stomach as she tried to reach her gun. Then he had her pistol and tossed it to the roadway in front of the light glare. He grabbed the lapel microphone and ripped it from her shirt, tearing it open.

"Greg! Stop!"

He pulled her toward the door of his pickup, filling the air with invectives.

Erica tried to wrestle free, but he held her with a powerful grip. She kicked and screamed.

He pushed her toward the open door of the pickup and backhanded her across the face. "Get in there you goddamn bitch! You're gonna pay."

With her back against the end of the seat, she kicked out with a hard contact to his groin. He bellowed in rage. The kick did not stop him; a fist landed on her stomach. He was pushing her onto the seat when a loud horn sounded from beyond the light glare.

-

Tom Morrison screeched to a stop behind the sheriff's vehicle and tried to assess the situation in front of him. He suddenly realized a female officer was being assaulted and he leaned on the horn to distract her attacker. As the horn blew, the assailant swung his arm to point a pistol toward Tom. He instinctively dove back into the truck cab and then fumbled for the pistol in the glove box. He heard the window in the open door shatter as the shot rang out. Running on adrenaline, Tom pushed open the passenger door. He waited for a couple of seconds but there was no other shot fired.

He slid out of the passenger door on his belly into the tall grass and weeds. Tom took a deep breath and ran around the back of his truck to kneel and keep the open driver's door as a shield. He could see that the assailant had the deputy on the ground next to the truck and was tying the deputy's arms with tape.

Tom heard her pleading with the assailant and then saw him hit her viciously. Tom muttered an oath and lay flat on the ground. He could see the man tying the woman's ankles with tape; otherwise, he could see only the black emptiness of the dirt road beyond. How could he stop what was happening before the attacker did even more harm to the woman? He saw the assailant turn towards him; glance his way for a couple of seconds before going back to tying the woman. He heard again the pleadings from the deputy as the man tried to pull her upright.Tom rose to his feet, holding the pistol in front of him in both hands, aimed at the large man still trying to get the deputy to stand up. “Hey! Asshole! Let her go!”

The man let go of the deputy and she dropped sideways onto the road next to the truck.

Tom saw him reach for the pistol jammed in his waist. “Get away from her!”

The man raised the pistol and Jim heard the woman yell, “Greg. No!”

His first shot went wild, clipping the door frame next to Tom. The second shot missed as well.

Tom slowly squeezed the trigger. He saw the man lurch and the pistol drop, even as he dropped to his knees. He looked down at his chest, and dropped face down onto the dusty road.

Tom began to tremble. His heart pounded in his chest. He went quickly to the fallen man and kicked the pistol away. Pressing the pistol against the back of the man’s head, he reached down and felt for a pulse at his neck. He couldn’t find one. He looked down at his hand holding the pistol, and tried to still the trembling. He heard a moan from the deputy, lying crumpled up against the rear wheel of the pickup.

“Oh, God . . . Greg.”

Tom called for help with his cell phone on 9-1-1. He then removed the tape from the deputy’s legs and wrists. Realizing that her shirt had been torn open in her struggle with the assailant, he put his jacket on her and closed the zipper, hiding her ivory breasts from view. She moaned and seemed to struggle for consciousness. Tom laid her flat on her back. The bruises on her otherwise lovely face angered him, but he resisted the urge to kick the assailant in the head.

He wondered if he had killed him. He hadn't intended to, but years of training had taken over his every instinct and move. He felt a wave of nausea and stood still until it passed, then with his shirt sleeve, wiped the bead of sweat from his brow. Tom pulled his kerchief from his back pocket, shook it out, and proceeded to wipe the dirt and blood carefully from the deputy's face. She opened her eyes, again as her head fell f checked her pulse. It w the flash of blue lights and stood up.

Chapter 2

The sheriff arrived with a deputy and stopped alongside Tom's pickup. Tom kept his hands open at shoulder level as the two officers approached with weapons drawn. The sheriff removed the pistol from the waistband at Tom's back and pushed Tom up against the hood of the red truck. While the deputy called for an ambulance, the sheriff put handcuffs on Tom and made him sit on the road leaning against the patrol car. The sheriff hadn't said much to Tom, but had handled him roughly.

Tom wondered how much trouble he was in. He watched as the sheriff spoke with the woman officer victim, made notes, then stuffed the notebook in his shirt pocket and stood up. Tom saw flashing red lights approaching. The deputy was taking photos of the scene, and picked up the pistol belonging to the woman's assailant, as well as Tom's pistol and placed them in evidence bags in the sheriff's vehicle.

When the ambulance left with the injured deputy, Tom saw another ambulance arrive followed by a car which Tom thought probably brought the medical examiner. He watched as the sheriff engaged in conversation with the attendants and the presumed medical examiner inspected the body for several minutes, before the deceased was loaded into a body bag and then into the ambulance. When the ambulance drove off, the medical examiner followed in his car.

The deputy who arrived with the sheriff stood and watched as the sheriff approached Tom. The sheriff helped Tom to his feet, and removed the cuffs. "I'm Sheriff Craig Stockton."

"She gonna be all right?" asked Tom.

"Yeah, they'll keep her overnight. Sorry for the cuffs, but I had no idea what was happening when I came up."

Tom nodded. "Glad she's okay. You're keeping my gun?"

"For a while. You *did* shoot someone."

"Am I gonna be arrested?" asked Tom.

"No. Deputy said that you probably saved her life. But I have protocol to follow. You can get your pistol back tomorrow afternoon if it checks out."

Tom nodded. "Okay."

"Where do you live?" asked the sheriff. "I haven't seen you around here before."

"I'm about three miles down this road. On the right there's a narrow track goes up to my place."

The sheriff looked steadily at Tom. "Morrison? Yeah. There were some old folks living up that way. Some years back."

"My grandparents. They passed away back in 2003. I'm looking after the place."

The sheriff nodded. "Come by the office tomorrow afternoon. I want to go over the details again."

"I'll be there."

It was just before 4 o'clock the following afternoon when Tom parked at the Sheriff's Station in Camden. The dispatcher pointed to the hallway when Tom asked for Sheriff Stockton.

He nodded and went looking for the office. It was at the end of the hall.

Tom tapped lightly on the door frame.

Sheriff Stockton looked up and gestured for Tom to enter. “Have a seat.” He pointed to the chairs in front of his desk. “Just been looking at these reports.”

“Okay.”

“I'm a little puzzled.” The sheriff looked up. “Its standard procedure in this office is to do a quick check on anyone involved in any way in a serious incident.” Sheriff Stockton stared at Tom. “When I do a search for Tom Morrison, all I get back is Social Security info, a Virginia driver’s license, the schools you attended - you majored in political science - and

The sheriff looked at Tom steadily for a few seconds. “Also, Mr. Morrison, I see you were issued a license to conceal carry in D.C. while you were attached to some outfit called Greenleaf. I can't find any mention of an organization called Greenleaf, governmental or otherwise. And, there is no mention of what you were doing after your Army stint.” He shook his head. “I gotta tell you, I'm a little puzzled by this. When I pull strings in D.C. all I get is that all records are classified.”

“Yeah, I had to sign non-disclosure agreements.”

“Well, at least there are no records of arrest.”

“Never even got a traffic ticket,” said Tom grinning.

“You have a current passport?”

Tom nodded.

“Name of Thomas Morrison?”

Tom frowned. “Yes.”

“There seems to be at least one other. Some sort of diplomatic passport. I couldn't get anymore on that.”

www.ingramcontent.com/pod-product-compliance
Lightning Source LLC
Chambersburg PA
CBHW060606310726
48982CB00008B/1249/J

* 9 7 8 1 6 2 5 7 0 0 4 5 2 *